A LITTLE WITCHING AT THE WALL

Margaret Bailey

A Little Witching at the Wall is a work of fiction. All characters and situations portrayed in the book are fictional. Historical places and events are depicted fictionally.

The Cast:

Lily Marcuso, left-over hippie and would-be witch

Eleanor Markeson, suicidal spinster, teacher of German

Martin Girelli, out-of-work salesman, would-be Mafioso

Phillip Redding, wealthy guitarist and philanthropist

Ursula Kimmig, East German guitarist

Wolfgang Barkov, East German secret police agent

Horst Bauer, West Berlin policeman

1

October 25, 1989

Lily Marcuso leaned back into the big maroon cushions that were almost the only furniture in her small, row-house apartment near downtown Denver. A faded and frayed gold tassel flopped into her face. She shoved it aside absently and frowned at Cody, sound asleep with his mouth open and his legs tangled in the sheets on the mattress, the only other furniture she owned.

"I want my space back, Cody," she whispered, wishing she had the guts to wake him up and shout it in his face. She'd do it, too, if he didn't always manage to send her on a guilt trip. She fixed her eyes on his forehead and whispered with all the intensity she could muster, "To be straight with you, I'm not digging this arrangement any more. You've been crashing here for, like, months already and haven't done a thing. Not a penny on the rent, not a dish washed, a shower scrubbed."

She watched his toes, which always twitched if he registered something from the outside world when sleeping. Nothing. Bummer. Okay, got to do this with more concentration. She'd meditate him out of her life.

She settled into her cushion-modified lotus position, closed her eyes, and began the *ahs* and *ooms* of her mantra. She visualized Cody waking up and smiling and saying, "I'm moving out now." She focused on planting that thought in his brain. After a few repetitions, she opened her left eye and checked the toes.

Nothing. He still sounded like a bulldozer snorting its way through the rainforest. His sleep was just too dense.

Lily gave up the meditation and stared at him.

The hair of his over-long mustache actually rose and fell with each snore. His breath was sleep-sour and tinged with the smell of dried ginger that he always had in his mouth to keep his sinuses clear. The rise and fall of his chest heaved the peace sign he'd once shaved out of the hair. The sign had grown back darker and thicker than the rest of his hair, and he was stuck with it now, a fuzzy tattoo to remind him of his peacenik days. Which was cool, but there was something about it that made her feel weird about him. Like he forgot to grow up or something. Yeah. Like still wearing a team jacket twenty years after you graduated.

The whole hippie lifestyle just didn't quite fit a forty-year-old.

Something twitched in her head, but Lily ignored it. Cody was enough to deal with right now. She rolled her eyes and sighed.

He made her feel crowded in her one room. Not that it was spacious to begin with. In the front corner stood her ironing board with all her books on it, the broken iron serving as bookend. Sticking out from under the ironing board was the sitar that Cody twanged to accompany the creative process of his far-out poetry. His glossy old suede jacket lay across the bigger bulb of the sitar. Under her one big window lay a small Guatemalan handloom with an unfinished woven belt in orange and yellow. And next to that stood her old portable stereo and her small collection of music, mostly Woodstock favorites. Some hand-washed underwear hung on a wooden drying rack, and a lot of other clothing lay about the flattened shag carpet, waiting for the next trip to the laundromat. Well, okay, it was messy, and a lot of the mess was hers. But she was clean, and at least she wasn't a leech.

The twitch she'd been ignoring sent a tingle to the back of her neck. So he was forty and still stuck in the Woodstock mode. Maybe she wasn't so different. Twenty-eight, just as hippie with her billowy clothes and beads and stuff. And she hadn't even been at Woodstock. Was she as stuck as he was?

Her father's voice rose from the tingle. "What're you going to do with your life, Lily? You going to spend the rest of it working in that weird shop for minimum wage and no benefits? What happens if you get sick or..."

She'd heard it all before, but the last time he'd given her the spiel, she hadn't been able to shake it. And looking at Cody the Mooch brought it all back. She was a mooch, too. She shook her head with the big "no" in her thought. After all, she could almost pay the rent with the small trust her grandmother had left her. And buy veggies with her part-time salary. Well, yeah, sometimes her father kicked in a little, like when she needed a filling or one of the cats had to go to the vet. Okay, she was a half-mooch. But something else was bothering her that she couldn't quite put her finger on.

As if on cue, the cats, Ying and Yang, jumped into her lap and fixed their sly blue Siamese eyes on hers, their tails pointing at Cody.

"Cool it, you guys," she whispered, scratching them under their chins. "I tried. I guess we'll have to come up with a spell to make him split, okay?"

The phone rang. The cats leapt aside, hissing, their tail hair straight out. Lily jumped, not because she was so startled, but because the ring had gone right to the vibes in her neck. That meant bad news. She didn't want to answer it. The ringer jangled into her neck again.

Cody twitched a couple of toes; the jangling had hit a stray brainwave. He'd be up gritching about the noise if she let it ring again. She reached over and grabbed the phone out of the old doggie basket.

She wasn't surprised to hear the deep bass of her father's voice. After all, hadn't he just been talking to her?

When he'd answered her questions about her mother, who had diabetes, he said, "Lily, you remember you asked me to give you some lead time when your trust was about to run out?"

Lily gulped. "Yeah?"

"Well, the end is coming. You have about three months left. And it looks like January's installment will be about half of the usual payment. After that, you're going to have to be on your own."

"January?" The word came out as a squeaky and fearful echo.

"Now, Lily, you've always known..."

"Jeez, yeah, Daddy, but I didn't think it was coming, like, so soon."

"You're going to have to do something, honey. It's not just that your money's running out. I'm going to retire at the end of the year. I'd like to keep working, but nobody's repairing typewriters any more. It's all computers now. There'll barely be enough for your mom and me, and if she gets any worse, the medical bills will wipe out our savings. So I'm not going to be able to bail you out any more."

"Aw, Daddy, why didn't you tell me you were so strung out about money? How long has this been going on?"

"A couple of years. I didn't say much because I thought you'd get on your own feet when you came back from California. But lately I'm beginning to wonder." He sighed. "I should have been harder on you, Lily, but I had my fling, too, and didn't grow up till I married your mother."

The half-mooch bit hit Lily full force and frothed in her stomach until it was a big old swirling glob of guilt. Her voice came out small and pathetic. "I'm sorry, Daddy. I should've asked how you were doing. If I'd known, I'd've given you some of the trust. And I'll help you when you need it. I'll ask Chrissie for a raise. I'll do something, I promise." Promise. Yeah, right. What was she going to do? Get a better job when she'd only gotten the one she had at Skyflower Books and Cures because she and the owner had discovered they shared all kinds of vibes?

Cody stretched and yawned and emitted the five grunts in descending pitch that he always let out to greet the world after sleep. He looked over at her and raised his brows, probably picking up on her tone that something was wrong.

He stretched again, scratched his peace sign, yawned wider, and then sat on the side of the mattress with the sheets still wrapped around his middle and his legs crossed on the floor. Well, there was at least one thing she could do. She could demand that he pay his share of the rent.

Her insides quivering over a scary future, she said as steadily as she could, "Don't worry, Daddy. I'll be fine, and you will, too. Say hi to Mom for me. Love you." She hung up.

Cody ran a hand through his long brown hair. "What's happening, babe? You look, like, real up tight."

"My money's running out, Cody. Soon."

His face went from fuzzed out to axe-sharp and his gray-blue eyes turned into laser lamps. "What? Like how soon, man?"

Lily bristled. What nerve. The only time he was ever, like, totally focused on her was when they talked about her grandmother's trust. Still, it was a good thing she hadn't already told him he should move out. Now it would help when he could pay his own way. "Soon enough," she said. "Look, Cody, you're a real cool guy, with all your poetry and your music and all, but I don't make enough bread for us both. You got to help with the rent."

Cody gave her a look that was all fuzzy again and stretched out on the mattress with his hands behind his head. "Listen, babe, that's something I been meaning to talk to you about. I been thinking, it's been a blast, you know, crashing with you. But I told you I might go back to San Fran someday. And the old scene's been, like, calling lately. Like I'm supposed to do this thing now. Groove with the bros for a while and then head up the coast. Maybe make the scene in Seattle. So, like I say, I been wanting to tell you that."

Lily stood up and glared down at him. "Yeah, for how long, Cody? The last three seconds? You never said one word about this. You class-one mooch. You've been using me the whole time, haven't you? You think I'm, like, too dopey to realize that? Well you can just split this very minute. I'd ask you to pay me back for all the food and stuff, but I know exactly what you got, 'cause you got it all from me, and it's not money. You got nothing, Cody. You're a developmentally retarded leech."

Cody jumped up and stepped toward her, dragging the wrinkled sheet with him.

YingYang leapt onto Cody's thighs, their claws through the sheet and into flesh. Cody slapped at them, but they dug in harder. They growled in unison.

"Jeez, awright, you stupid animals, I'm cool," he shouted.

Lily lifted the cats and held them at her chest, where they continued to stare at Cody, growling in a rumble that came from their stomachs, their tails twitching wildly.

"I'm splitting, man," Cody yelled. "The hell with you and your sorry pad." He threw the sheets off, lunged naked for his jacket and sitar, snatched his suede pants off the floor, and reached for the door. He turned back and hissed at her, "I'll make you sorry you did this!"

"Oh yeah? And how are you going to do that from 'San Fran'?" she asked, giving the sawed off city a nasal drawl.

He slammed the door behind him.

She heard him drop the sitar on the tiny concrete porch and assumed he was pulling on his pants.

"And don't you come back," she shouted at the door. "Everything in this room belongs to me now. I paid for it." She sat down hard on the mattress, still looking at the door. "Just go do your stupid scene. I don't need you!"

When her adrenaline rush evaporated, she rocked forward and back, clasping her arms around her chest and moaning, "Aw, bummer, man, now what am I going to do?"

2

Eleanor Markeson felt as if she were driving through a black, freezing hell instead of down the Boulder turnpike. The shifty demon-wind blasting across the highway buffeted her boxy VW camper, making her careen left and right. Damn. It'd take everything she had to make herself crash into the bridge support she'd chosen; with the stupid wind she'd even have a hard time aiming at it.

She'd been an idiot, planning her suicide on the way home from the seminar instead of on the way to it. Hadn't the weatherman said a cold front was moving in?

The wind shoved her toward the stripes and she fought to stay in the right lane. What on earth had possessed her to sign up for a seminar on the Boulder campus, anyway? As if she could teach a single post-Romantic novelist to high school German students who couldn't read live novelists, much less dead ones.

She heaved a great sigh. Time to join them.

The dead ones. Yeah, death, how she needed it. She'd contemplated it often enough in the last few years, wishing for the nothing-matters state. No more broken love affairs. No more pining for the baby she'd never had.

A sniff followed that thought. It sounded like the last water struggling through a clogged drain. She felt in her purse for a tissue but found none. Yeah, death. No more recurrences of the lovely dream—the kind, faceless man standing next to her with his left arm around her shoulder, making her feel sheltered, not alone. Everybody knew if you hadn't found that kind of happiness by forty, you never would. And today was her birthday, the one that shoved her over the hill and into the valley of no hope.

Where was that underpass? Exit 18? She'd just passed mile marker 19. Soon. Snuff the pain right out. She moved into the left lane, obeying the call of the massive concrete pylons coming into view.

A Volvo station wagon streaked past her on the right going about eighty, the driver honking angrily.

"The hell with you, buddy. This is *my* death. Looks like you'll meet yours a few years early, anyway." Nearly on the interchange, she commanded her hands to merge metal and flesh with concrete. She heard the warning ridges under her left wheels. Oh, damn. She'd forgotten to unbuckle her belt. She reached for the buckle; the camper veered onto the dirt and back onto the pavement. The pylons flashed by on her left and into her rear-view mirror.

Eleanor moaned. Damn, damn, damn. She eased back into the right lane. The Volvo was already over the long hill ahead of her. Maybe some kind of overdose.

She shifted down as the incline increased. How many Valiums would you need to relax yourself to death? Near the top she picked up speed again and crested the hill. A family of raccoons was crossing the road. They froze in the headlights. She slammed on the brake and swerved as much as she dared, but something hard went under the right tires.

"Aaah," she groaned, pulling onto the emergency lane. She slumped over the wheel and sobbed without bothering to wipe away the tears. How could she kill a raccoon when she couldn't even get her own death right?

Jumping out of the car on the passenger side, she glimpsed a dark figure at the top of next exit, just ahead. He stood with his back to the wind, watching the ramp, his head pulled into his collar, his coat flapping around his legs. He started down the ramp at a run. Hitchhiker. She'd barely have time to check the animal and leave before he reached her.

Eleanor ran to the back of the car. The wind tore hair from her French bun and whipped mouse-colored strands into her wet face.

There were no more raccoons on the road, just one black, lopsided animal-lump, dead still. Its ringed tail, highlighted by oncoming headlights, rose and fell in the wind.

She moaned and ran back to the VW. The hitchhiker was barely thirty yards away, coming at a dead run, his coat flapping like bat wings in a horror movie.

She turned the key. The passenger door flew open. A small skinny man reached in and grabbed the panic bar on the dashboard. She jerked her foot off the clutch and gunned the motor. The car lurched forward. The door slammed into him as he reached for the far side of the seat.

"Oof. This is a hijacking!" he yelled, pulling the rest of his body in and settling lopsided on the seat. "Hijacking," he shouted again. Even at that volume his voice was unsteady. "Drive me to downtown Denver."

Aw, shit, thought Eleanor, stomping on the clutch for second gear. This is all I need. "No," she said. The VW was picking up speed going down the hill now.

"What?" he yelled. His voice cracked like a teenager's.

Eleanor glanced at him. Somewhere in his twenties. Incredibly immature. "You heard me."

"Listen, lady, I got a gun here." He pulled at the right side of his coat and swore at a brief ripping sound. In a second a gun with a scrap of fabric hanging from the hammer wobbled in front of her face.

"So?" She shifted up to fourth.

He whipped the scrap off and flicked it to the floor. "So?" he squawked. "So I could kill you right now, that's what."

Eleanor snorted and had to sniff again. Then she exhaled a series harsh, bitter breaths that had started out to be a laugh.

He shoved the gun into her side. "Look, you, I mean it."

"You just go ahead." Sniff.

He inhaled in shock. The gun trembled against her ribs.

What a twit. The thing probably wasn't even loaded. Angry now, she grabbed his hand and moved the gun to her right temple. "Well, do it. 'Course, I'm going...," she peered at the speedometer, "almost sixty now. You go right ahead." She glanced at his contorted, wild face. "You don't look like much of a loss to the world either."

His shaky voice got louder still. "Lady, you don't seem to understand what's going on...going down here."

"I understand perfectly, young man." She hesitated a moment. But so what if this cretin knew? "Just go ahead and do me the favor. I just tried to drive into the last bridge support and kill myself."

The carjacker slumped into the seat and his bravado slithered to the floor.

"Shit, just my luck," he said, his voice steady now. "I hijack a broad who'd love it if I took her out." He was silent for a few minutes. Eleanor shifted into third for the next rise.

"Listen, lady, couldn't you just drop me off at 17th and Downing where I li...so they can see me get out of the car? I'll never get in the Mafia this way."

"Certainly not. I'm going home."

"Great. Where's home?"

"Southeast. Down by Denver University."

The carjacker crossed his arms over his chest, the gun dangling from his right hand and pointing into the seat. He stared out the window.

Eleanor glanced at him. Bony nose. Weak chin. She shook her head. "You're doing this as some kind of test? Whatever for? You're not the Mafia type. Look at all those thugs in the movies. They're not all hulks of men, but they all have a ruthless air about them. There's nothing ruthless about you. Desperate, maybe, but definitely not ruthless. If you want to join their ranks, you'd better read up on the Mafia. Check the public library. They have books on everything."

He faced her with his mouth hanging open. "You're gonna lecture me on getting...? Maybe you ought to check out a how-to book on suicide. You ever think of that?" He shook his head. "Jeez. I got a vivid picture: *The Field Guide to Mafia Acceptance. In with the Mob in Five Easy Lessons.* Yeah, right."

"There's no need for sarcasm. You ought to be ashamed of yourself, anyway. What do you want to join the Mafia for? There're plenty of honest jobs, you know."

"Yeah, and I suppose you got one."

"Certainly, I'm a high school teacher."

"Well, now, ain't that great? Must be a barrel of fun. A regular get-rich-quick job, too. You just love it so much you tried to off yourself."

Eleanor sighed and sniffed.

"Not me, no way," he went on. "I need excitement, danger." He looked at her in the oncoming headlights.

She heard something that was a cross between a cough and a moan.

"Okay," he said, "what I need is the money. I got laid off from my last job."

When he didn't continue, Eleanor prompted, "Which was...?"

"Shoe salesman at Penney's. And don't tell me I can aim for anything brainier than that."

"Nonsense. All of us demand far less of ourselves than our potential."

He raised his non-gun hand in a gesture of helplessness. "Yep, you're a school teacher, all right. Anyway, I'm sick to death of getting turned down. And about a week away from living on the streets."

Sniff. "You wouldn't have a Kleenex on you, I suppose."

"What? No."

Neither of them spoke again until several green exit signs had passed in and out of the headlights. His silent, awkward presence pressed at her like a stifling foam.

"You're sitting on my purse," she said.

He clicked with his tongue, opened the door, jerked the end of his coat inside, and tugged at the purse. The strap caught on something; he heaved up, yanked it loose, and laid it on top of the hand brake between the seats. He went back to staring out the window and brooding.

The rest of the long ride to and down I-25 was silent. At the first stop light after the Interstate, Eleanor expected him to jump out, but he stayed in the car. At the next, she said, pointedly separating the words, "You…can…get…out…now."

He didn't seem to hear.

She pulled into her parking place behind the apartment building.

He followed her toward the entrance, breathing in her collar.

"Good-night," she said, and stopped.

He ran into her from behind. "Listen, I could still kill you." He almost seemed to be pleading.

She turned and looked him in the eye. "No, you couldn't," she said sadly, taking in his acne-scarred face and his lank brown hair. "You're not the killer type. And even if you were, every action has its moment. Your moment passed out there on the turnpike, and I'm afraid mine did, too. Go hijack somebody else."

"Where am I gonna get a car around here at this time of night?"

"That's not my problem. Just get out of my sight. And if you have a brain in your head, you'll give up the whole stupid idea."

He made an unseemly sound, turned, and walked back down the driveway between the buildings, head down, hands jammed into the pockets of his dark tan trench coat.

Eleanor watched him trudge away. She should feel relieved. Instead, she felt—what? Stupid. She should have gotten him to pull the trigger.

In bed several hours later but miles from sleep,

Eleanor rolled over and felt the sheet pull across her right thigh and left shoulder. Throwing off the blanket and spread, she yanked at the sheet until it lay flat again. She jerked the covers back up and closed her eyes. It was no good. That idiot carjacker had gotten her all wound up. Oh, baloney, who was she kidding? She hadn't slept in ages, even on nights when there weren't any attempts on her life. Her eyes flew open and she shot bolt upright. "Of course," she said aloud.

She stared into the dark, vaguely aware of the turning of the red digit-minutes on the clock on the dresser. Her heart was racing now, beating the clock at about a thousand to one. She could take out a contract. Death wouldn't require any courage at all. It would come right out of the blue in the middle of a normal day. If she could arrange it. How on earth did a person buy a contract? What would it cost?

At 2:30 she got up, took her guitar out of its case and ran a few scales, softly, so as not to disturb old Miss Wiemers downstairs. When she'd calmed herself enough, she played the lilting, sad melody of the Vivaldi *Concierto* in D that everybody was playing these days. It had been Hal's favorite. He'd even worked up a little jazzy sax accompaniment to play with her. At least, he said he had. Only he'd broken up with her before they ever tried it out.

A few tears dropped onto the shoulder of the

guitar. She wiped them off and put the guitar back in its plush case.

As she stood the guitar back in its corner, she went over the plan again. One day next week she'd go up to Colfax Avenue. Lots of sleazy bars there, the kind of place where those types hung out. Of course, it might take a couple of tries before she found someone.

She stared at her drawn, strict face and too-big nose, red now from the tears that wouldn't stop. Why didn't they tell you when you were growing up that it turned out like this? That life was nothing but a chain of broken, wrenching relationships. It just wasn't worth it.

She could go ahead and hit the bars tonight, only there was that guitar convention in Berlin. It was only a couple of weeks away. She could do two more weeks—a breeze after the endless months of pain she'd already endured. She sighed and wiped away a few more tears. Why had she signed up for the thing in the first place, requested a whole week off "for her sister's surgery"? Why hadn't she realized back then, in the time of stupid hope in July, that Hal would leave her just like all the rest? Still, she might as well go since she'd botched her suicide and the school had already approved the leave. Besides, it'd be a shame to waste all the money she'd forked out for the plane ticket and the hotel.

Sitting on the bed, she took the brochure off her night table and read the line-up of competitions, concerts and workshops for the hundredth time. At least she would enjoy the immersion in music for a few days and when she got back she would definitely make the arrangements.

A new thought struck. "Oh, my God, yes!" she said aloud, throwing the brochure back on the night stand.

Ten minutes later, she drove out of the parking lot and headed toward Colfax.

Martin Girelli, failed carjacker, paced his one-room apartment on 17th and Downing, grinding his teeth and muttering. Stupid woman ready to off herself. Just his luck. Now he'd have to explain it to Sonny tomorrow and get a drop-off point for another try. If they even gave him a second chance. Damn.

He grabbed his five-pound weights off the bathroom shelf and pumped the iron until he was out of breath. He checked himself in the long mirror, flexing his biceps. They didn't look any different from yesterday. He gripped his hands across his prominent ribs and struck a Charles Atlas pose. Pathetic. Like everything else about him. He ran a hot bath to relax himself.

With a sigh, he removed his gold watch, the only nice thing he owned, and laid it on a stool he'd sneaked from a dumpster and repaired with a couple of odd screws. If he didn't end up on the streets next week, he'd sand it down and paint it, make it look real nice, like the dresser and the sofa table he'd salvaged. He stripped off his faded red boxers, climbed in the bathtub, and slid under the warm water.

As he emerged and lathered his hair, he allowed himself to dream. A plush apartment with a balcony overlooking a park would be nice. A shower. Maybe a Jacuzzi. He slid down again and came up through the layer of suds, snorting at his own stupidity. Scrap all that. Never gonna happen if something didn't change. What a life. What a loser. Not even the army wanted him, with his severe bunions on both feet.

He wiped his eyes and looked across at the gold watch, radiant as the sun on the chipped gray paint of the old stool. Seven years of selling shoes and that's all he had to show for it. His big blowout purchase—a week before his pink slip. Well, no more. Something was gonna change, all right. Next time he wouldn't fail. His heart beat faster.

Somewhere, deep inside, a fold in his psyche tried to open. A tiny glimmer of guilt sparked through the opening. He pinched it shut.

3

October 26, 1989

Stepping behind her friend Francine up to the old brownstone house, Lily squirmed as vibes of resistance slithered faster up and down her spine. This house, of all the houses in Denver. Hadn't it always given her the willies when she walked past it on the way to and from work? So what was bringing her here? Why now?

The whole evening had felt out of sync. She'd never been to a guitar concert before in her life, much less a classical one. She wouldn't have gone to this one either if Chrissie, her boss at Skyflower Books and Cures, hadn't given her the tickets because her new hot guy didn't dig square music. And Lily would certainly never have gone into this house. But wait a minute. There was a secondary vibe here. Not nearly so spooky.

She whispered to Francine's back. "You sure somebody actually, like, lives in this old crate?"

Francine turned with her long broom skirt

lifted to clear the steps. "'Course I'm sure."

"What'd you say his name was?"

"Phillip Redding. You know, the Redding family that owns that glass factory out south of town? They're, like, practically the richest people in Denver."

"Never heard of them." Lily's shoulders twitched as she passed under the graceless roof over the bare, rectangular porch that ran across the front of the house until it met a round, windowed turret at the corner. "How can anybody live here? I mean, it's only the ugliest house in the whole city. And it gives me the creeps. Like it won't let me out or something. I look away every time I go by it."

Francine nodded. "Like, Drabsville. I guess they didn't believe in curves or color in those days," she said, flipping her long, unfettered red hair over her shoulder with a heavily beringed hand. "All I know is, this is where he has the receptions after guitar concerts. He gives them all the time, you know."

They stepped through the hall, past a dark stairway and into the already crowded living-dining room. Two chandeliers hung about twenty feet apart in the huge space, and lamps brightened several of the small tables against the walls, but the corners remained gloomy and inhospitable.

"That's him," said Francine, giving Lily an elbow jab and pointing at the tallest man in the room, who was just emerging from what was probably the kitchen.

Something arced between her and the man, something powerful and flashy, like sparkles in the green band of a rainbow, and so fast it hit her like a stun gun. Lily froze in her tracks. The floor beneath her rocked. She groped at a table for support. Her hand landed on a coaster and slid to the wall, but she never took her eyes from his face. What had hit her? Destiny binding them? She shook her head in quick jerks and stared. Slowly, his aura began to glow, green swirling gently into blue. It was beautiful and wistfully longing—and all wrong in this horrible box of a house.

The Phillip person hadn't taken two steps into the reception room before he was surrounded by women. Only his head rode above them, but in the shifting gaps, Lily watched his aura shrink away from them and turn yellow around the edges. Stress. Far out. A cool looking guy like that stressed out over a bunch of old maids whose body language was so clear they might as well be shouting. They wanted him. Desperately.

Nice looking, but—well, he was old. Like way off the charts old. Easily in his forties. Maybe even fifties. Why would he be so uncomfortable around women? Hmm. His aura didn't have that tinge of purple that gay guys' auras always had. He didn't even look rich. And Lily was connected to him in some way. That was clear by the vibes racing all over her back and the floor that was still shaking under her feet.

Francine elbowed her. "What're you staring at?"

When Lily didn't answer, she said, "You're flipping out over Phillip Redding? Are you off your tofu or something? Every single woman in town has had a go at him, and a lot who weren't so single. You got no chance, Lily."

Lily tore her eyes from Phillip for a second to answer Francine, but nothing came out. She went back to ogling him, unwilling to lose a minute of that beautiful, struggling aura.

Phillip stretched his neck like a threatened giraffe, mumbled something to the women, and squeezed sideways through them to shake hands with the evening's guitarist, who had just pushed into the room behind Lily and Francine.

As Phillip passed Lily, he looked directly into her eyes and said, "Welcome. Please help yourself to whatever you like."

Vibes spun like a gyroscope in Lily's stomach. She scooped air with her hand, as if she could capture a little of that gorgeous color and breathe it in, but she could hardly breathe at all. When Phillip moved toward other guests, her knees gave way and she grabbed Francine's arm for support.

October 27, 1989

Lily sat down cross-legged on her cushions. She shoved the crust of a cream cheese and alfalfa sprout sandwich aside. YingYang jumped into her lap. She reached over them for the Denver *Sentinel* and read the article about Phillip in the "Out and About" section for the eighth time, skipping the opening paragraphs about the concert and the reception:

> Redding, Denver's most eligible bachelor, co-owner of the Redding Glass Works, is planning to celebrate his 45th birthday while attending the Fourth International Guitar Convention in Berlin, November 7-9. Asked whether he was planning to participate in the competition, Redding smiled and said he was only going to listen; competition was not his thing.
>
> Well known for his love for music and his unstinting support of guitarists of all kinds, Redding is sometimes criticized for his lifestyle, which seems to consist of music and little else. "He's never worked a day in his life," complains one acquaintance. Still, Denver's female singles seem to find him...

Lily threw the paper on the brown carpet, shooed the cats off her lap, and lay back with her hands entwined in the back of her thick, wavy black hair. She gazed absently at the filmy, dusty blue parachute fabric that billowed from the center of the ceiling to the corners, softening the rude right angles of the room.

"'Denver's female singles,'" she mused. She'd gotten an eyeful of them last night. She'd even checked the women's hands, and every one of them had short nails on the left hand and carefully shaped ones on the right, just as Francine had explained before the concert. Guitarists, one and all. Against them, Lily really didn't have a chance. Francine was right.

But they fried his aura, right? And she was in his karma, right? Wasn't that why his aura had been so visible to her when Francine hadn't even seen it? Hadn't his aura spoken directly to hers? Didn't he live just a few blocks from her? She had to give it a try. Anyway, maybe she had an ace in the hole.

Ying jumped onto her chest and nudged her chin. Idly scratching him behind the ears, she looked into the black slits of his pupils. "I know, Ying, 'Denver's female singles' are one up on me, digging the guitar and all."

She sat up, put the cat in her lap, and regarded her peasant blouse embroidered in faded primary colors and the thin, slightly frayed brown and rose paisley skirt that tickled her ankles when she walked. A wave of dismay rolled over her, but she let it pass.

"Okay, maybe they're two up on me. They're, like, more presentable," she said, stroking Ying, feeling his back arch and vibrate with purring. "I suppose you'd call these 'shirttail-hippie clothes,' just like Mom. As if I didn't know hippies are, like, practically prehistoric. Everybody knows that. Still, it was a gas being a hippie, even if I only got in on the last few gasps before the movement died."

Dolefully fingering the silver ankh dangling from one ear and the slender pink crystal hanging from the other, she glanced across the room at the flea-market Yamaha guitar she'd just bought and at the book open on the floor. *Beginning Guitar.*

"Okay, I can learn to dig the guitar, and beginners belong on the list of 'guitarists of all kinds,' too, don't you think?" she asked Ying. "I know! I'll ask Phillip to teach me. If he says yes, I'll take some money out of my savings account. I must have about $500 in there. I'll get some new threads and dress nicer for him. He'll fall in love with me. That's in our stars. Later I can get a better job, help Daddy and Mom, and get a new life."

She ran her hands from her shoulders to her wrists, as if she could shed the old life like a snake skin. It didn't make her feel different. The old life was stuck to her like Cody's peace sign.

But a new life was what she'd really dig.

Right on. She needed to settle on something meaningful. That thought pulsed in her head for a minute. Something to...what? Put a little good in the world. Yeah, that was it. Send some good vibes out there. This business of doing your own thing, letting it all hang out, had lost its cool. All it had brought her was the feeling that she wasn't much use. She didn't have a root down anywhere.

Not that she hadn't had a blast.

Yang joined Ying on her lap again.

"Hey, guys, you should have made that scene in Haight-Ashbury in '82."

YingYang fixed their four blue eyes on her.

"You trying to tell me you did, in one of your eighteen lives? Okay, that's cool."

Right after Haight was the Zen trip. And then that witchcraft class down on Seventeenth and Downing, practically in Phillip's back yard. She remembered Shalmon, the black dude who'd conducted the witching sessions. That talisman. With the memory came a deep, quiet moment in her head. The ace in the hole.

She picked the newspaper up again and smiled at the picture of Phillip Redding, filling in the colors from memory. Sandy hair, gray eyes, a rather weak chin, and a button of a nose just red enough to speak of too many receptions. Her future man, generous as a pauper. And, like, totally marriage-resistant, according to Francine.

She ran her finger down the picture.

"It's not that I want to, like, use you, man," she said. "I just know it's supposed to happen. And when we get together, I'll work at making you happy. 'Course, you don't seem to be unhappy now, but I'll really try to be good for you."

Turning the cats off her lap, she pushed up from the cushions. She kicked aside the doggie basket, giving a long, sad sigh for Siddhartha, the puppy that had run away to escape YingYang. She stepped over a plastic sack of granola and in two more steps knelt in front of the ironing board, spreading her skirt over the floor to keep the tinkly fake brass coins around the hem from getting under her knees.

"I know I bought a book from Shalmon," she said aloud, running her finger along the bindings. From *Clock- and Counterclockwise: What Crystals Tell You*, through her high school French book, to *Only Eat What Doesn't Have a Mother*, there wasn't a single title that reminded her of the witchcraft class. "Burn out!" she said. "I know it had a little flask inside a pentagram on the cover."

She brushed her teeth to clear her mind and returned to the cushions. "It'll turn up," she said, settling into her yoga position. *Ah oom*, she chanted, starting her mantra.

In a few minutes she realized she wasn't getting into it the way she should. She focused her mind on incoming vibes.

Something prickly but also soft and pliable.

She turned her head in the direction of the vibes and opened her eyes. The doggie basket. She jumped up and grabbed the old blanket out of it.

A book fell to the floor, a slender paperback with a pentagram on the front, enclosing a little brown vial. *Parsley, Sage, Rosemary and Mandrake Root: Witchcraft from Your Windowsill.* The last bit of the title was chewed away.

"Far out!" she crowed. "That was fast." She went back to the ironing board and grabbed the astrology chart for 1989. November. They'd even given his birthday in the article, or pretty close. She flipped through the worn pages and found Scorpio.

Unexpected sources bring great changes in your life just before your birthday, not without some danger. Be open to suggestion.

Lily sat cross legged on the cushions again, laid the witchcraft book on the astrology book and lit a candle behind the pile. She laid the picture on top of the books. "You see, Phillip? It's in your karma."

A negative vibe poked at her, and she closed her eyes to examine it. Witchcraft was the wrong way to go about it? Well, if there were any other way that would work for sure, fine. But Phillip was a rich man; every old maid in town wanted him. The idea that he might look past all their lovely guitar-playing hands and discover Lily with her ten stubby fingernails and her clunker guitar was just too far out. Too risky.

The vibe wasn't convinced. Give up the whole unworthy idea.

Give it up? What was unworthy about it? All she wanted to do was make him happy and feel she could contribute something positive. What was wrong with that? No, the situation was desperate. She had to come up with a radical plan. Several radical plans. Because it was his aura that spoke to her, and wasn't that, like, already in the spheres, where magic hung out and things like guitars and money and age didn't matter? Not to mention the fact that her witchcraft was white magic, not the other kind. Harmless. Aimed at good things, in fact.

She smiled down at Phillip Redding's head lying atop her little pile of hope. "You'll never get out of town," she crooned, running her hands over the arching backs of YingYang.

4

October 27, 1989

Phillip Redding squirmed in his chair and wished Allison, his sister-in-law, had chosen different seating for her dinner. Directly across from him, without so much as a flower arrangement to buffer them, sat Glenda Lessing, another one of Allison's colleagues and the date he hadn't even known about. She'd moved to Denver at the beginning of the school year. She was a tall, prim, and not unattractive divorcee whose fiercely pedagogic eyes were fastened on him like chalk on a blackboard.

He glanced at Allison at the head of the table, her face aglow with approval, and fantasized a swift kick under the table. Already the comfortable evening with family was a bust.

Glenda dabbed at her pretty pink mouth with the corner of her napkin, never taking her eyes from him. "Allison tells me you have part ownership in a glass works," she said. "That's fascinating. I visualize a whole family tradition of artisans, whose latest generation blow glass art works like I saw in Mexico."

Phillip and Roger both laughed aloud.

Roger answered her. "Think window panes, Glenda, and mirrors and industrial glass. We haven't had a glass blower in the plant for half a century."

"Aha," she said. "And what is it you do at the plant?" she asked Phillip, smiling brightly.

Phillip stretched his neck in his collar and pulled at his tie, wondering which of the two female types this one would turn out to be. "I...ah...keep an office there."

"You're the vice president or something?"

"Well, nominally. I just get my income from the works."

"So what do you do?"

The pivotal question. Now for the pivotal answer. "I play the guitar, I read a lot, sometimes I travel..." He trailed off, knowing he was adding concrete to the foundation under his playboy reputation.

Glenda paused through a millisecond of shock. "So you don't have any kind of job? Then why do you have an office in the glass works?" she asked across the glittering silverware and cut glass goblets. Her gray eyes had just hardened to the same glitter.

"Uh, no to the first question." Phillip shoved at something orange on his plate. "As to the second, I think they're storing silica in there at the moment." He turned to Roger for confirmation.

Roger swallowed quickly and laid his fork back on his plate. He nodded. "I'm afraid we all agreed several years ago, Glenda, that Phillip has no real head for business."

"None," agreed Phillip. "Believe me, the plant runs a whole lot better when I steer clear of it. At the university, I tried studying business, but that first year was such a flagellation of spirit that I finally dropped that major and switched to arts. I guess you might say I came out as a Bachelor of Dabbling. I never did settle on any one art, although now my interest runs to music..."

Glenda backed away slightly, without curving her ruler-straight spine. "Guitar music, yes, you said that. How interesting. So how do you spend all your time, if you don't work? I hope you don't mind my asking."

Phillip stretched his neck again. "Look, I live easily on my income from the plant. I have more than enough money, and I don't spend my time trying to scrape more of it together."

Allison put down her wine glass and said, "Don't sell yourself so short, Phillip. What he really does, Glenda, is look for ways to spend part of his money where it does some good. He's one of the world's few real Samaritans. He's just very modest about it."

Glenda aligned her knife and fork neatly on her nearly empty plate and pushed it two inches from the edge of the table. "Really. So you're basically a philanthropist."

Allison answered before Phillip could react. "I guess Phillip is a sort of Renaissance man *cum* humanist *cum* guitarist. His current project is some colored glass for the new low-income housing."

Glenda's eyes widened and her right brow rose a little. "Stained glass windows? In a housing project? It'll be broken within a week."

"That's what I told him," said Roger.

Phillip turned to his brother. "One more vote for your side, Roger. Well, maybe I should consider something else. Some monster-proof equipment for the playground?"

Glenda said though a tight smile, "Probably much more practical." She shook her head and regarded him like a student she'd just caught cheating. "I just can't imagine not working. I've been working my whole adult life."

Allison rose and began collecting plates. "Are we ready for coffee and dessert?"

Phillip jumped up. "Let me help," he rushed to say, waving the half-risen Glenda back into her seat. He grabbed his plate and a serving bowl and followed Allie into the kitchen.

When the door swung closed behind him, he whispered hoarsely, "I'm furious with you, Allie. I asked you not to do this again."

She turned from the sink and her face was soft with concern. "What, help you find a wife so you don't have to live the rest of your life like a hermit in that old box of a house downtown? I'm just trying to make you happy, Phillip."

"Who says I'm not happy now? Look, Allie, it wouldn't be so bad if all these blind dates you come up with were anybody but your colleagues. Teachers just don't sit well with me. You being the exception, of course. Although I'm rethinking that. I may just look for a different favorite sister-in-law."

"Ha. I'm your one shot at a sister-in-law, buster. So what's wrong with teachers?"

"They're all so—I don't know. Spinstery or something. Predatory. I've seen that stalking look turned on me too many times not to recognize it. It makes me all gawky. And if they don't stalk me, they invariably disapprove of me. You saw that on her face. I'm just not willing to justify my existence to her or any of them."

"But..."

"No buts. Believe me, a teacher is the last kind of person I want to get mixed up with. And in my experience there's only one other kind of woman in the world. So I have a choice between the teacher-types and the gold-diggers. I don't want either one. My life is just fine the way it is. All I really wanted when I came tonight was a nice dinner with you and Roger before I leave for Berlin. And that's still all I want." He started for the door.

"But..."

Phillip turned, raised an index finger, and flashed a stern warning from his eyes. "If I want a wife, I'll choose her myself, thank you."

Allison pointed her own threatening index finger at him. "You're doomed to marriage, favorite brother-in-law. And somebody else is going to have to find her for you. You wait and see."

On his way back from Roger and Allison's comfortable home in the suburbs, Phillip heard Allison's caring voice say the word *wife* again and again. It vibrated like a huge tuning fork in his stomach as he drove onto the small parking lot that had been his main reason for buying the old Westover Mansion. Here his receptions got no complaints from neighbors about lack of parking, since the lawyers, their staffs, and the civil servants who worked in the area cleared out at five.

He picked up a plastic cup that was still rattling around the lot, even though he thought he'd picked all of them up this morning. He unlocked his front door, and for the first time in a long time, he noticed the stale beer and wine.

Really, the place smelled like a bar after closing time.

Wife. Ping went the tuning fork.

He walked into the living-dining room, which he'd left for Lupe to clean tomorrow. It looked like the aftermath of a demented musicians' picnic. Lipstick blots puckered at him from napkins that littered the table tops, along with used *hors d'oeurves* toothpicks, plastic glasses, and paper plates with olive pits and half-eaten Swedish meatballs. Sheet music had served as coasters on most of the tables. A music stand lay on the floor in front of two chairs. A scratched guitar lay on the turret window seat, its D string missing. The string was hanging from the chandelier over the dining table.

Wife. Ping. A woman in this house—would hate it. Definitely not a great house to live in. The roar of one-way traffic from downtown intruded almost without interruption. The carpets showed more wine stains and cigarette burns than Turkish design. The dark curtains made the house gloomy at all times.

The stolid mansion itself, built in the plainest of taste, squatted among the skyscrapers like an old brown rock in a crystal showcase, too ugly to be of interest even to the Colorado Historical Foundation.

His house was only good for giving parties.

He could sell it. Or keep it for the parties and live someplace nicer. That kind of life with a wife wouldn't be so bad. They could travel. They? Ha. It took two to make a "they." And his choices were teacher or gold digger. He'd never met any other types. The tuning fork in his gut swung in the other direction. A wife? God no. Too much of a complication in simple and happy life.

Phillip put a flamenco CD by Paco de Lucia on the player and let the music take over. He went upstairs, bouncing to the rhythm of a light-hearted *guajiras*.

5

November 1, 1989

Ten feet tall and a man with a future like a great big rainbow, Martin Girelli, successful carjacker, strolled through Sonny Levinsky's used car lot on Colfax. He couldn't wait for Sonny to tell him. He was in. No more shoe sales for him. No more poking at the bottom of his pockets for bus change. No more picking cast-offs out of dumpsters for his furniture.

Well, okay, he'd enjoyed refinishing that stool. Maybe he could do that kinda work as a hobby when he was rich. But he'd have a lot of nice new stuff, too.

He entered Sonny's trailer-office and sat down in front of the grungy old metal desk. His elation fizzled a little at the sight of his contact: Sonny's biceps, so huge they strained his skin allotment, bulged out of the arms of his black Trans-Am T-shirt. No taller than Martin, he threatened by sheer mass of muscle and obvious willingness to use it.

His face menaced with heavy black whiskers that bristled darkly just below the skin and refused to be shaved below a five o'clock shadow.

"I told you I could do it," Martin said, grinning to hide the struggle to hang onto his new stature.

Sonny drew his heavy brows into a long, skinny black brush. "Well, yeah. But three attempts at a car-jacking ain't so hot, Marty, I gotta tell you."

"I know, I think my bio-rhythms were down for the first two."

Sonny didn't look as if "bio-rhythms" hit home anywhere.

"Bad luck," Martin explained. "I mean, that one broad was already trying to off herself, and the old man was stone deaf. You gotta admit, that last one was a doozy, though. A Blood in Blood turf." He wouldn't add that the Blood had been so high on dope when he grabbed him in front of the Seven-Eleven that Martin had convinced him he was a taxi driver, and when they got to the appointed corner, he'd told the doper to get his bags out of the trunk. The Blood had passed out opening the door, rolled out, and lain with his head on the pavement, his feet still in the car, and his red cap shining in the streetlight like a railroad signal.

Sonny waved away the glorious memory. "So,

okay. The bosses still wanna give you one more test."

Martin's shoulders sagged.

Sonny sat up a little straighter and cocked his head on his almost neckless shoulders. "Is this gonna be a problem?"

"No, oh, no. Not at all." Martin squeezed his hands together between his knees to get the squeak out of his voice. "Me, I'm up to anything."

"Okay, so here's what goes down. We got a real easy contract."

"A contract?!" It was a whisper, but at least it didn't squeak.

Sonny cocked his head to the other side. "Is this gonna be a problem?"

"Uh, no, I just thought contracts were something you, uh, worked your way up to."

"Well, yeah. I only done a few so far myself." Sonny leaned back in his swivel chair and put both hands behind his head. His pecs and biceps curved obscenely. In the little indentation between muscles just below his sleeve was a tattoo of a skeleton in a coffin. "It's just that this one is a total pushover. Some old broad. Somebody wants her took out in Berlin." He leaned forward again. "So here's the deal. You gotta get to Berlin by November 6. You check into this hotel." He shoved a yellow post-it note across the desk and then a second. "You go to this address and you get your info and some tools from this contact."

Martin tried to control his hands as he took the papers. "So they gonna spring for the airfare, right?"

"Naw. That's part of the test," he said with a frown. "I gotta tell you, Marty, I don't think they got much faith in you."

Martin stuffed the notes in his trench coat pockets to hide his trembling, and stood up. "You tell 'em don't worry about a thing. I can handle it."

He walked blindly out onto Colfax on legs too wobbly to support him and sat down in a coffee spill on a bus bench, staring at the two memos in his hands. *Guitar convention, Berlin, Hotel am Zoo, November 7-9,* read the one in his left hand. *Breitenhofstrasse 23, November 7 or 8, ask for Max,* read the other.

"Where am I going to get air fare to Berlin?" he asked aloud into the din of traffic. He didn't quite drown out the voice that was coming out of the fold in his psyche, wide open now, like a mouth screaming, "Oh, my God, this is murder. I can't do it."

A Colfax bus ground to a stop in a cloud of diesel exhaust and gutter dust. The door opened. One second later the driver shouted, "Hey, buddy, you gettin' on or what?"

Martin jerked his head up. "No, sorry."

As the bus roared off, he looked at the date on

the memo again. November 7. He looked at the date on his beautiful gold watch. November 1.

6

November 1, 1989

Lily moved the spout of the watering can from the potted St. John's Wort to the baby gingko tree that her boss was so proud of. She hummed sweetly at its strange, fan-shaped leaves, which some customer had told her were the missing link between needle and leaf trees. Usually she could stroke the leaves and practically meditate herself into the beginning of time with the gingko, the oldest surviving tree in the world, but today she couldn't get into it at all.

She turned her head back to the front of Skyflower Books and Cures. Where was Chrissie? Two days now Lily had been covering for her, and Chrissie hadn't even told her why. She didn't sound sick. She sounded downright dreamy and happy whenever she called to check on things. Practically spaced out. Was she smoking something special?

"I don't, like, care a flip about what she does,"

Lily told the gingko. "I just got something important to do now, and I need time to be sure it comes out right." She hadn't even opened the witchcraft book because the shop left her no energy for working out the plan. And every day got closer to the time when Phillip would leave for Berlin. Bum that Chrissie, anyway.

The tiny wind chime above the front door tinkled.

"Hi, Lily," said Chrissie, stepping in and stopping with her back to the doorjamb. Her presence radiated tension, but Lily couldn't read her aura because the hanging plants blocked one side and the other was against the light of the front window.

"Chrisseee," Lily shrilled. "Where've you been? I need to go home and start on my plan."

"Plan?" asked Chrissie vaguely, fingering the pink quartz crystal that hung around her neck.

"I gotta find a way into Phillip Redding's life. Make him like me. I told you that on the phone yesterday."

"Oh, yeah." Chrissie's head raised and her long blond hair fell over her eyes. "What about Cody?"

"Cody? Cody's gone. I haven't even thought about him for two days."

"Listen, Lily, I, uh, I should've told you, Cody's not gone. He came by my place. I guess it was right after you threw him out. That's why I didn't go to the concert. We're gonna be crashing together for a while."

Lily's brows pinched together. She strode through the vitamin aisle to the front and turned Chrissie until she could see the aura. Aha. Crashing was, like, the wrong word. Thrashing was more like it.

"Don't do this, Chrissie. I don't care for me, 'cause I got something else on my mind now, but Cody's a leech. He'll, like, clean you out. I don't know why I didn't see it a lot sooner."

Chrissie smiled a sly but dreamy smile. "You just don't know him the way I do. He's gonna come in the shop and play while he writes."

Lily stepped back and frowned at her. "That's what he told you? He doesn't write, Chrissie. All he does is scribble out like a million versions of this senseless poem about a poppy plant that has flowers shaped like Korea or someplace. And as for his playing—you ever listen to him? The sitar sounds like a cat fight."

Chrissie narrowed her eyes. "He said you'd be mean. But he promised me. And he says his playing will help the business, so I can pay him something. He's starting right after lunch."

"Cody's coming? With both of us in the shop?"

"Oh." Chrissie shoved her hair behind her

ears. The dreaminess disappeared from her face
and she kept her eyes on the fern plant to her left.
"No. The thing is, Lily, since I'm going to be
paying Cody, I can't afford to keep you on."

Lily's heart crashed into her pelvic bone.
"You're firing me?"

"No, I think it's called 'laying off.' Isn't that
what they do when they can't afford to pay the
workers anymore?"

"Don't do this Chrissie. He's gonna make you
sorry in the end. You'll see..."

"Look, as soon as the business picks up like
Cody says it will, I'll call you to come back. To
give us a break. Sorry, Lily, that's just the way
bells chime right now."

Lily grabbed her Madras tote bag with the
spangles sewed in the pattern and stalked out
without saying another word. She walked hard on
her heels to beat out the anger. Cody had made
good on his threat, after all. And Chrissie, well
Chrissie was just being as stupid as Lily had been.
Burn out. Here she was with the trust fund
running out and no job. She had to do something.
Man, she was in Desperationville.

When she passed Phillip's house, she didn't
avert her eyes, as she used to. She checked every
window for a glimmer of that lovely aura. Okay,
he wasn't there now. Maybe in a couple of hours.

At home, she threw herself on the mattress

and took several deep breaths to calm her anger at Cody and Chrissie, who'd just handed her a big blank future. In-breath: *huh huh huh huh*, out: *ph ph ph ph*.   When her heart stopped flopping, she thumbed through *Parsley, Sage, Rosemary and Mandrake Root: Witchcraft from Your Windowsill.* Fingering the many pages that were half torn out or badly mangled by sharp puppy teeth, she muttered, "Geez, Siddhartha, I didn't know you were this fond of printer's ink."

Gathering YingYang to her, she stretched out on her cushions and flipped languidly through the chapter on "Curses."

The cats peered into the book with her, purring in stereo.

Here and there, her eye snagged on an ingredient of interest—toad's venom, donkey's lung, tomb dust, even the fat of an unbaptized baby. Huh. She certainly didn't have any of those on her windowsill.

She read through one recipe that called for holding hog's dung and charnel in the left hand, pricking them three times with a knife, then pricking the underside of a table three times and leaving the knife sticking in it. The last part of the spell was missing. "Worse curse for the witch than the witchee," she told the cats. "I wonder if it was supposed to make the victim turn into a pig or a table. Or charnel, whatever that is."

Meowing, YingYang jumped over the book onto the floor. They circled each other for a minute before jumping back on her chest, where they crouched in their stalking mode, intensely focused on the book.

Lily's eyes popped open wide. "Hey, you guys, cool it. What do you think this is, a séance? You'd think you were really into witchcraft or something."

YingYangs' heads turned, their four blue eyes as intent on her as they'd been on the book.

"Hey, guys, I'm not into curses," she said.

YingYang lost interest and stalked off, their tails in the air.

Lily went back to her research. The chapters were alphabetized, with "Flight" listed next, its invocation calling for thorn apple fruit, monkshood, belladonna, and hemlock. "Flight into the next world, no doubt. This stuff is, like, heavee, more serious than I thought."

Lily skipped "Healing," inserted a finger at the beginning of the "Love" chapter and stopped at the next, "Protection." She was holding about half the book between her fingers. "Well, this is encouraging," she said, "even if most of the pages are half shredded. Gotta be, like, something in here I can use."

Actually, only one recipe was still intact. It called for powdered periwinkle to be mixed with ground worms and disguised in a meat dish. Jeez, who had ground worms on a windowsill? Anyway, it was much too risky. She'd never get Phillip to dine alone with her, and a crowded restaurant meant the mix could end up in the wrong hands. Besides, she'd have to eat it herself. Her vegetarian stomach lurched. No, it had to be a potion, something she could hand him personally and they could drink together. Not that she'd figured out that part of the plan yet.

Page 47 started a new recipe: "...otion for the Inducing of L..."

Was that Lotion or Potion, Love or Lust?

At the bottom of the page were the riddled remains of the instructions: "Mix thoro---k while intoning---chant. The---er will fall irrev---in love with the next ---use of rose oil to enhan---your own pow---beauty, and aura---"

So it was love, and the "...otion" must be potion, since the person administering a lotion would automatically be the next person the administeree would see, right? And the "k" must be "drink."

The last word on the page was "Caution:..." Page 48-49 was missing. Caution what? Maybe the ingredients would offer a clue.

Castor oil. No way. Even if she went out and bought some for the potion, she'd never be able to gag it down herself. Olive oil, maybe. No, there was that nice coconut scented massage oil in the medicine chest. That ought to do it. After all, oil was oil.

Jasper. "I thought that was, like, some kind of petrified wood," she muttered. A mineral of some kind probably. Maybe zinc would do. Aloe wood and root. No problem.

Cinnamon, nutmeg, long pepper. What on earth was long pepper? She could use some of the dried ginger root bits that Cody hadn't chewed on. That was pungent. And ginger was a long root.

It was all to be mixed with one part brandy and one part water. Rose oil was no problem. What chant were you supposed to do? Of course, she only knew one, anyway.

Lily thumbed on through the recipes, stopping a long time at the one that called for mandrake root. Judging by the fragmented text, it was supposed to affect sex in some way. Mandrake root. Wasn't that a poison? Maybe only in large doses. Probably had to be special ordered, anyway. She could get some if she could find the people who ran the bookstore where the witchcraft class had met. 'Course, the last time she'd been by there, the store had been shut down with yellow police tape stretched across the door and the broken window.

There were other types of spells that had nothing to do with things that grew on her windowsill, and she flushed wide-eyed when she read them. Way too personal for this stage of the game. Still, she could use one or two later if the first one didn't work or started to wear off.

Tossing the book aside, she pulled at a hank of hair and said to the cats, "This is, like, way far out, man. I ought to ask someone for advice." But she'd lost Shalmon's phone number ages ago, and she'd never seen any of the other people from the class again.

"Hey, YingYang, you think I should give it up? Maybe just walk right up to Phillip and, like, tell him I love him?"

The cats stared.

"Right, he'd laugh in my face. Besides, that'd be a lie. I don't love him. Yet."

She read through page 47 again, then stripped, washed, brushed her teeth, and rubbed herself down with rose oil, fully intending to do the mixing and chanting naked. However, the fall chill was in her apartment. She donned her fuzzy Sears robe, looped the rubber-lined colorful wooden rings in her long, thick black hair so that it fell around her shoulders like a macramé work, and took the coconut scented oil to the kitchen alcove. She lit all the candles she could find in spite of the southern sun streaming in the tiny kitchen window.

She set out a clean plastic milk container and

then changed her mind. "Got to be something natural," she said, taking out a ceramic oil jar with a cork. No, too small, and it smelled rancid when she uncorked it. She settled on an old green Coke bottle and a wine cork.

She opened the refrigerator and pushed cranberry juice and milk containers aside looking for the brandy she'd shoved in there after the Solstice party last summer. The bottle said Bailey's Irish Cream. Bummer. She looked again, sure there must be some brandy. She could get dressed and go buy some, but the time was getting short. There was no telling when Phillip was leaving and she had still to plan a way of slipping the potion to him.

The watered down Irish Cream did not look appetizing. She added some ground cloves to give it more color and took a whiff. She shrugged. "Oops, the chant," she remembered, and began the *ah*, *oom* she'd learned in the witchcraft class. She smashed the ginger root, aloe, and zinc tablet under her heaviest glass, and added them to the mix, along with cinnamon and nutmeg. She took another whiff and said "Hmmm," between an *ah* and an *oom*. At last the coconut scented oil went in; she corked it all and shook the bottle gently.

The oil did not want to mix with the Irish Cream.

She turned it upside down and shook

vigorously.

The oil blended by giving up its ghost in small bubbles that rose to the top and let off little wisps of smoke or steam.

She stared into the bottle for a long moment, then backed away and sat down on the cushions. "I'll never get him to drink it," she said aloud. "Him, heck, I don't think I can get myself to drink it." A minute later, she added, "Of course, if I don't test it first, and it's too awful to drink, I lose my one shot at Phillip."

She approached it again and uncorked it. It gave a tiny "whoosh," and she sniffed. She cocked her head and knitted her brow. She took the glass she'd used to smash the ingredients and filled it with water. She tipped the bottle very slowly and let the tiniest amount touch her upper lip. Nothing happened. She licked at it, the water glass in hand, ready to wash it out of her mouth instantly. Nothing happened. It didn't even taste too bad. Sorta like a gingerbread latte. With a gritty texture. "I'd better wait a few minutes," she thought.

Ten minutes later she took a small swig, and in a few minutes another. "Wow, this stuff grows on you." She smiled and picked up the recipe book again, looking for an indication how much of the potion she was supposed to drink. "Well, I guess I get half and he gets half."

She took a few more swigs, and soon the bottle

was half empty.

"Oh, man, what've I done? I don't even have a plan for getting Phillip to drink it yet." Keeping her eyes on the floor, she stepped over and closed the front curtain lest she fall for some passerby. "Anything could happen. I'll go there now and see if he's home. If he's not, I just have to wait and keep my eyes on the ground till he comes. Jeez, just my luck, I'll fall in love with an ant or a squirrel or something."

Yang was suddenly at the corner of her vision.

She shut her eyes tight and turned toward a stack of recently folded clothes. Groping, she found her long wool skirt and a sweat shirt with a few scraps of flowers still embroidered on it. Her eyes still closed, she put on her coat and a big floppy tam, grabbed the corked bottle, and left. Outside, she rushed down Seventeenth toward Phillip's house, her head down, eyes barely open.

At the corner of Downing she ran full tilt into a thin man only slightly taller than she. They grabbed each other to keep from falling and looked briefly in each other's eyes. Lily felt little bubbles rise inside her and give up all her resistance in little wisps of smoke or steam. A wrinkle passed down her vision, like a pleat in time, and left her rigid. The Coke bottle smashed to the pavement.

The man mumbled something and rushed away, pulling at a dark, wet stain on the back of his trench coat.

She stood like a stone pillar for a minute, staring after him, and then looked down at the brown potion oozing toward the gutter, hissing as it went. Here and there its bubbles were smoking. Next to it lay a yellow memo sheet. She reached down and picked it up as if it were an injured bird.

It read, "Guitar convention, Berlin, Hotel am Zoo, Nov. 7-9." Her head spun. She closed her eyes and the face came back to her, all tormented and—what?—panicky or something. The brown eyes set close together and the wispy brown hair, the acne scars—the most beautiful face she had ever seen.

Her head was aswirl. That face. It set her all squishy. But Phillip. He was in her Karma. Like, for sure. Determined, she tried to turn in the direction of his house, only a few blocks away.

Her feet had taken root in the pavement.

That face. The guitar convention. What did this beautiful new man have to do with it? Same place where Phillip was supposed to go. Same date. Were they both in her Karma? She flashed on an old Laugh-in re-run she'd seen on TV. The Fickle Finger of Fate. It was pointing at her. If it would just quit wobbling like that...

Absently, she threw the largest pieces of broken glass into her purse and shoved the rest into the cracks with her shoe. The cork had disappeared. Maybe he'd kicked it someplace.

Half an hour later Lily squeezed through the door of her bank just as the guard tried to close for the day. She cleaned out her small savings account. At home, she called Francine, her guitar friend, for information, wrote a $50 deposit check to the International Classical Guitar Society Convention, and reserved a plane ticket to Berlin, arriving on November 5.

7

In Weimar, German Democratic Republic, Ursula Kimmig lugged her guitar up the three flights of stairs to her home. Tension stretched between her heart and her head, taut as an E-string and more uncomfortable than the damp autumn cold. She'd just played the Bach "Chaconne" for some of the other students, a trial run before the competition. She'd made mistakes she hadn't made for years— buzzing frets, wrecking the rhythm, missing notes and barely covering the lapses. She hadn't realized how scared she was of the competition.

She shoved the guitar case through the living room door and crowded in after it. The door struck the china cabinet, as usual. She turned right and squeezed her thin frame between the dining room table and the baby grand piano on which her father gave lessons. She laid the guitar case on her day bed by the front wall. She'd get something to drink and practice the fugue again. While both parents were still at the Academy, she'd have a couple of hours of practice time to iron out those rough spots.

Her heart skipped a beat at the thought of the competition, barely a week away now. Had the years at the music academy really prepared her for this? All those Westerners listening, people from all over the world. In Berlin. *West* Berlin. They would certainly make her a lot more nervous than a few colleagues, and today she'd played like a chimpanzee. But other nerves were buzzing like a missed fret, too, over something that had nothing to do with the competition. She couldn't quite get the cause to surface. She stifled the buzz and focused on the "Chaconne." Thank God she had the next few hours alone.

Just outside the door footsteps scraped to a stop, followed by a loud, demanding knock.

Her heart sank. Joachim. Even if it weren't too early for him to be off shift, she'd know by his heavy boot-walk that he was still in his gray People's Police uniform. *Volkspolizei*. One of the feared *Vopos*. Well, she wouldn't let him in. She opened the door a crack.

He shoved in without waiting for an invitation, forcing her to retreat from the door.

Annoyed, she checked her anger. That was one of the things one never did in East Germany— show anger to a *Vopo*. Or defiance. Instead of closing the door in his face, she backed into the path between the china cabinet and the table.

"What are you doing here, Joachim? Aren't you supposed to be working?

He took off his cap and ran his hand through his straight brown hair. "You mean you didn't hear me?"

"Hear you?"

"I called you twice. I've been following you almost since you left the Academy."

"I just gave a bad performance of my competition piece, and I'm worried about it. I need to practice now, if you don't mind..."

"I see." His hazel eyes turned hard and his thin mouth stretched into a straight line. "Why do you always put me off this way, Ursula? You know how I feel about you. And you know I don't like the idea of your going on the other side of the Wall like this."

"It's only a couple of days, just a competition, Joachim."

He went on as if she hadn't spoken. "I suppose you heard over West Radio or something about all those Russians demonstrating with their stupid candles and leaving on trains because that idiot Gorbachev let them go. Who knows what those capitalists on the other side might do now that they've heard that? I want you to stay here. Or go play in a Russian competition. Why are you doing this anyway? You know we..."

He was headed right for his usual subject.

Why did he assume there was anything between them just because they'd known each other forever? "Joachim, you know I can't back out now. Remember what it took for me to get permission to go?   All those forms, all those interrogation sessions.   But couldn't we please talk about this when I get back?   Right now I really need to concentrate..."

He closed the door and leaned against it with one foot crossed over the other, staring straight at her.

She saw in his eyes the power to stop her if he wanted to, and saw him deciding whether to use it. She knew he'd refrained from blocking her application, a fact he'd obliquely reminded her of several times.

Finally he smiled. "All right, take your trip to the West. But don't put me off any longer. You know we'll marry sooner or later. It's obvious to everybody. I've known you since the *Kinderhort*." He reached out and pulled a strand of her blond hair forward. "What were you, three, the first time I saw you with your school bag practically pulling you over backwards?" He let the hair go and put his large, cold hand on her face, so like the rest of him, cold and calculating, using the party for his own gain, but professing belief in the socialistic ideal.

She stiffened and drew away, sensing the

imposing frame of his whole body, realizing that even if he were stark naked, she'd still see him in the *Vopo* uniform, a man of power. A man to keep away from. She knew her voice would shake, but she said, "I'm not going to marry anybody until I see whether I can make a name for myself as a concert guitarist. And the only way I can do that is to compare myself to guitarists from the other side. Besides, I don't think any degenerate capitalists are going to kidnap me."

Frowning now, he went on as if she hadn't spoken. "We'll have it easy. We won't have to live with my parents more than three or four years, I promise. We'll have our own apartment in record time."

Ursula laughed in spite of her nerves. "You think so? And how will you manage that?"

His face darkened with her laughter and gave her the feel of an icy nail scraping her spine. She felt like shoving him out onto the landing, but he was blocking the door.

His hand moved to her neck. "I'm going places in the Party, I told you that. I'll have influence."

He was going to stand there and elaborate with his thumb on her Adam's apple. Frustrated, she gave up getting rid of him and slipped out of his grasp into the tiny kitchen. She found two glasses and lifted a bottle of mineral water from the crate under the sink. "I thought you told me you didn't believe in using the party for individual gain." She poured him a glass and handed it to him.

"I don't, but if it will get you to say..."

The telephone rang. She jumped and sloshed water from her glass onto the floor.

Joachim started and paled. "What's that?"

"A telephone. Just a minute. I have to answer it."

She slid past him again, between the cabinet and the table, to her parents' bedroom. The telephone stood on the window sill in the far corner.

After she picked up the receiver, she got a long moment of dead line and then a click. Another student had told her it was a *Stasi* wiretap, but she found that hard to believe. Why on earth would the State Security Service, the *Staatssicherheitsdienst*, want to listen in on their conversations? None of them was a security risk. Still, the thought made her feel flattened by a hostile weight.

When her mother's voice came over the line, it sounded hollow. "Uschi, isn't it nice to have a phone? It makes things so much easier." The sound of a truck came over the line. She must be in the one functioning phone booth in front of the academy, avoiding the monitoring for personal calls from her office. "I need you to do two things.

Meyers has chickens today, each family can have half of one. Run over there first before they're all gone."

"But Mutti..." she said over another truck noise.

Her mother went on, "Also, I saw new toilet seats being delivered to the plumber down the street. Go see if you can get one or two. We'll offer one to *Herr* Reitler to fix the light fixture over the piano."

"Mutti, I have to practice..."

"You can practice later. You have to get those things done. Otherwise, there's nothing for supper."

When she hung up, Ursula sighed, sitting on the edge of the bed with her shoulders drooping and her knees touching the wall under the window sill. The practicing would have to wait, as usual. There was always something. By the time she stood in line at the butcher's and waited at the plumber's, her father would have returned and begun his lessons and her mother would be playing her cello in the bedroom. The kitchen was too small to accommodate a seated musician; the bathroom was unheated. She'd have to work on her essay on socialistic overtones in the Pachelbel "Canon" until they were finished. If she ever got rid of Joachim. And she needed to get rid of him for good. She could not marry a man she would always fear.

He was backing away from the bedroom door when she returned. "Why didn't you tell me you had a phone? When did you get it?"

Angry at his eavesdropping, she barely managed to stifle a frown. "Last week. You can't imagine how surprised we were. Father ordered it the day after I was born because I was so premature. It took them twenty years to deliver it. Every time it rings, we all think it's some kind of alarm."

Joachim took a small notebook from inside his jacket. "What's the number? Maybe I won't have to chase you all over the streets to talk to you."

No, he was not going to get the number. "Listen, Joachim, I have to go now. Mother wants me to run some errands."

Annoyed, he shoved the notebook back into this jacket. "I'll walk you down, but I'll come back and get it later."

When she'd gotten away from Joachim and started up Klopstock Street, Ursula let her mind wander back to the telephone. Did West Germans have to wait twenty years for a phone, fifteen years for a car, and forever for an apartment? Well, of course they didn't. You could tell by West German television, bad as the reception was with the blocking, that things just went faster on the other side of the Wall.

It was nearly nine before she could pull the guitar out from behind the piano. She turned two dining chairs around, laid her sheet music across them, set up her footstool, and began with some warm-up exercises, simple arpeggio patterns for the right hand.

The noise of running water and clanking dishes in the kitchen and the radio in the bedroom battered at her concentration. She closed her eyes in a search for patience, and when she opened them, she was staring at the wall opposite her. Suddenly it seemed scarcely a meter away, squashing everything in front of her into a collage of polished wood, mattress, piano strings, keyboard, chair legs, and tabletop. She could barely breathe.

It must be the thought of going to the West, the realization that in a week she'd be on the other side. What would it be like? Were the people really as grasping and violent as the papers said? Would they jeer an East German guitarist? Or were they like her, only not afraid, not looking over their shoulders all the time? Her heart beat faster; her hands began to shake and perspire. She skipped the scales she normally ran and went right to the Bach to see how she would play when she was this nervous.

Her left hand dragged and squeaked on the bass strings. Her right fingers, sticky with nervous perspiration, snapped off the strings before the stroke was well placed. She missed every modulation. She sounded like a beginner trying to tune up. At the corners of her mind a thought was nudging through to consciousness: space, she needed space. A place where she could breathe, could practice any time she wanted, could pass another person in a room without having to climb over the furniture. She had no hope for such a place. She closed her eyes and played an old etude from memory. It didn't sound much better.

Now the nervous buzz from before rattled at the edges of her concentration and then exploded into her brain with such terrifying clarity that both hands froze in position.

Stay in the West.

Her heart stopped. Great God. Her parents. Reprisals. Her plans. The danger. An uncertain future over there. She tried to put the thought far away, but it lay about her like a bubble of light that pushed the crowded room into the distance.

Stay in the West.

Ursula put the guitar away and went into the kitchen. Her whole body was still shaking.

"That didn't even sound like you playing," commented *Frau* Kimmig, drying her hands on the dish towel and laying it over the dishes in the rack.

"I know. I sounded horrible. I guess I'm just nervous about the competition. I think I'll go down and take a walk to clear my head."

She stepped through the outside door that had been hanging by a single hinge for two years. Tsking at it, she let it stand for all the disrepair and neglect of the city around her. No new hinges, no work in the factories for lack of parts, no one to pick up the broken bicycles and umbrella frames that littered the streets.

She hardly noticed the chill fog as she retraced her steps past the plumber's shop, the street lit only by the dim windows of the buildings that were still livable. She crossed the open triangle between the Schiller and Goethe houses and walked toward the center of town. Cranach Square in front of the Hotel *Elefant* and around the corner from the Academy was the only place lit at this time of night.

She stepped into the pool of misted light and looked at the Lucas Cranach house and the neighboring houses with their brightly colored Renaissance gables. She peered in the other direction toward the buildings lost in the fog. She knew them like her own pockets. Their roofs sagged; the half-timbering and the old bricks showed through the crumbling stucco like mange. She looked again at the bright side of the square. The restored houses, their restoration touted as the beginning of a city-wide renewal project twenty years ago, were a sham, a showpiece for the tourists who stayed in the Hotel *Elefant*, which was far too expensive for East Germans to frequent.

The two sets of houses were just like the promise of the Party—and its delivery. The reality was that nothing worked, nothing ever got done; and the Party praised itself incessantly. Pachelbel as a socialist, indeed. He was a musician. Like her. Not interested in politics but in music. All she wanted to do was play beautiful music for others to enjoy.

She strode past the Academy, where both her parents taught music. She knew they had believed in socialism. They would never have been promoted to department heads or have gotten such a good apartment if they were not true party-liners. They'd waited all their lives for the showcase prosperity that was always coming. Did they still believe? If not, did they confide their disappointment to one another? What went on in their heads when they heard the rumors of the great changes Gorbachev had been initiating? Were they just rumors or reality?

Stay in the West. Even if she could consider it, how could it be done? Could she find a West Berliner to marry? She breathed out a quick laugh at the idea. She would have less than four days there. Maybe there would be Americans at the convention. They were supposed to be pretty rash people. But who wanted to go to the race wars and the endless poverty that made up America? Anyway, the thought was as unworthy as it was ridiculous. She could no more marry a man she didn't love than she could marry one she feared.

She was in the darkness of Klopstock Street again, lost in thought, when a voice seemed to shout in her ear, and a hand touched her arm.

Startled, she looked back. "Joachim. Where did you come from?"

"What do you mean? I must have called your name five times since Schiller Street." He got off his bike to walk with her.

"Sorry, I didn't hear you."

He looked at her sharply. "That's the second time today." His face softened. "You're really scared, aren't you? I would be, too, if I were going over there."

"The practicing didn't go well," she said. "I'm more tense about the competition than I thought."

He dismissed her nerves with a flap of his hand. "I'm sure you'll perform beautifully, just like always. Did you read the paper about Egon Krenz's new measures? How do you think things will go?"

Ursula put her head down and shrugged. She could not look at him. He wanted to talk politics, as usual, wanted her to agree with his views. She knew he didn't like the radical policies of Gorbachev. Joachim posed as such a political idealist, as if he believed the future of humanity lay in socialism.

"Come on," he said, "are you so nervous you can't even talk?" He wheeled his bicycle in front of her, took her head in his hand and lifted it, trying to see into her eyes.

She knew she'd closed her face to him and was thankful for the darkness. He jerked back if she had slapped him, moved away, and walked next to her in silence. Had he been able to read her thoughts, the decision she had to make?

They said goodnight in front of his building and she went home, thankful that he'd forgotten about the telephone in all his political talk. For the first time she understood the veil that always seemed to cover the eyes of her countrymen. A small flame of mistrust, fanned by fear, became a ring of fire that kept you alone with your most painful decisions.

She didn't know where her parents stood and couldn't confide in them. Did they ever look each other in the eye anymore? She remembered them at supper. They hadn't even talked about music, only the necessities of the table. Suddenly she could not remember the last time her parents had chatted with each other or laughed. Or even smiled at each other. Did life become such a dreary routine in the West?

The old assumption surfaced as she climbed

the wooden stairs that smelled of cabbage and old potato peels: if she stayed here, eventually she would marry someone and they would enter the life of all young couples—years of living with one set of parents or the other, with luck a one-room apartment by the time they were thirty. The thought squeezed the breath out of her.

At home again she went into the bathroom and lit the water heater hanging on the wall over the tub. The gas jets hissed around the copper tubing. She turned on the one tap and the water ran scalding hot out of the water heater into the tub. In a few minutes she turned the gas off and let the water run, cold now, until she had a temperature she could stand. By habit, she thanked her parents mentally for the convenient bathroom. In Joachim's building they still had to haul buckets of coal from the basement to fire up the water heater that took up half the bathroom. It was unbearable in the summer, and often she could tell he hadn't bothered.

She slid as much of her body as she could under the warm water in the short, deep tub. She massaged her shoulders and tried to think about anything but the West. Even as she concentrated on relaxation, the sentence she'd been trying to shut off began a rhythmic and terrifying loop in her head.

Stay in the West. Stay in the West.

She went to her bed in the dining-living-music room with a blinding light in her head and a boulder in her heart.

8

November 4, 1989

Eleanor Markeson sat in a train nearing the border between East and West Germany, fighting the urge to jiggle her knee. Why hadn't she flown straight into Berlin instead of booking a four-day jaunt through the East before the conference? Idiot, she'd told them about this, so the hit man could even be on the train, endangering the other passengers. What on earth had she been thinking? Of course the hit man might have better sense than to commit murder on a train, where his only escape was into East Germany.

She sighed and glanced out at the no-man's-land that stretched into the distance. Beyond it, dreariness. The mud-gray buildings she remembered from the last trip, the abandoned trucks and cars dotting the landscape, the hideous factories of urban East Germany in the gloom of November would do little to lift her spirits. Of course, she'd booked the trip before the depression hit bottom.

Anyway, maybe she only had these four days left. That was a comforting thought. And even if the hit man didn't find her on the first day of the convention, at least in West Berlin she'd be in a musical environment. Still, the slowing train made her antsy. Border crossings were always long and scary. What if something happened and she missed the hit? Her heart shriveled at the thought.

The train screeched and clanked to a stop next to a platform backed by a long screen of dirty corrugated fiberglass. Across from her an obvious West German, nattily dressed and looking superior to the rest of humanity, rose and opened the window to air out the crowded compartment. The dank cold of winter in Germany swept in across her, stabbing through the knit of her sweater.

Outside, the *Vopos*, *Volkspolizei*, the dreaded "people's police," checked the underside of the train with exaggerated dentist's mirrors, looking for stowaways or contraband. Now who on earth would stowaway on a train headed for East Germany? On the side away from the platform guards stood with their German shepherds, making sure that no one got off onto the tracks. Well, it was one way to keep people employed.

For forty minutes, Eleanor endured the frigid air, wishing for the nerve to shut the window herself. She was about two seconds away from asking the fresh-air-fiend to shut it when the first of the border officials stepped into the compartment, the money changer. Now she cursed herself for not having changed her money in the West, where she could have bought the East marks for ten to one instead of one to one. But the risk of being detained as a smuggler had made her cautious, scared the hit man would give up and leave. She took out the forty West marks she had and handed them over, receiving four limp and dingy blue ten East mark bills.

The money changer left without exchanging a word with anyone. Another hour went by, and Eleanor shrank more into the seat, trying to get the velour to warm her rather than sap her body heat.

The *Vopo* came in at last, a gaunt man whose uniform hung about him like a limp gray flag on cold steel pole. Without a word, he checked the visas of the other passengers, comparing faces with passports, and then snapped his hand toward Eleanor.

Eleanor faltered. She had no visa because the East German travel agent she'd booked with in San Francisco had assured her the room voucher he'd sent would serve as a visa. Her hand shaking, she surrendered both the voucher and her passport.

He checked the picture against her face and took out the voucher. Squinting, he sneered at one side, turned it over, and sneered at the other.

"What is this?" he growled.

Eleanor felt herself shrink into the seat. "It's an *official* room voucher from the *official* East German Travel Agency. It's as good as a visa," she said in the shakiest language she had spoken since German 101. Even to her own ears, she sounded like a smuggler and a spy.

"You must obtain a visa," he said, slapping the passport back into her hand. The tone of his voice brooked no protest.

"Where?" asked Eleanor, fearful she'd have to go all the way to Bonn.

"In the office at the end of the platform."

"Will it take long? My travel agent assured me I was booked on this train through to Eisenach. Will I make it back on time?"

"*Ja.*"

He stepped out and Eleanor grabbed her purse to do the same.

"You should take everything with you," said the fresh-air-fiend. The rest nodded.

"I guess you're right. Thanks. I should've known it wouldn't be easy. The last time I crossed the border, I was detained for seven hours." Still, the *Vopo* had said she'd make it. It'd be a mess if she didn't, because she was booked into the travel program they'd assigned her. And they didn't allow deviation.

She hauled her suitcase and her guitar down

from the rack and squeezed out of the train. In front of her the dirty fiberglass partition blocked her view of everything but her train and her platform. An elevated passageway at each end spanned what must be a large number of tracks. *Vopos* paced the passageways, their guard dogs straining at short leashes. One turned to stare at her. She stopped. Who knew where the Mafia had contacts? He could be the hit man. He turned and continued his patrol.

The "office" was a vast room with a single desk at one end, approachable only through a mazed barricade, as if the guards were expecting an unruly crowd of refugees from the West. The woman at the desk, also in *Vopo* garb, stared long and hard at an apparently gripping blank form before indicating that Eleanor should sit down.

"I need a visa," Eleanor started.

The woman shoved the blank form at her without glancing up. Eleanor filled it out.

The woman gave it a perfunctory glance and said, "Fifteen marks."

Eleanor took out twenty marks.

"I can't take that. You have to give me West marks."

"I don't have any more. I already changed them on the train."

"Then you have to change them back."

"Where?"

The woman motioned over her shoulder toward Eleanor's right. "Cashier."

Eleanor got up and went around a corner to the cashier's window. Looking through it she saw the same office and the same woman. There was no one else present. The woman stared long and hard at some other entertaining paper and finally came to the window. Resentfully, she gave Eleanor fifteen West marks and five East marks for the twenty East marks, then went back to her seat.

Shaking her head, Eleanor went back to the desk, handed her the fifteen marks, and waited again while the woman ruminated and finally rubber-stamped the form in about twenty places.

Her visa in hand, Eleanor asked, "Can I get back on the train now?"

"Go through customs."

"Where?"

"Past the cashier."

She found the customs window, closed and dark. Behind her she heard a whistle followed by a shuffing and a rattly rhythm that increased as her train picked up speed.

Dammit. Now she'd probably be detained in Eisenach. Would she even make it to Berlin in time for the conference? For the contract? Because the hit man might still be on the train.

9

November 5, 1989

Wolfgang Barkov, a mid-rank official of the *Staatssicherheitsdienst*, the State Security Service, hung his gray overcoat on a wall peg in the tiny, unheated foyer of his Dresden apartment. Dropping his *Stasi* identification onto the narrow table, he noticed that his wife's was there. Damn, she was home already. And he'd been hoping for a few minutes' peace to go over the day's strange events—or lack of them. Most of the day, he, along with his colleagues, had sat absently over transcripts of wire taps, hunched nervously under the foreboding of this evening's rumored demonstration.

Rubbing his hands against the cold, he went into the living room, closing the glass door behind him.

Helga sat at the table, stolid as a stump. She didn't bother to look up from the newspaper she'd spread before her. "Go light the water heater, Wolfgang. I want to bathe before we eat."

"Good evening," said Wolfgang with as much sweet sarcasm as he dared put in his voice.

"There's nothing good about it that I can see," she snapped. "Or didn't you notice anything in your department today? You'd think the world was coming to an end just because a few dissidents take to the streets. Well, we'll just have to whip them back into line before they put a lot of idiotic ideas in people's heads."

"Seems to me they've already had the ideas for weeks. You saw the West reports of all those people leaving through Hungary and Czech..."

She gave him that ego-clawing look, which she used whenever he disagreed with her.

He threw up his hands and started for the bathroom. Devil take her anyway. He was at least as smart as she was, and a hell of a lot craftier when it came to using the Party to get what he wanted. Just not as much of a bully. And never quite as decisive under stress, which was why she outranked him. He admitted that. But did she have to bludgeon her way through everything in life? Couldn't she ever just relax and be pleasant? He was desperately tired of living under her thumb.

While she bathed, he set the supper table with a little sausage from the tiny refrigerator, brown bread, butter, and Chinese beer. He worked quickly, his mind busy with the demonstrations again. Idiots. What on earth were they protesting against? A government that guaranteed them life-long employment and a comfortable old age? Try to find that in the dog-eat-dog West.

Why didn't Krenz act? Call out martial law or something? He hadn't accomplished a thing as parliamentary chief since replacing Honneker. What was he waiting for, the winds of the *perestroika* to blow the Wall right over? That moron Gorbachev. As if people were capable of governing themselves. They needed a strong hand to keep them in line.

They should've dispatched Helga to the Hungarian border, Wolfgang thought. She'd have sent them home with their tails between their legs, damn them. Or maybe she'd have gotten trampled in a stampede for the Austrian trains. He grinned.

But no, they weren't sending her anywhere, just him. His colonel had come to his desk with a distracted, forgetful air and ordered him to "escort" some group of musicians from Weimar to West Berlin on Tuesday, four days away. Guitarists, at that, unproductive ninnies. He'd have to herd them out of Weimar Monday night to get to Berlin by the morning of the seventh. But at least he'd have a few days away from Helga.

It was nearly eight when she came in, wearing her black robe with the huge purple flowers on it, her graying hair limp around her square face.

"Why didn't you turn on the news?" she demanded, sitting at the table. "Do it."

Wolfgang turned on the television set. After a minute the fanfare of the *Tagesschau*, the news from West Berlin, blared into the room. No picture appeared on the screen.

"Go fiddle with the antenna," she said, already spreading butter over her bread, out to the very last crumb in every corner, as always.

"I know, Helga." Wolfgang opened the window and jiggled a special de-scrambling antenna on the sill. "Is that better?"

"Keep turning. No, too much. Go back. Stop. Stop, I said. You went too far. Stop. Now leave it before you mess it up again."

He passed behind her to his place at the table and aimed a chopping motion at her neck. It made him feel better.

As he settled to watch the news, his anger gave way to the feeling of triumph his TV set always gave him, even if he'd had it twenty years—longer than he'd had Helga. It was the first thing he'd gotten by using his *Stasi* rank to move his name to the head of a waiting list. At the time, the wait had been two years, but he'd had his in three weeks. *Esel*, jackasses, the people who hadn't learned to use the system to their advantage. He slapped a slice of sausage on his bread as the moderator began speaking.

"*Die Nachrichten am Samstag, dem 4. November.*" "The news for Saturday, November 4. We begin this evening with a live report from the *Alexanderplatz* in East Berlin," the speaker began.

The picture switched to the *Platz*, where it panned the crowd.

Wolfgang sucked in his breath, nearly choking on his bread. Helga's jaw clamped shut and her eyes disappeared into a vicious squint at the screen.

"The demonstration is estimated at about a million people," the speaker continued. They were standing in the Square, silent as a grave in the light of a million candles. The huge bulb atop the radio tower and the lighted red tower of the City Hall, gray on his black and white set, rose like monuments to lost patience in the background. "In Leipzig, Dresden, and Kiev candlelight demonstrations are in progress as well..."

Wolfgang's mouth fell open. They weren't doing a thing. Just standing there with all those candles. His heart skipped a beat as he realized what they were doing was a lot more forceful than storming some barricade. And it was here in Dresden, too. What's more, it was on international television.

Helga slammed her hand down on the table. "That idiot Gorbachev," she shouted. "Look what he's started. He's handed every East Bloc government a noose."

"My God, there are so many of th..."

"Dresden, too," she shouted. "They have to be in front of the opera house. Get out there, Wolfgang. Go help break them up."

He jerked onto the back of his chair. Get out there with all those dissidents? Not in this life he wouldn't. There were probably as many here as in Berlin, and their sheer numbers made him the dissident, a hated dissident, at that. The demonstration was a hell of a lot more dangerous for him than for them. "For what? They're not doing a damn thing. It's not against the law to stand around with a candle."

"I don't care. Go."

"No."

She turned her piggish glare to him and he waited for her to pull rank and force him to go. But all she did was mouth the word *Feige*. Coward.

"Go yourse...," he started.

She turned back to the news. "Shut up. I can't hear what he's saying."

The *Tagesschau* continued with a summary of events since Honneker's collapse at the Warsaw Pact Meeting in Bucharest in July. It reran clips of the exodus through the Hungarian border crossings to Austria in August and September, the fleeing traitors running hunched over as if to dodge bullets, glancing back often in disbelief. It showed the thousands who'd left the West German embassies in Prague and Warsaw on special trains at the end of September, and ended with the prognosis for the "regime" of East Germany's Socialist Unity Party.

The foreboding he'd felt all through his work day was gone, wiped out by certainty, certainty of doom. Wolfgang did not need some West German idiot to tell him the end was near. He jumped up and went in the kitchen to get away from Helga. His breath came in quick gasps and his heart was trying to gallop out through his ribs. He ran his left hand through his thinning blond hair and down his narrow, sharp face.

It was going to fall. And when it did, those who had held things together would be blamed for every ill that had befallen the country since Hitler. He felt his face go ashen. The *Staatssicherheitsdienst*, the *Stasi*, would be the scapegoat. Everyone hated them under the surface because no one knew for sure who the agents were. No one liked the fact that neighbors were encouraged, sometimes forced, to inform to the *Stasi*, even if the "information" was fabricated. No one liked the universal wiretapping.

He needed to do something. Cover his *Stasi* activities. He needed time, but they'd ordered him to Weimar and West Berlin.

No, wait! His face relaxed suddenly and then he smiled. Weimar was exactly where he needed to go. And Berlin, too. The trip couldn't have come at a better time.

He grabbed another beer and started to rejoin Helga but stopped dead at the door. Now he knew how to get rid of her, too.

10

Eleanor dragged herself into the Hotel *Cäcilienhof* after a day of sightseeing in Potsdam, formerly the western suburb of Berlin. Now it was walled off like all the other suburbs, leaving West Berlin an island in the sea of East Germany. After the frustration of the border crossing, the constant fear that any misstep would land her in a remote prison, and the lonely sightseeing in Dresden, she wanted nothing more than to get out of the East. Perhaps there was a border crossing between Potsdam and West Berlin. Of course, she had a ticket for tomorrow's train to East Berlin, but maybe she could change it.

She stepped to the reception desk and waited for the clerk to notice her so she could call the East Berlin hotel and cancel her reservation. Like everyone else in the East, he seemed closed off to her by some brooding fence. Was it the political uncertainties, or were these people so accustomed to suspicion that they were as implacable as the Wall itself? Had they not noticed the breath of free air pulsing farther east? Or had they simply not been exposed to it on their news networks?

Her shoulder drooped under the weight of her camera. While the clerk sat and stared at the switchboard, she listened to murmured, reverential Russian conversations behind her in the half-timbered lobby. She tried to feel a bit of their awe to be standing in the place where Truman, Churchill, and Stalin had met to divide Germany into four "spheres of influence," but her aching feet did not feel awed. What she'd seen in the last three days was the mess the communists had made of their "sphere."

The Russians can flock here to walk on hallowed ground all they want, she grumbled to herself. They could at least demand toilets on every floor. So what if this was where Stalin gave the Soviet Union a leg up to world power? I bet even he had to go to the bathroom in the middle of the night. It was ridiculous having to go downstairs and across the building in her bathrobe.

She cleared her throat. She saw the muscles in the clerk's jaw tense, but otherwise he might as well have been a corpse in sitting rigor mortis. She plopped her camera on the counter next to a notice of an amateur soccer tournament in Potsdam the next day. Still he stared at the switchboard.

It had been like this everywhere. She'd arrived at Eisenach eight hours late, with no time left visit even the Bach house. Officials everywhere were curt and had never heard of the word *helpful*. The feeling of being a pesky or suspicious intruder had worn her down. Her spoken German was in a tailspin, and when she did try to talk to people, they constantly looked over their shoulders. The requirement to register at the police station in every town; the cold, crowded train rides; the inconvenience—none of it had changed since the last time she'd spent a week traveling in the East.

So much for all the talk about new winds blowing. These people wouldn't know how to enjoy freedom if it blew right up their noses. Eleanor had had enough. If she had to pay a king's ransom for an extra night in West Berlin, so what? She wouldn't be needing the money after next week. A small smile curved the corners of her mouth and gave her courage. Maybe the hit man was already there. The thought pulled her through time to the guitar convention. Only she had to get there first. She shuffled her feet and dropped her purse on the counter with a thud.

The clerk turned slowly in his swivel chair but said nothing.

"Could you please place a call to the *InterHotel* in East Berlin for me?"

The clerk tugged at his dark green uniform vest without bothering to get up. He looked terribly put-upon but gestured toward the back of the lobby. "It's a long distance call. I have to put it through to the booth there."

"Why would it be long distance? The hotel can't be more than—what?—twenty five kilometers from here."

The clerk tightened his lips into a thin line. "The wires go around both East and West Berlin."

"Aha." Well, of course, that explained everything. Eleanor dragged her belongings to the booth as he returned to the switchboard.

The *InterHotel* answered in the form of a very efficient, cool, female voice. Thank heaven, this would be a little easier.

"*Guten Abend.* Good evening. This is Eleanor Markeson. I want to cancel my reservation there for tomorrow night."

"You cannot cancel it."

"I beg your pardon." She felt her shackles rise. "I made the reservation. I can certainly cancel it."

The voice was icy now. "The East German Travel Agency made the reservation. Only they can cancel it."

Too annoyed to be polite, Eleanor said, "Well, you just make a note that the room is going to be free. I'll call the Travel Agency tomorrow morning and get my money back. You'll hear from them." She hung up, angry but relieved. Tomorrow— West Berlin!

At seven the next morning she was at the train station, along with most of the population of Potsdam, as the train rattled in. It was already so crowded she gave up the hope of finding a seat and stood in the corner of an open space at the end of her car with her guitar standing on top of her suitcase against the wall.

The train stopped every ten or fifteen minutes, and by the third stop, Eleanor was squashed in like an asparagus in a can, unable to move anything but her eyes. For an hour she rode that way. Then the train stopped again and a voice over a loud-speaker said, "This train ends here. Everything gets off."

"'Everything?'" Eleanor whispered to herself. She waited for the car to empty out enough for her manage her luggage. When she looked out the door of the train, she thought, My God, it's a purée of human flesh. From one end of the platform to the other, tightly packed bodies shoved each other toward the center stairway.

Beyond her platform were countless others. A single pedestrian bridge spanned them all across the middle. Past the tracks shorn fields stretched as far as she could see in the lifting fog. There was no building of any sort, nor any signs to orient passengers. In the distance she heard a jet take off, and then she realized they had skirted both Berlins completely and were near the East Berlin airport,

Schönefeld.

She watched the crowd for a second before being shoved from behind. There was not a thing she could do but join the mass. She was struggling to insert her guitar case into the slow stream of bodies when a train arrived behind hers and the loudspeaker said, "This train ends here. Everything gets off." Another arrived several tracks over, to the same squawked announcement. Someone shoving past her by using her suitcase as a horizontal slide remarked that the trains were bringing people to transfer to this train, which was returning to Potsdam for the soccer tournament.

Eleanor was near panic. She looked up at the one stairway that led to the overpass. There were four people abreast going up the stairs and one row struggling to make its way down. The stairway was about fifty feet away, but it took her twenty minutes to reach it because other people kept shoving past. By the time she stood at the bottom step, there were four rows of people lumbering down the stairs, carrying baby carriages, huge net bags of soccer balls, picnic baskets, even bicycles. There was one row elbowing and shoving its way to the top.

There was no room on the stairway for her suitcase or her guitar. Using both arms, she hung them over the railing on her right and started up, stepping sideways. Without the pressure from behind, she would not have made it up the first step.

About four steps from the top, she noticed a man with a huge beer-belly standing at the corner where the steps met the bridge. The crush of people behind him was so great that his stomach hung far out over the railing. Ow, that must hurt, shot through her head. Why was he just standing there? Hit man? Her heart slammed against her ribs. No, surely not here in this crush. He grimaced, eying her luggage. She gave him a weak and guilty smile, hauled the guitar and suitcase over the railing, and squeezed them in front of her so as not to hit him.

When she was directly behind him, he put his hands on the railing and shoved backwards with all his might.

She was lifted off the concrete and lost all control of her movements.

"*Ach, bitte,*" she wailed. In her mind she saw herself go down, trampled to a bloody stain on the bridge, her guitar smashed to a mass of splinters and tangled strings. Not death by squashing, use a gun, her mind pleaded. Not now, not here. No one in the entire world knows where I am at this moment. Tears started. Not that anyone cares.

She still had not found the ground under foot again when a short, bald man came elbowing his way through the crowd, yelling, "*Lassen Sie mich durch*!" "Let me through." The pressure of the crowd diminished slightly, and Eleanor's right toe hit the bridge. The man took her guitar out of her hand, turned around, and shoved it out in front of himself like a battering ram. *"Kommen Sie mit*!" he commanded over his shoulder.

Eleanor's mouth dropped open, but she couldn't muster a single word. She had no choice but to follow—he had her guitar. She held her suitcase in front of her to keep the channel open and followed.

He plowed the crowd with the guitar all the way to last stairway, went down it, and then put the guitar back in her hand. "This is where you catch the train to East Berlin," he said. He turned on his heel, and disappeared into the throng.

Eleanor, her mouth agape, could not summon the presence of mind to say "thank you."

Who was he? she asked when her mind stopped reeling. Oh, my God, *Stasi*! Her heart skipped several beats. I don't believe this. They must have gotten suspicious when I tried to cancel the room. He was sent out to watch me; then he must have taken pity on me instead. A *Stasi* agent with a heart? Do they make them like that?

Still shaking, she remembered: he'd said East Berlin. She wanted to go the West Berlin. She looked around for a map of the train line to see how she could get to a border crossing. There was none. Nor a schedule of departures. Frustration and depression reamed a pulsing black hole in the middle of her back that vacuumed up her strength. It was too much: the crowds, the luggage, the cold—when all she wanted was to get where the hit man was, if he hadn't already given up and gone home. She couldn't deal with this kind of complication. I'm just going to ride to the end of the line and then take a taxi to the Travel Agency. At least the worst part of exiting the "German Democratic Republic" is over, she told herself. She was almost right.

In the East Berlin train, crowded as the first one, Eleanor rode to a huge station in the middle of the city. The loudspeaker said, "This train ends here. Everything gets off."

Eleanor looked out the smudged window from her seat in the farthest corner of the car. There was no sign to tell which station it was. She looked around at the others, shoving slowly toward the exit. They were all very well dressed, like East Germans who'd gotten permission to visit relatives in the West, or West Germans on their way home. That meant that this might be the main Berlin border crossing, *Friedrichstrasse*. A fellow passenger confirmed where she was, and Eleanor gave up the idea of going to the Travel Agency if she was already this close to getting out. Taxis were almost non-existent, anyway, and where there were any, the line of people waiting was a great deal longer than the line of taxis.

She allowed herself to be swept down the steps, out of the building, and around the corner to a large concrete square in front of a plain building. A rumor circulated among the crowd that the doors didn't open until noon. She glanced at her watch. It was just after eleven. She tried all three telephone booths on the side of the square to call about having her money refunded. Not one of them worked.

When the doors opened, Eleanor found herself in the middle of the crowd. As before, other passengers glided by on her slippery cases. She was among the last to go in.

Inside, the checkpoint was divided into two main sections, one for East and West Germans, one for everybody else, both fronted by mazed barricades. Inching through the maze, she watched as the one official checked the hundreds of foreigners through. He never smiled, never uttered an unnecessary or friendly word; but he scrutinized every traveler, checking faces against passport pictures. Most of them he waved on around a corner of the counter and down a hall. Every once in a while he'd point in another direction and the people would disappear behind a divider.

Eleanor handed him her passport. He glared

at her, checked for her name on a list, shoved her passport through a little window in the wall at his side, and said, "Wait over there," pointing to the holding area behind the divider.

She stood among the Turks, the Arabs, and the Indians, all of whom were clearly spies or assassins. Without her passport she felt like a political amputee. Her legs were so tired she had to lean against the wall for support. Her feet hurt, she was exhausted, and her stomach was growling loudly enough to make the spies and murderers glance at her and grin at each other.

One by one the thugs were called back, received their papers and went on. A few new ones took their places. Then there were no more people coming in. And still she waited, cursing herself for the whole stupid jaunt through the East.

Finally the passport slid back through the window, the guard motioned her over, and told her to go through customs.

Eleanor grabbed her passport, picked up her luggage and trudged through a passageway to a room where several customs officials were pulling everything out of suitcases, feeling the linings, opening books and cosmetic bags. Only one was free. She started toward him, staggered slightly, and he waved her on. I must look even worse than I feel, she thought, and smiled wanly at him.

Before her was a double door. And behind

that was West Berlin. The knowledge lifted her spirits. She used her suitcase to push the right door open, fully expecting to see the *Kaiser-Wilhelm-Gedächtniskirche* a hundred feet away. Instead, she was looking at a flight of metal-edged concrete steps. She climbed them, and at the top she found the same train she had gotten off of two hours earlier. Her suitcase dropped to the floor, her shoulders sagged, and tears burned her eyes. "Hit man, where are you?" she said aloud.

The whistle blew and the few people remaining on the platform hurried into the train. Eleanor grabbed her suitcase and ran after them. She found a place to stand right outside the restroom at the end of a car. "If I begin to see landmarks of West Berlin, I'll make it to the convention," she thought. "If not, I'll lock myself in the rest room, get out my pocket knife, and to hell with the hit man."

11

November 6, 1989

Horst Bauer stood at the window of the West Berlin police station with a ham sandwich in hand, staring absently out at the fog. In his mind he was staring out at the incredible panorama of the sun drenched Rocky Mountains behind Denver, where he had spent six months exchanging information and training on organized crime. He dreamed of going back to that sunny, spacious land someday, where you could drive for an hour and be alone in the mountains, so hidden in the forest that you felt the "civilized" world, with its crowded, stinking, noisy cities, was only the product of some hideous dementia.

Of course, he was stuck here; they didn't hire German police in Denver, much less in the mountains, where he had spent almost every free day skiing. But vacations... The *swoosh* of skis turning on powder was whispering in his ears as he bit into his fingers. He looked down and realized he had finished the sandwich without knowing it.

He downed the last of his coffee, threw his trash away, and headed back to his desk to write up a report on the afternoon's patrol. What a waste of time, both the activity and the report. He'd checked the vendor's licenses of all the over-aged hippies and the Turks, Africans, and Indians selling junk jewelry to the tourists on the *Kurfürstendamm*, had run a few off, and gathered a little useless information.

A message lay on top of his stack of forms, a call from Scott Donahue, his mentor in Denver, who'd become his great friend. With a smile he checked his watch for the eight hour difference and decided to call Scottie at home. Sunday morning. Just barely a decent hour. If he wasn't off skiing, he'd be getting ready to watch one of those strange, brutal American football games on television.

"Hey, Horst!" Scottie shouted into the phone. "How ya doin'?"

"Great. You need not to yell. I can hear you as if you were here standing. It is very good to hear your voice."

"Yeah, likewise." Horst could hear the smile in his voice.

"Shines the sun over there?"

"Of course. But I think there was a little snow in the mountains yesterday. Anyway, Keystone's getting one run open next week."

Horst sighed.

"Listen, buddy, there's a reason why I called. Word's on the street here that there's a contract out on some woman who's gonna be taken out in Berlin. You know anything about a guitar meeting over there in the next few days?"

"No."

"Well, that's where it's supposed to go down. I couldn't find out anything about the woman, but I got a description of the hit man. And get this, he's supposed to be some amateur who doesn't have a record for so much as glass bottles in City Park. A real dork."

"What means '*dork*,' please?"

"That's somebody who can't ever do anything right."

Horst wrote the word down, *dorck*, and said it three times.

"Here's what I got on the hit man," Scottie continued. "Brown hair, brown eyes, pitted face, maybe five foot six, skinny, thirty or so."

"Five foot six. Is that tall or small."

"Real short for an American."

"It sounds like about fifty percent of the German men."

"Sounds like an easy bust, too. Listen, we want to talk to this guy if possible. We're pretty sure he's someone trying to break into the Mafia.

He won't have had contact with anybody big, but maybe we could work our way up from the contact he had, who we arrested yesterday. We'd give him witness protection, if you can get him before he does any harm."

"Okay, I'll see what we can do here."

They talked a few more minutes about Scottie's cabin in the mountains and the friends Horst had made, then said good-bye. Horst hung up and walked down to his captain's office, not seeing the straight, sterile gray halls or hearing the sounds of keyboards and interrogations. He was hiking from the cabin to the lake with a fishing pole in hand. But as he passed Rainer Moltke's desk, he was jolted back. Rainer played the guitar. Horst stopped and waited a second for him to get off the phone.

"You know anything about a guitar class in Berlin in the next days?" he asked.

"What kind of guitar?"

"I don't know anything about guitars. How many kinds are there?"

"Well, electric, acoustic, and then they're divided into folk, rock, classical, jazz."

Horst screwed up his face and scratched his cheek. "Hmm. What kind do you play?"

"Jazz, mostly."

"Well, if a woman goes to a guitar meeting, which kind would she most likely choose?"

Rainer shrugged. "Classical or folk, I guess."

"Anything going on in those areas?"

"I can ask around."

12

His suitcase in the small trunk of his *Trabant*, Wolfgang Barkov drove down his street, trying to find smooth passage along the two rutted strips that had been torn up years ago, one for the laying of a sewer pipe and the other for a cable to the municipal TV antenna out on the hill. No one had ever bothered to replace the cobblestones; it was impossible to get both sets of tires on the stones in the middle, and the sandy mud was dotted with deep puddles. He clucked in annoyance all the way down. Sometimes the failures of the regime made him feel like demonstrating, too.

He drove quickly through Dresden, jolting over the noisy, uneven cobblestone streets, past cyclists, clanging streetcars, and *Trabis* exactly like his with their clouds of stinking blue exhaust. He yielded only to the expensive *Wartburgs*, which cost more than most houses and for which the waiting period was fifteen years.

His mood was as dreary as the city around him. Heavy smoke of brown coal rose from a thousand chimneys and mixed with the foggy drizzle, shutting his apprehension in the tiny *Trabi* with him.

For the first time in years he noticed the gutted cars, washing machine drums, and mangled bicycles that blighted the city. This was the way the world would see Dresden when the government fell. Well, let them. He wasn't going to take any blame for it.

The *Stasi* offices were in a mud-gray building with flaking stucco that had been built after the war. It was the same color as every other post-war building in the country, unadorned by a single cornice, a speck of color, or even a sign. He went directly to the car pool office and requisitioned a *Wartburg* for the long trip he had planned. He certainly wasn't going to jolt the teeth right out of his head driving a *Trabi* on the so-called *Autobahn*, which went without warning from two-lane cobblestone roads to uneven four-lane highways, on which there were still one-lane bridges.

"I'm going to Weimar to do some background checks on the musicians," he told his superior. "I'll just stay there to escort them tomorrow night."

The colonel gave him a long look but said nothing. That look rattled him more than the *Autobahn* as he left town.

Impatient with his slow speed in the fog, Barkov drove to Erfurt, where the *Stasi* active files and archives were housed, thankful it was only a few kilometers from Weimar and he would not have to explain any discrepancy in the kilometers he drove. As soon as he reached the outskirts of Erfurt, he parked the car out of sight on a side street, grabbed his new Italian brown leather briefcase, and rode the streetcar to the center of town along with somber children and drab, unsmiling women carrying shopping bags. The archive building was so much like his own office building that he would have recognized it even without an address.

He shoved his *Stasi* card through the bottom of the bullet-proof window just to the right of the wide metal door to the basement. "Captain Barkov to investigate the file of Ursula Kimmig, Rainer Bloss, Sandra Peter, Uta Bartholdt, and Manfred Streit," he growled, reading off the list of Weimar guitarists.

The guard, a gaunt man who had been at his job long enough not to question Barkov's aggressive authority, logged him in by name, ID number, date, hour, minute, and second. Then he shoved the card back, and punched the buzzer to the heavy door into the stacks.

Wolfgang strode through it and down the stairs, his shoulders heavy with fear. No one was allowed to examine his own files, much less tamper with them. If he were caught, he'd be disciplined within an inch of his life and probably sent to the Polish border.

The room, by far the longest he'd ever seen, contained endless rows of shelves, all housing fat, two-ring binders with finger holes in the spines to allow removal from the shelf. For years he had been complaining about having to write up reports instead of entering them in a master computer. Now he was grateful there was a file he could alter. He repeated aloud the one name on his list that was close to his own in spelling as he made his way through the stacks. "Bartholdt, Bartholdt..."

He turned into the second aisle labeled B, squeezed past a stolid woman who was evidently updating a file. Pretending to search, he watched her out of the corner of his eye. She moved the top file to the bottom so that the files were in chronological order, except the latest, which she laid on the top. "Bartholdt," he said again, running his finger along the binders until he came to Barkov, Wolfgang. His file was far thicker than he'd imagined.

He glanced past the woman and across the aisle to the N files, where several other women were working. He hadn't known so many people would be down here. And they were *Stasi*, people who knew the rules and would be commended if they caught him and turned him in. For the first time he felt the fear of the *Stasi* that the schmucks felt.

He couldn't risk standing here with his own file in hand. He needed a place to work unseen. At the end of his row, another agent had papers and binders spread all over a table. Barkov took his binder and walked slowly down the side aisle until he found a table at the end of the X-Z row, where no one else was working. His heart thrumping against his rib cage, he opened the binder.

The first item in his file was his supervisor's report on his last assignment, his recruitment of Walther Resweber as informant. It had been an easy assignment. Resweber had run over a young woman not two hundred meters from the opera house in Dresden and been convicted of drunk driving. Wolfgang had offered to have the affair stricken from his record and his sentence revoked if he would report on conversations he heard around him at the construction sites where he worked. No names need be mentioned.

At least not at first. Wolfgang laughed grimly. They were always so gullible.

A new realization choked the silent laugh. His work with Resweber was only three days ago. His hands shook. If the filing was that fast, he was in a race with time.

Behind him, a paper rustled. It was so close, he jumped. He glanced around.

A squat woman with a face like a toad was directly behind him, staring as if she expected him to vacate the table immediately. She stood solidly with her weight on her left foot and her mouth turned down on the left side. The stance of authority.

He bluffed. "I need at least another half hour," he growled and turned his back to her.

She sniffed and moved away but glanced back in anger.

It was too risky, spreading his file out. He'd have to take the whole damn thing with him. The thought stopped his breath. Stealing a file was a whole different matter. He wouldn't be sent to some political mudhole. He'd go to prison.

Would someone discover that his file was missing or would the government fall first? Either way, he stood to lose. But this was Monday. In a few hours he would be in Weimar to escort the musicians to the West. By tomorrow night he would be safely away and could find a way to burn or destroy the file.

He took all the papers from his briefcase, mostly blank forms, and inserted them in the binder, leaving the last page of his file on top, an innocuous report on his interrogation of a suspected dissident. He closed his file in the briefcase and took the binder back to the shelf much thinner than it had been before.

Next he pulled Helga's file from the shelf and thumbed to the back. If it wasn't damning, he'd find a way to add something. But as soon as he'd read the last four or five reports, he realized it wouldn't be necessary. She'd been praised consistently for her work in "defection prevention." She'd sent a lot of people to prison. Or shot them.

For a moment, Wolfgang stood and stared blankly at the files. He'd always sensed there was some reason why she'd suddenly been transferred from Berlin in the mid-seventies. Had she been the border guard who'd shot the man approaching the wall because his little boy's ball had rolled into the no-man's-land? The international outrage had gone on for days, and the government had thought it prudent to move the guard. There'd been a rumor the guard was a woman.

He'd never known exactly what she was involved in, but he knew she'd taken a dutiful pleasure in it. Now it was clear why she'd been so upset at the thousands defecting over the Hungarian and Czech borders, where there were no standing orders to shoot to kill. Well, the dissidents and the West would just love this when they got their hands on the archives.

There was no doubt about it—as soon as the government collapsed, Helga would become a pariah. She'd either go into hiding or get caught.

Either way, she'd be out of his hair forever. If necessary, he'd see to it that the people knew about her file.

Not until he was sitting in the streetcar again, the briefcase weighing on his lap like a time bomb, did it occur to him to wonder what he would do after his world fell apart.

13

Lily sprawled in one of the maroon leatherette chairs in the lobby of the Hotel *am* Zoo, her stocking feet on the polished table, her duffel bag on the floor next to her. She'd registered and been told she was in a room with another American woman who'd wanted to save on her stay. That was cool. At least the room wouldn't cost so much.

A glance at herself in the mirrored column beyond the table told just what she'd suspected— no aura. Burn out, she thought, I need a nice long meditation. If her long skirt weren't so narrow, she'd draw her legs up on the chair and assume her lotus position.

Her eyes felt grainy and her brain floaty. She was still vibrating from the rough flight over the Atlantic. It had been too bumpy to eat, read or watch the film. Even the stewardesses had looked green when they weren't strapped in their funny seats. And then there was the flight from Frankfurt to Berlin, which had been like a flight from Denver to Colorado Springs, barely clearing the power lines and going straight from take-off to landing. She hated both.

She was waiting for the wonderful man with the yellow memo. Now her confidence in their karma faltered. Maybe she was in the wrong place. Or maybe the memo he'd dropped was for somebody else and he was just delivering it. Or maybe it was for last year. Or next year. Bummer. Here she'd spent all the money she had left to be with him and he wasn't even here. She closed her eyes and replayed their crashing into one another on the corner in Denver. Surely that wasn't an accident. Was it? Her heart constricted. Please, karma, let him come in now.

The door swung open and a balding man with a very important aura walked in like he owned the hotel.

Burn out. But before she could lament any more, her stomach let out a gurgling growl. Though it was late afternoon in Germany, her stomach demanded breakfast. Not that she could afford to eat in the hotel. Still, how much could they charge her for a yogurt with a little granola thrown in? She gazed around the lobby looking for something that resembled a restaurant.

Beyond the reception desk on her left was the entrance to the bar. Opposite that stood a bulletin board on an easel in front of what must be the conference rooms, covered with lists and glossy black-and-whites of guitarists obviously far out into their music.

She was just getting up to go ask about a restaurant when he walked in carrying a bag not unlike hers and wearing a dark tan trench coat. He looked cold and scruffy and divine. His aura was definitely missing, too. He stood in the doorway for a minute, staring around as if he'd just arrived from Uranus, while bell boys and guests milled past him, shoving him aside.

Lily's spirit rose like helium.

When the traffic thinned, he moved along the front wall to the counter, put his left elbow on it, and walked along it to the first receptionist. She gave him a big, phony smile.

Lily moved behind him in time to hear him say, "...a few days, maybe till Thursday." The voice quavered and squeaked, and it made her swoon. She wanted to run her fingers through the shaggy hair that hung half in and half out of his turtleneck.

"Two hundred thirty-eight marks the night," said the coolly attractive receptionist, a *Frl. Geduld*, Lily read on the nametag that rode shotgun on the beautifully controlled bosom.

The man gulped. "That would be about..."

"Approximately $169."

His hands clamped around the edge of the counter, his knuckles turning white. "Uh, can I pay for the first night and then pay the rest when I check out?"

"Certainly, sir."

Lily moved so that she was standing next to him. He took two hundred-mark notes and a fifty out of his billfold. From the corner of her eye, Lily could see there was only a five dollar bill left. She thought of the twenty-eight marks and the three dollars left in her purse. A wave of empathy rolled over her, followed by a wave of self-pity for the loss of kind, rich Phillip.

The receptionist shoved a registration card at him and turned to answer the phone. He took up the pen and bent over the form, his hand shaking. Then he paused, his brow furrowed. He looked around at posters displayed at the end of the counter.

Lily followed his glance. The largest poster showed that famous mountain in Switzerland. The text was in seven languages, and shortly she heard him whisper, "Craggy." He said it several more times, and then it became "Craig." Quickly he wrote "Craig" in the name slot of the registration card, and next to it, after a minute's pause and a shrug, "George."

Like wow, he's more out of it than I am, she thought. George? She tried the name out in her mind, as if saying "Percival" or "Chauncey." Oh, well, maybe he had a quirky middle name.

Her palms were sweaty, her right eye twitched, and she knew her face had turned that horrible splotchy red it always got when she was nervous. She was finally going to speak to him. She opened her mouth just as the receptionist handed him his key.

He picked up his bag and headed for the elevators at the back of the lobby.

She tagged after him.

He looked at the number on the heavy wooden key holder with its rubber ring around the middle and then punched the up button.

"Hi," she said. "Clunky, aren't they?"

He glanced around a minute and stared at her, surprised. "Are you talking to me?"

"Yeah. The keys here. I guess they want to be sure you don't walk out with them."

He looked at the key again. "Yeah, it looks that way."

The elevator swung open and he stepped in. Lily started to follow and then remembered her bag. "I'll be right back," she said, beaming at him.

When she got back, the elevator had nearly closed. She shoved her hand in between the doors and they slid open again.

Her karma-man didn't even look at her as he moved aside.

Like bummer, she thought. "What floor are you on?" she asked, her heart banging too loudly for her to hear her own words.

He didn't answer but his vibes sent out a kind of panicky warning.

When the car stopped on fifth floor, he stepped out ahead of her and walked away.

Lily stood in the hall watching his retreating back, fighting tears. "Aw, burn out," she muttered. "He doesn't even know I exist." For a minute she stood after he'd entered a room, a puddle of misery in the corridor of a foreign hotel. But then the memory of bumping into him popped up again, she straightened her shoulders and looked for her own room. "Same floor. See? It's gonna work out. Even if I have to do something drastic."

14

Comfortably settled in the Hotel *am* Zoo after her ordeal exiting East Germany, Eleanor adjusted the showerhead to spray onto her tight shoulder muscles and tried to pretend she was less depressed in the West. Ha. In the morning she'd walked all the way to the Berlin museum of musical instruments and found it closed. Idiot. She should've remembered German museums were closed on Mondays. And she should've known right then how the day would turn out.

She'd strolled up and down the *Kurfürsten-damm* until she'd seen every bead of wiry hippie jewelry and every scrap of Indian Madras fabric laid out on the sidewalks. Her feet had gotten cold and sore. The horrible awareness of being alone had followed her everywhere, like a cold, murky breath from hell. She'd tried to get her mind off it in a sound-dubbed movie, Crocodile Dundee; but without the Australian accent, the story didn't seem to amount to much. Any museum would have been better. A lot of people went alone to museums.

Her stomach flopped with hunger, though she couldn't hear it growl with the shower running. She could go down to the hotel restaurant, but this was Europe, and she knew that even if she found an empty table, inevitably some loving couple would come and ask whether the other seats were "free." Then they'd sit there mooning over each other and making her feel like disagreeable air. Maybe she'd go out and buy something from a sausage vendor on the street.

She shuddered and tried to relax in the hot stream of water. In a minute she would get out. She should go downstairs, even if not to eat. There was no point in staying up here if someone was looking for her to—to carry out the contract. Her heart thrumped in fear. She should have told the contact in Denver she wanted it to be painless. She could just stay in the room. No, if she did, in the end she'd just have to go home and face the same old emptiness. She turned off the water, determined to go down to the lobby, where she'd be visible.

Almost immediately, she heard a key in the lock and the hall door opened. The hit man! He had a key? And here she was, stark naked!

She grabbed her robe and wrapped it around her wet body. Pushing her hair out of her face, she opened the door and stood with her eyes closed, waiting.

Nothing happened. She stepped out into the room.

A woman smaller and younger than she with long, strangely woven black hair and very dark eyes that glittered under the jet lag was just heaving a duffel bag onto the bed. She gave Eleanor a big smile. "Hi, I'm Lily," she said, shrugging out of an ancient pea coat. She had on a long gray and pink plaid wool skirt cut on the diagonal and an old turquoise turtle-neck with "Let it aaaallll hang out" sprawled across the front in silver letters that had long since lost their polish.

Eleanor glared at her. Damn. If there was anyone in the world who didn't look like a hit man, this was it. Who in the hell did she think she was, coming into somebody else's room?

Lily backed away from her. "Hey, listen, they said at the desk you'd written with your reservation that you'd share a room. So they put me with you when I showed up for the conference."

Eleanor backed against the bathroom door for support. "You're a roommate?"

"Well, like, yeah."

"Oh." Damn. Why had she ever written such a stupid thing? Of course, that was back in the time of Hal when she hadn't even thought about a contract. Now what? Suppose the hit man only had the room number and took Lily out instead of her?

"Oh," she said again. "I'm sorry. I thought you were someone else. I'm Eleanor. You registered for the conference at the last minute, I guess."

"Yeah, it was a spur-of-the-moment decision."

"No guitar? I guess you're not here for the competition."

Lily laughed. "Me? In a guitar competition? Like, hardly!" A shadow passed across her face. "In fact, I knocked myself out of the running for a lot of stuff. Which bed is yours?"

"The running? The other bed's mine," Eleanor answered, trying to make sense of the slight derailment in the girl's train of thought.

Lily sat down on her bed, shoved the pillow back to the wall and leaned against it. "I'm way out starving," she said, pulling a huge jar of peanut butter and a spoon out of the duffle bag that had sunk almost out of sight in the feather quilt. She dug into the peanut butter and began eating.

Eleanor toweled her hair. "Is that lunch or supper?"

Lily worked her mouth free. "Breakfast. Or actually all of them. Lots of protein in this stuff, you know."

"There's a restaurant on the second floor." Eleanor stopped, realizing why Lily had brought the peanut butter with her. "It serves as breakfast room, too. You know breakfast is included in the price of the room. It's a generous buffet."

"Really? Wow, that's, like, cool. I'll have to find a way to tell..." Her face went all dreamy, but she didn't say whom she wanted to tell.

Eleanor combed her hair back and started pinning it in her French bun.

Watching her, Lily stopped mouthing the peanut butter. "Hey, I know you," she mumbled around it. "Like, wow! This is so far out. You're from Denver, aren't you?"

Eleanor stopped in mid-jab with a pin. "Yes. How did you know?"

"You took a witchcraft class a few years ago, didn't you?"

Eleanor plopped on her quilt and felt it push up around her hips. "My God, I knew that would come home to roost one day. Were you in there, too? I can't believe this."

Lily's face slid into nostalgia, her spoon drooping several inches away under a heavy dollop. "Yeah, that was a gas, wasn't it?" She shook her head and popped the peanut butter into her mouth.

"I guess that's one way to put it. Funniest thing I ever did in my life. And one of the dumbest."

Lily cocked her head to her left and squinted.

"Why'd you do it if it was so dumb?"

"I had a young friend then. I loved him more than life, but I wasn't in love with him, if you know what I mean. He dared me to take the class. He was in medical school then and never had time for anything like that. I would've dropped out after the first session—remember the woman holding the snake against her chest and petting it? She scared the living daylights out of me. But Randall got a huge charge out of it when I told him. After that, I didn't have the heart to quit."

Lily held the jar toward her. "You want some?"

"No, thanks."

Lily busied herself with putting her food away.

Eleanor fell silent and let Randall's face hover before her, his wavy black hair and his Irish blue eyes. It was the loss that always came back with the most painful impact. They had both been sure that their love, uncomplicated by sex, would last forever, regardless of her love affairs or his. Randall was gay.

She could still see his impish smile as he shoved the catalogue from the Denver Free University across the table in the Mexican restaurant.

"Check the page I dog-eared," he said.

Eleanor stared at the items he'd highlighted,

and her mouth fell open. "History of Witchcraft, Theory and Practice of Wi...? You're going to take classes in witchcraft? How are you going to fit...?"

"Not me, you. It'll be a blast." His grin was pure mischief.

"You can't be serious." Eleanor read the blurb aloud. "'Students are expected to provide their own working materials.' Did you check out these 'materials'? I can just see myself running all over Denver, asking for eye of newt. Not me, sorry."

In the end, of course, he'd talked her into taking the history class.

Lily's voice intruded on the memory. "So you took the class on a dare, practically."

Eleanor nodded, coming back to the present. "Actually, I went when the history class was scheduled, but I never heard anyone say a word about history. I'll never forget that first time. Every face in the room did a double take when I walked in wearing my schoolmarm clothes."

"Hey, I remember when you came in. You looked like you'd just stepped out of your car onto Pluto or something. I was standing on the steps that went up that that loft where they sold the really weird stuff. Oh, man, I loved that class. Remember chanting in the park?"

Eleanor smiled at the memory of the fifty or so students trying to make a circle in the miniscule triangular "park" where Seventeenth crossed the diagonal Park Avenue. "Are you kidding? I kept my nose in the grass the whole time while we *aahed* and *oomed*. I knew perfectly well every student I had was driving by, exclaiming about the lunatics in the park. Did you ever hear about the woman in the hospital we tried to send those vibes to?"

"She died."

"Figures."

A grin spread across Lily's face. "Oh, man, I shouldn't laugh. It's not funny."

Eleanor snickered. "I know." She bit her lip. "You still have that talisman we made?"

"Sure. I don't wear it any more though. I got a rash too soon to tell if it would ward off bad vibes like Shalmon said it would."

"I carried mine around in my purse for a while." So silly, she thought now. And it certainly hadn't warded off the bad vibes as far as Randall was concerned. The night she'd told him about it was the same night it had been clear that Randall's new affair with Joel from San Jose wasn't going to be a passing thing, and eventually Joel's influence on Randall took him down roads where Eleanor would not follow.

Lily was laughing, and Eleanor put the nostalgia aside. "Randall thought the consecration of the talisman was the funniest thing he'd ever heard," she continued. "So phallic, stroking that white candle with oil from the middle to the end in both directions." She repeated the motions with her hands until they were both giggling. "What powers did you concentrate on while we were chanting the talisman into usefulness?"

Lily snorted and searched the ceiling for an answer. "Man, I don't remember. I was just out of Zen at the time, so maybe it was inner peace. What about you?"

"I concentrated on a healthy liver for a man in Germany I'd met during the summer. He'd contracted hepatitis in Spain."

"Did it work?"

"Not exactly. Actually, I never knew. He quit writing."

They were both holding their sides now.

The laughter made Eleanor feel lighter somehow, in spite of the memory of Karl. "The talisman was good for some things, though. I could hold it in my hand and drive the whole length of University Boulevard without hitting a single red light."

"Far out!" Lily shrieked, kicking the air with both feet.

Eleanor was hardly able to talk now for the giggles. "And it was great at starting cars. One day one of my students came back into the building while I was on last period supervision in the hall. It was about twenty below outside and she couldn't get her car started. 'You go back out and try once more, Linda,' I said. 'I promise you it'll start this time.' She gave me a weird look, but she went. And—I'm not making this up—in a few minutes, holding the talisman in my hand, I actually felt the car start."

"Like, wow! Maybe it jumpstarted your German friend's liver to his wrist. No wonder he quit writing." She roared and slapped at the quilt.

Eleanor was taken aback for a second then lay back on the bed and howled.

"Does it still work?" asked Lily, catching her breath.

"I don't know. I lost it, I guess. I lost Randall, too, in California. I wouldn't mind finding the talisman again, though."

After a minute in which they both stared at the past, Eleanor asked, "What about you? Did you do anything more with the witchcraft? Did you join Shalmon's coven after the class?"

Lily rested her head against the wall. "No. Geez, I'd forgotten he asked me. It turned out they were looking for a female Aries. But I have, like, dabbled a bit in potions. So far they haven't exactly turned out the way I wanted." Her face showed frustration for a second and then she said, "Man, I am so zonked." She turned to rummage in her bag again. Taking out a plastic grocery bag, she went into the bathroom. In a minute the swishy sound of her toothbrush came through the door.

Eleanor dressed to go find a street vendor and maybe a hit man.

When Lily came back, she dumped the duffel bag on the floor, stripped to her ragged underwear, and arranged herself on top of the feather quilt. After a few seconds, her head came up again. "Bummer," she said. "They make you sleep on pillows. Don't they give you any blankets around here?"

Eleanor looked around and laughed. "That's the blanket," she said. "You sleep under it, not on it."

Lily got up again, pulled at the quilt and found the edge that had been folded under. "Man, this thing is heavy. You really sleep under it?"

"Well, I always flip all the feathers to one side and sleep on the very edge of the bed under the thinner side. If I get cold in the night, I just reach out and slap some more feathers over me. Here, let me help you." She took the quilt and shook it vigorously. Lily lay down and Eleanor heaved the quilt until the far side of the bed was a mountain of feathers and a thin layer lay on top of Lily.

Lily closed her eyes. "Later, Eleanor."

Eleanor took her key and walked down to the elevator, the image of Randall before her face, squashing her spirits down again after the laugh. His psychologist lover, Joel, typical of those who tamper with the minds of others, believed in a healthy ego-centrism as the only viable basis for relationships. He taught Randall that whatever he wanted to do was right, regardless of whether it hurt other people. Eleanor had found Joel's views, like so much that comes from California, to be unripe.

"Joel says that 99% of the time it pleases me to please other people," Randall had explained. "And that one percent, when it doesn't please me, I have the right to please myself."

Eleanor thought about that dictum for a minute. "It sounds to me like you please yourself 100% of the time that way, leaving no room for sacrifice."

It wasn't long before the depth of Joel's influence hit home. Christmas was a few weeks away. She couldn't face another holiday season with either of her sisters' families. The laughing children made her feel hollow inside.

"What are you doing for Christmas?" she asked him.

"Going out to be with Joel in San Jose."

She hoped he might say, "Why don't you come out for a day or two?" The unspoken invitation hung palpably in the air between them. It was not forthcoming.

Desperate not to face another Christmas walking alone in Washington Park, she asked,

"Would it be all right if I joined you for a day or so?"

"No."

Not "No, Joel's having his family there," or "No, I need this time with him." Just "No." The blare of that one syllable still echoed in her heart. Not long after that they had parted. Was he in San Jose now? Did he ever remember her? She sighed as she left the hotel.

A little later, the fatty meat of a Bratwurst heavy as a rock in her stomach, Eleanor went to the conference room to see whether any guitarists had gathered yet. If the hit man had arrived, he would probably seek her out among the musicians.

A few French guitarists were jamming and talking. She sat several feet away from them with her hands on her lap, the long right nails and the short left ones clearly visible. But the young Frenchmen chattered away in their own language and made no effort to include her. After a couple of glances they obviously dismissed her as non-French. Or just too old to matter. She listened to the music for a while and then left. Alone in the elevator, she massaged the wrinkles around her eyes.

Lily was on her stomach, sleeping badly with one leg hanging over the side of the bed and the other under the mound of feathers, along with everything else but her nose. She was mumbling, almost chanting, something about steam in the cream and potions and lotions.

Must be some hippie song, Eleanor thought. Should she try to put the girl's leg back on the bed and move the feathers again?

Just then Lily did a push-up, grabbed the pillow, beat it vigorously, and flopped back down without waking, her head facing in the other direction. "George? What kind of name is that?" she mumbled. Then she fell silent.

Eleanor shook her head. The name reminded her of something. She put on her nightgown and quietly opened the drawers in the dresser until she found the Berlin telephone book. She was thumbing through it when Lily turned and sat up, looking as if she had just wakened from a hundred-year coma. She stared red-eyed around the room for a few seconds.

"Oh, yeah," she said, "I'm in Berlin, right?"

Eleanor smiled and nodded. Lily got up and brushed her teeth. By the time she got back Eleanor was putting away the book.

"You want to call somebody? I can leave if you want to talk in private."

"Oh, no, I didn't have any intention to make a phone call. It's just a thing I have. Every time I visit a city, I look in the telephone book for a certain name, the man who was the first of my many sorry experiences with men."

"Who was he?"

"Well, just some guy who phoned our house once when I was about fifteen and asked for Eleanor. When I went to the phone, he said he was my long-lost brother John. And when I didn't believe that, he said his name was George Craig."

"Who?!" gasped Lily, sitting hard on the bed.

"George Craig. Then he..."

"This is so far out."

"...said he was a soldier stationed out at the base and he and his buddies had just been playing a kind of telephone game, dialing numbers at random and asking for Eleanor. After we'd talked a while, he said wanted to meet me. So we had a date for Friday night."

"You had a date with George Craig?" Lily whispered.

"Well, that might not have been his real name either."

Lily's bloodshot eyes were staring right at her, but they were focused on something else. "Aw, man, I hope you're right."

Eleanor narrowed her eyes and shook her head; Lily's thread of the conversation didn't seem to twine with hers but to run in loops parallel to it. "Anyway, he stood me up. Which would've been the end of it except for my little sister. About two weeks later, early on a Saturday morning, the doorbell rang, and Ruthie ran to see who it was. It was a strange young man. Ruthie slammed the door in his face and came galloping back through the house screaming, "Eleanor, Eleanor, George Craig is here! George Craig is at the door!"

Lily was hanging on to every word, and Eleanor settled on her bed to continue. She hadn't had such an avid listener for a long time. "By the time Ruthie got upstairs, my mother was at the door.

"'Well, George Craig, it's about time you got here,' she growled at him.

"'I'm not George Craig,' he said.

"'Oh, I suppose you changed your name again? I guess you're not John any more either?'

"'No, ma'am, John's the one who drives us to our routes. I just sell the magazines.'

"My mother was already laughing when she let him in, too embarrassed to send him away.

"About that time my older sister came down. "Well, George, it sure took you a long time to find the house.'

"'I'm really not George Craig,' he said.

"Lottie looked at Mother for an explanation, but she was biting her lips and couldn't talk.

"'Were you expecting a George Craig?' he asked.

"Mother and Lottie could only look at each other and laugh.

"'No,' one of them managed to stammer.

"'Oh. Well, you *know* a George Craig?'

"'No.'

"That did it. Neither of them could explain, they were laughing so hard, but about that time Ruthie came back.

"'Boy, George, was Eleanor ever mad when you stood her up. I guess she's really going to let you have it.'

"I came in right behind her, dressed in my finest clothes, but all buttoned wrong, my lipstick completely askew. 'Well, George, I'm so happy to meet you at last,' I gushed.

"'I'm not George Craig, I'm not George Craig,' he shouted at me, standing up. He gathered up all his magazine materials and rushed out the door. We never saw him again."

Lily was still staring as if Eleanor were telling her the most gripping tale ever told. "And you were fifteen? Uh, how old was this George Craig?" She didn't appear to see the humor in the story.

"Which one, the first one who wasn't or the second?"

"The first—I think."

"I don't know, maybe twenty, since he was a soldier. Of course, I never saw that one. Anyway, it got to be a family joke. Every time I go to another town, one of my sisters will ask me whether I found George Craig. So in every city I check the phone book."

Lily regarded her with a hard, almost hostile stare. "What would you do if you ever found him?"

Her brows went up and she scratched at her earlobe. "I don't know. Back then I'd have called him up and given him one of the more unpleasant pieces of my mind. But I never found a single George Craig. Funny, you wouldn't think it was such an uncommon name. Now it's more of a joke than a need to find him."

"You're never going to believe this. There's a George Craig registered at the hotel. I saw him. I'm sure he can't be the same one, though."

Eleanor's jaw fell open but she couldn't form a word.

Through a perfectly inane smile, Lily added, "I'll show him to you. He's, like, gorgeous. He's got a wonderful soul. I think. Hey, what time is it?"

Eleanor looked at her watch. Maybe after the three conference days she'd get used to the leaps of focus. "Nearly ten."

Lily glanced at the drawn curtain. "Morning or night?"

"Night."

"Burn out! I'm as wide awake now as the middle of the afternoon. I think I'll go walk around a little while. Can you see my aura?"

Eleanor's mind stumbled over the strange

question. "Your aura? No, I don't see any. Did you leave it somewhere?"

"Well, no, but see, when you fly your aura can't keep up. That's why you have jet lag."

"I see."

"Oh, geez, I hope mine didn't get on the wrong plane in Chicago and end up in Peru or something. Bummer." Lily dragged a clean but monstrously wrinkled peasant blouse out of her duffle bag, put on the long skirt, and shrugged into the pea coat. She gave Eleanor a wave, a warm smile, and a "Later," as she moved toward the door.

"Wait!" Eleanor cried. She pulled Lily back, opened the door, and checked the hall for her hit man. "Sorry," she said when she found the hall clear. "I was just..."

Lily waited for her to finish. When nothing further came, she smiled uncertainly and left.

"Okay, I looked like an idiot," she said to the door. "I guess she'll understand soon enough."

She put the phone book back in the drawer. Well, that would be something else—to find George Craig after all this time. Or would it? There was some weird connection between Lily and that name.

Why would he turn up here? Now? She shook her head but a dark vibration buzzed at her nerves.

15

November 7, 1989

Lily turned onto her left side, vaguely aware of being in the fuzzy zone between waking and sleeping. The face of the man who called himself George Craig was plastered all over the inside of her eyelids. She forced it away and pasted up the face of Phillip Redding. It refused to come into focus, and in a few seconds the sharper nose of George poked through and slowly replaced Phillip's round one. The scruffy face kept coming. She tried to reach up and erase it, but a great weight pinned her arm against her side. She rolled onto her back again, and the weight pressed down on her whole body.

Annoyed, she opened her eyes and looked down. A great mound of white lay across her, like a giant jelly doughnut. When she pushed at it, her hand sank out of sight. In a moment's panic, she feared she'd never get rid of the weight, nor of the certainty that Phillip was the man of her karma, not that George person, beautiful though he was.

She caught herself sliding into a syrupy memory of his scraggly hair and his rumpled trench coat. He was so...

Get out of my head! she commanded. Had she screwed her chances already, trying to get a man who didn't know she existed and trying not to get another one who didn't know she existed, either? The whole thing was cosmically stupid. Or was it just a test of some kind?

And the weight? It was nothing but that ridiculous feather quilt. She kicked the unwieldy quilt aside. "Geez, I'm drenched with sweat," she said as goose bumps prickled her damp body in the cool air.

The other bed was a great amorphous hump of feathers, too, and Eleanor was gone.

She leaped from the bed and into the shower in two steps.

When she returned her head was clear. She dressed in the same clothes she'd put on last night, visited the restaurant, packed a lot of food into her napkin for later, and wandered around the conference, looking for George. She poked her head into every room. Well, those guys were sure into their stuff, all right. Whole rooms of people digging the two guitarists on the stage. Looked like one was a teacher and one a student. No George, though.

"Just as well," she murmured when she was

back in the room. "Like, I need a little quiet to figure out if I can fix this bummer. There's just got to be a chapter on cancellation of potions." She hoisted the duffel bag onto the bed, rummaged in it, and drew out *Parsley, Sage, Rosemary, and Mandrake Root.* The newspaper picture of Phillip fluttered to the floor. She started to pick it up but said to it, "No, I'm just going to let you lie there. 'Cause I'm, like, trying to figure out what to do with you."

She focused on the book and ran her finger down the table of contents. Then, just to be sure, she looked through every item in the short index.

"Aw, man," she sighed, finding nothing on the undoing of the done. "I guess it isn't going to wear off, either. How long has it been now, a whole week? This is a major burn-out." She picked up the picture. "It's a shame about you," she said to the thousands of dots. "You just have to be in my karma somewhere. 'Course, if you were, you'd, like, at least know I exist by now."

Lily sat on the bed in her lotus position with the book and the picture held at eye level. She couldn't make the dots coalesce into a picture of Phillip's face now. They were just dots. It was a sign. "So if you're not my karma, how come your horoscope said there were some changes coming just before your birthday, and maybe some danger? Somebody's supposed to get you if I'm hooked on this George character. And it ought to be somebody who deserves you. Like Eleanor. Seems like she's had nothing but bad luck with men."

She dropped the book into her lap. "Far out!" she whooped, watching the picture waft to the floor again. "That's it. And I know it'll work, too. Best idea I've had since taking the witchcraft class!" She started to leap from the bed.

A small vibration at the base of her neck caught her off guard.

"What?" she asked, sitting back down. Did she have the right to meddle in Phillip's affairs? Of course she did. Anybody could see she was in his karma. Just not as his mate. So what else was she supposed to do?

But what about Eleanor? Now that was a lady in sad shape. She had practically no aura at all. Just a little weak rose and yellow, a sure sign of loneliness and fright. But there was more. The whole aura was surrounded by a layer of gray. It looked like death closing in. But that was silly. She sure looked healthy enough.

Lily ran her hand through her tangled hair. Hmmm. So okay, Eleanor could use some help, even if she hadn't shown up specifically in Phillip's horoscope. But then, she hadn't read Eleanor's. Maybe it was clearer there. And anyway, what harm could it do to hitch up the two of them? If there was anybody who needed a kind man, it was Eleanor. Every little curve and jerk of her body language, every blank stare as she slid into memories said she was, like, way out depressed. Man, they were made for each other.

"Besides, the last time I did this, it was for my own good. Now it's for somebody else," Lily said aloud. "Gotta be right, right? I'll be doing them both the biggest favor of, like, their whole lives," she declared with pretty much complete conviction.

Fumbling in the bag again, she pulled out the coconut oil and a Baggie containing the spices, aloe, zinc tablets, and ginger root.

"And now, the *piéce de résistance*," she announced, plucking a split of real brandy from the airplane out of her tapestry purse and drawing a five pointed star in the air with it.

An empty water bottle stood on the dresser. She used it to grind the zinc and ginger on the edge of the bathtub, *ahing* and *ooming* wholeheartedly. She mixed it all in the brandy with a little tap water, and put half back into the split bottle, leaving half in the water bottle.

She looked again into the split bottle. The oil wasn't combining with the rest. Nor was it giving off little wisps of steam or smoke. It lay like gleaming, slimy castor oil on top of the brandy-water-spice mix. "Uh-oh," she said. "Well, maybe it's because of the brandy. I'll just have to keep shaking it. Like Italian dressing, right?"

Ten minutes later, dressed in heavy black tights under her paisley skirt and a lilac turtle neck under the peasant blouse, she took up both bottles and started to put them in her purse. "Two potionees coming up," she tittered.

The water bottle stopped in mid-air. "Uh-uh, the way things are going, I'd better do one at the time. I could end up with Eleanor in love with me!" She put the water bottle into the duffel bag and ventured out to find Phillip.

16

Ursula Kimmig woke with a start when the bumping and swaying of the small bus stopped. She looked out at the glaring light of the border crossing and then beyond to the gray of the beginning day. That tense *Herr* Barkov, the "tour guide," who had sat surrounded by empty seats, was just getting up. She knew, and she knew the others did, too, that he was *Stasi*. Sometimes there was no mistaking them.

He hoisted the briefcase he'd held on his lap the whole way.

She wasn't surprised to see it was exactly like hers, since the only place to buy foreign goods was in the *Intershops*, which all carried the same things.

He turned to the back, and said, "Get out your papers now," without looking at anyone directly.

She ran her hand over the top of the beautifully made Italian leather briefcase her parents had given her for making it to the competition. Their faces had been so proud, so eager for her to play well. With a dark spot where her heart should be, she fingered the stitching. It was a costly gift, coming from the *Intershop* in the *Elefant*, the elegant and expensive tourist hotel on Cranach Square. She'd felt guilty about accepting it, knowing they'd sacrificed at least two month's salaries to buy it with West marks. She'd almost wept over the gift that only she knew was the last one they'd ever give her, determined as she was to find a way to stay in the West.

She opened it and took out her passport and her exit permit, which was limited to West Berlin and to three and a half days.

She climbed out of the mini-bus with the other four guitarists and watched as the *Vopo* began his inspection. He reached for *Herr* Barkov's briefcase. *Herr* Barkov jerked the briefcase away, pulled out a paper, and hissed something at the guard.

The *Vopo* reddened and went on to the first guitarist. He emptied every guitar case and every piece of luggage, probed the linings, and left the contents to be repacked by the owners.

What does he think we are? Aliens trying to smuggle things out of the country? she thought. Ha, as if we had anything the Westerners could possibly want. She masked her face with indifference and let the process wash over her.

When the inspection was finished and a host from the conference had joined them, the bus moved to the West checkpoint, where the guards did little beyond matching faces with passports. Then the bus drove into the soft light of a misty morning in West Berlin. Ursula was fascinated, taking in the incredible number of taxis and the variety of cars, all of them bigger than even the *Wartburg*.

The bus was thankfully slow in the rush-hour traffic, giving the host plenty of time to point out the sights. They drove past the *Siegessäule*, with the gold statue of Winged Victory at the top; past the classical Tomb of the Russian Unknown Soldier, hastily erected in white marble before the dividing line between East and West Berlin had been established. Already, Russian soldiers were guarding it, goose-stepping slowly, reverentially across its length.

What a different message it gave from the monument that was later built in East Berlin, which was in no way reverential, being more a monument to war and intimidation.

They passed the strange oyster-shaped concert hall and entered an area of shops and hotels. Past the pagoda-like entrance to a zoo on the left and an amazing line of taxis parked at the curb on the right, they pulled up in front of the Hotel *am* Zoo. *Herr* Barkov jumped out and waited while the guitarists headed for the entrance. He almost smiled when Ursula passed him. She cringed mentally. She certainly didn't want him paying her special attention.

A porter came with a cart and started unloading the luggage. The group went up to the reception counter and waited while a receptionist talked to a small, thin man in a dark tan trench coat. Ursula stood behind the rest of the guitarists; but they moved back to the end of the line, one by one, their faces drawn in disgust, until only *Herr* Barkov stood before her. She stepped aside to put some space between them and got the scent from the man at the counter—stale coffee and a general lack of clean clothes.

It looked as if this was going to take a while. Wishing she had the nerve to move away from the smell, too, which Barkov might interpret as rejection or fear of him, she set her briefcase down on her left.

Barkov stepped beside her and put his on the floor between his feet.

At the desk, the small man was almost shouting
at the clerk. "Is there someplace around here to get some breakfast?" Even Ursula could understand him.

The doll-like clerk backed away slightly and said, "I speak English, *Herr* Craig." She looked with undisguised distaste from his rumpled coat to his scraggly hair. "Perhaps you don't know this, but breakfast is included in the price of your room."

At this the man drew himself up to his full scrawny stature. "Of course I knew that. Thank you."

The receptionist continued, "The breakfast room is on the second floor. You can't miss it, the doors will be open."

"Well, I'll just go on up there then." He turned too close to Barkov, at the same time shoving the sleeve of his coat up as if to check the time. Where a watch should be, there was only a pale stripe around his wrist. His face registered dismay just as he caught his toe on the front end of *Herr* Barkov's briefcase and fell into him.

Barkov lost his balance and fell into Ursula.

She tried to catch him but the three of them went down in a heap.

Barkov shoved the American aside and grabbed his briefcase.

The small man helped Ursula up, collected the second briefcase, started to hand it to *Herr* Barkov and then put it in Ursula's hand.

Barkov blanched and stared hard at both briefcases. He started to say something, started to reach for her case, but stopped himself.

The thin man mumbled something apologetic that Ursula didn't understand, clapped Barkov on the arm, smiled with his pitted face, and hurried off to the elevators at the back of the lobby.

Barkov turned to Ursula again, his face twisted with...what? Anger?

Before he could say anything, Ursula moved to the back of the group. Repulsive man, she thought. I have to keep him away from me.

Half an hour later Ursula left her room to go down to the convention hall. From the turn in the corridor she heard the elevator door open and saw *Herr* Barkov waiting, holding his briefcase. Two people with guitars got on, but he let them ride down without him. He looked more tense than ever. Ursula nodded at him but did not look him in the eye as another guitarist joined them. A third guitarist just squeezed in as the door closed.

In the lobby, Ursula walked as close to the other guitarists as she could.

Barkov stayed right on her heels as she entered the hall where the stage was set up for the performances. Hotel workers were still setting up chairs, but the room was full of guitarists. Ursula smiled, feeling suddenly at home. Some things knew no borders, after all.

Everywhere musicians were holding their right arms up as fingerboards, running scales up and down them, or showing their companions a new fingering. Others were using the fingers on their left hands as strings to demonstrate right hand technique. Still others were comparing fingernails on their right hands, holding them palms out toward the viewers to show off the shape of the nails in relation to the fingertips. Many were sitting alone, facing the wall, practicing. The gentle din of half a hundred guitars playing different pieces droned about her ears, and Ursula forgot *Herr* Barkov completely.

She went to the front of the room and leaned against the stage, around which workers had just finished hanging a dark blue skirt. She could see a few of the name tags from here, could make out the countries represented. There were Africans chatting with Italians, South Americans with Japanese, Americans with Germans. They all looked relaxed with each other. Not wary. They looked directly into each other's eyes and laughed. Surely, they couldn't all be friends already. How could they be so open, so trusting?

She looked around for her companions. Three of them were seated in a small knot, staring, not talking, even to each other. Somehow, it looked dark where they were sitting. She looked back at the Westerners. The light that had exploded into her head eight days ago and never quite gone out seemed to merge with the light she felt emanating from the laughing, relaxed people from this side of the Wall. She breathed deeply and felt as if she had taken their light into her lungs. Stay in the West.

Unable to stop herself, she began to inspect the men. She dismissed most of the younger ones; appealing as many of them were, they were clearly in no position to marry. Ursula slapped herself mentally for such a self-serving thought, and continued to look.

There was an older man across the room, seated next to a very slight young woman. Ursula threaded her way through the chairs and sat down near them but not close enough to intrude. They were both from the USA, the girl from something that started with an O and the man from Col... She checked both his hands; Americans were supposed to wear their wedding bands on the left. He was not wearing one. She tried to listen without being obvious. He had sandy hair, a small chin, gray eyes, and a kind of button nose, slightly red.

He caught her looking at him and smiled. He even said something, but it was too fast. He beckoned her over. Ursula put her hands up and shook her head. He stood up and came to her. He spoke to her again, but she could not understand. She read the name Phillip and something that started with an R. Her face flushed. She looked around for *Herr* Barkov. He was standing right behind her. A shot of adrenaline propelled her out of the chair.

In German she said, "I think I'll go look at the music displays before the next master class." She looked neither at Barkov nor at the American. She left the room. Near the door were two more men, young ones who didn't look as if they'd come for the guitar convention. Probably agents of some kind, too, she thought. Maybe the West was full of spies, too.

17

Horst Bauer walked into the Hotel *am Zoo* with Rainer Moltke, whom he had requested for this assignment as the colleague most likely to recognize a non-guitarist in the crowd. He let his raincoat slide down his arms. The hem of it dragged through the dirty water already puddling the floor of the fancy hotel. He jerked it back and slung the coat over his arm. "Damn, I wish I were anywhere else, away from this gloomy Berlin soup-sky." He didn't mention his longing for Colorado, with which he'd plagued his colleagues for months.

"Right. A nice trip to Spain." Rainer shook off his umbrella and headed to the letter board at the back of the lobby.

They found the conference room, where guitarists were sitting in clusters doing the most curious things with their hands—plucking at thin air, fingering their left arms with their right hands, holding their hands out to each other with the palms out.

Horst stopped dead at the entrance and stared,

wondering if they'd happened onto a gathering of lunatics. "Is this normal?" he asked.

Rainer looked at him and then back at the gathering. "What?"

"I guess it is, then."

They circulated, looking for a hit man. Rainer elbowed him and pointed at a lean, grim man with thinning blond hair, a narrow face, and an air of cold calculation about him. Horst shook his head.

"He certainly isn't a guitarist," said Rainer.

"No, but our man is small and has brown hair. Besides, he's supposed to be a real amateur. That one's either KGB or *Stasi*, guaranteed."

Horst followed the feral stare of the KGB agent and found a young woman leaning on the edge of the stage. She was gazing transfixed at the guitarists. Not beautiful, but definitely attractive, with short blond hair and a lovely figure under a plain blue blouse and a gray pleated skirt. Horst couldn't tell the color of her eyes from his side of the room, but it was the face that riveted him. She had that look of longing that he understood, the desire for escape, for a sunnier place. She scanned the gathering as if an outsider who desperately wanted in.

Horst watched as the KGB agent moved in her direction. She was under surveillance. Maybe in danger. It was none of his affair, certainly none of his assignment. He scanned the crowd again for a face that seemed out of place—other than the KGB agent.   He glanced at Rainer, who wasn't registering interest in anyone, either. He found the girl again.

He started to move closer, but he'd only taken a couple of steps when she walked to the far end of the room and sat down near a man and a young woman who had her back to Horst. The man, middle aged with a slightly red button nose, was very likely American, judging by the open smile he gave the newcomer.

The KGB agent moved behind her.

The American leaned toward her and said something.   The girl froze, as if she hadn't understood.   Then KGB bent down.   The girl noticed him, jumped up, and rushed past Horst out of the room.

She glanced at Horst as she left but didn't look in his eyes.

Horst's smile had hardly begun to fade when the agent rushed past, slowing for a second to give him a suspicious stare. There was power in his eyes, but there was fear, too. Horst watched him catch up with the girl at the elevator. He started to join them, but Rainer was suddenly at his elbow.

"Where are you going?"

"Oh. Nowhere."

"There's nothing out of the ordinary here. Come, let's see what we can find out from the receptionist."

Horst nodded absently. Why would he have gotten on the elevator with the girl? Because he had an absurd desire to shield her from that snake.

18

Ursula bent forward on her chair in the front row of the master class. She strained to understand the English conversation between Jules Fortier, the aging Canadian master, and the student who was playing a Fernando Sor serenade. She'd never seen anyone perform like Fortier, though he played only sections of the piece to demonstrate his advice. He seemed to be torn between dancing in his chair and playing the guitar. He drooped with the melody, bounced with the beat, and soared with each scale passage. Shocking. Far beyond the bounds of musical interpretation or good taste.

Still, he gave such an unassuming, sincere impression when he wasn't playing; he had such a kind air about him that she was drawn to his almost unlined face and his halo of wavy, silver hair. He smiled at the student, encouraged him, helped him overcome his nervousness, and praised him when he improved. Each time the student repeated a phrase following Fortier's suggestions, the music sang with new intensity.

She'd often sat in on her father's piano lessons because she had nowhere else to go, but now they were dry in memory. And suddenly she grieved for the warmth that had never flowed between him and the student. Nor between the student and the music. Nor between the music and the listener. Dry music. Mathematically precise.

Her attention came back to the stage. Fortier had stopped talking to the student and was addressing the audience.

"I always try to let go of my ego," he said. "The important thing here is not me but the music, the black dots on white paper that represent someone's attempt to speak directly from his heart to yours. Between you and the composer there is an instrument. And that is me with my guitar. If I put my ego aside and see myself as the composer's instrument, then the creator and the audience are of equal importance, and I can concentrate on them. If I don't, I'm what's important. I fall into the competition trap, comparing myself to other guitarists and other performances of my own. This misses the whole point of music. The thing is, each instrument sings differently, and the special, particular message it can deliver in a special, particular moment is the beauty of music."

Ursula was still translating in the appreciative silence that followed the short speech, when he added, "Assuming, of course, that I don't botch the whole piece." The audience broke into laughter and applauded. She wished she had understood better.

She heard little of the rest of the class. It was a socialistic thought, actually, letting go of the self for the benefit of others. Why did she hear it put this way for the first time in the West? Why did the music she had heard all her life suddenly feel like ashes of sound? If she stayed in the West, would she find someone like Fortier, who could show her how to make such warmth flow from her fingers? Stay in the West. The thought sent her heart into *molto agitato*. She clamped her hands together in her lap until the knuckles were white.

When the class was over, she left the room with the other East Germans, heavy at heart and full of an aching awareness of things she should have learned all along, things that might now be beyond her reach.

As she moved to the back of the room, she saw *Herr* Barkov lurking at the door. He'd disappeared after he'd seen her settle into the class. What did he want, anyway? Why wasn't he following any of the others? They could be halfway to Paris by now for all he knew.

She looked at her schedule as an excuse to ignore him. She had to report to room 112 to pick up the score of the new piece that had been composed for the competition. None of the contestants could see it before today. That gave them two days to prepare it before the final round of the competition, at least those who made it that far.

She thought again of Jules Fortier. He would say that a competition automatically imposed the ego of the performer between the composer and the audience. He was right. It forced the audience to listen for who was best, not what the composer meant. It defeated the purpose of making music.

She collected the new piece and started back to her room to examine it.

Herr Barkov, with his skinny, tense face, got in the elevator with Ursula, an Oriental guitarist and a strict looking woman with her hair in a vertical bun at the back of her head. Ursula pretended to ignore him by thumbing through the new score. The Asian got off on fourth.

The new composition was one of those arhythmical, aleatory things, with wavy lines and zig-zags where notes ought to be. It called for strumming the strings above the nut, banging on the bridge, running the thumbnail up and down the bass string. She heaved a disgusted sigh and shut the folder just as the elevator door opened. Barkov followed her down the hall, with the strict woman not far behind them. Ursula walked faster to put more space between herself and Barkov. She turned the corner and ran.

She had her key in the room door when he caught up to her.

"Miss Kimmig, you have..."

The woman from the elevator was directly across the hall, and though she appeared to have trouble with her key, Ursula could tell she was listening. It emboldened her. Barkov wouldn't do anything rash with a witness half a meter away.

"If you don't mind, *Herr* Barkov, I have to practice for the competition." She went in and shut the door in his face, her heart thrumming. No one slammed the door in the face of the *Stasi*. She listened. Across the hall the woman's door closed, but if Barkov walked away, she couldn't hear his feet on the carpet. Probably he'd be waiting right there when she went down for the next class. She made up her mind to be more subtle in rejecting his advances. Why had he focused on her? That girl from Potsdam was prettier.

She shoved her quilt aside and stretched out on the bed with the new music. Her mother had taught her to read through a score with her eyes before trying it on the guitar. Once she had even said, "Make friends with the music." That was as close as she ever got to saying, "Play from the heart."

Ursula ran her eyes over the score. It contained patches of recognizable notes here and there, but in other places there was not even a staff, much less a clef sign. There was no way to become friends with it; at most she could try to make it less inimical so the guitar would survive the attack. She could make the strings above the nut sound like the laughter of impish children. Dragging a nail down a bound bass string always gave her the feeling of being in a dentist's chair. If she tilted her finger and added a little flesh to the stroke, she could make it sound like a whispering wind.

Composer, audience—and performer as the instrument between them. What was the composer trying to say with this rubble of thought? Did he want to scream at the audience? Ursula knew the other guitarists would play it that way—it was too discordant to believe he was speaking serenely. Did she owe it to him to take his strident message to the audience? Or did she owe it to the audience to play her own special message? She could play it as memories from the grave. She would lose the competition. But then, who was to say she had any real chance of winning it, anyway, with people like Jules Fortier on the panel?

She took her guitar out and began to look for the memories.

19

In the lobby, Lily sat in a maroon leather chair facing the conference area, focused on getting Phillip and Eleanor to appear. She'd been tempted to peek into all the rooms down that hall until she knew where they were, but that would have been rude. Too bad. She could have directed her vibes a lot better.

And speaking of rude, there was that Ms. *Geduld* over at the desk, looking as if she'd swallowed a packet of needles. Well, Lily was a guest in the hotel, wasn't she, and didn't she have the right to sit in the lobby? Hmmph.

Still, this was no good at all. That receptionist was distracting her, making her concentration too weak to have any effect on Eleanor's appearance in the lobby, much less Phillip's. She wanted them close together, but not too close. Phillip first.

She laid her purse on the floor and drew her feet up into her lotus position. Immediately she felt a stiffening of the air in the direction of Ms. *Geduld*. She turned her back to it, closed her eyes, and faced straight in the direction of the conference entrance. *Ah-oom*, she started, certainly not loud enough to bother any of the other guests sitting nearby. Well, okay, some of them were staring. Germans were, like, *known* for that, right? So they'd probably stare even if she just sat quietly. *Ah, ah.* Deep breath in. *Oom.* Long breath out. Again. Good, now she was getting into it. A few more breaths and she was almost there. But not quite.

Sighing, she stretched out with her feet on a table so that she was nearly horizontal. She drew her chakra crystal from her pocket and began dangling it over the head chakra. Yep. It circled in the wrong direction. She forced the crystal to circle in the right direction and felt a bit more focused. The crystal slowed and reversed direction. Bummer.

Okay, there was still something wrong. What was she missing? Oh, yeah, a plan. Panic shot through her, even in deep meditation. She sat up again. Burn out! Why hadn't she thought of this? How was she going to get Phillip to drink that potion stuff? It looked about as appetizing as gutter water.

Lily thought for a few minutes, never missing an *ah* or an *oom*, until she'd come up with a plan. Okay, it was, like, a pretty sorry plan, but nothing else popped into her head. Still, now she could do the vibes to get Phillip and Eleanor to come out in the right order. She stretched out, shut her eyes gently, and sent out very smooth vibes visualizing Phillip emerging and Eleanor coming out about a minute behind him.

Now what? Vibes were bouncing back. All jagged and bumpy.

Lily opened her eyes.

There towered Ms. *Geduld*, blocking the view to the conference area, her aura orange with purple and brown lightning streaks, her face pained as if the needles were rushing back up her esophagus. She forced a smile, and around her eyes, cracks opened in the make-up that held her face together. "Are you qvite all right?" she asked.

Lily blinked. "Of course I'm all right. Why?"

The little face-quake progressed by a quarter inch at the eyes and opened a new fault line on her forehead. "Becauss you seem very discomfortable. Iss your bed in your room not all right? We do not take the siesta..."

Lily leaned to look past her. "No, everything's fine. I'm just watching for someone."

Ms. *Geduld* folded her arms across her chest— an entire paragraph in body language that was hardly necessary, considering the steely nature of her uniformed bosom. "Perhaps..."

"There he is." Lily jumped up, nearly knocking the implacable Ms. *Geduld* to the carpet.

"Gotta go. See you." She stepped around her.

He wasn't alone. In fact, he was surrounded by women, just the way he'd been at the party in Denver. Bummer. That only made things worse. What if he actually drank the potion and then the wrong woman got into his field of vision. Man, this was going to be hard.

"Phillip," she yelled as she grabbed back for her purse with the split bottle in it.

He stopped and looked around, obviously surprised and confused.

Lily ran up to him, elbowing aside a woman who looked as if she thought Phillip was her one and only karma.

"Hey, Phillip, remember me?" she asked, knowing he wouldn't. "I was at that great party you gave for some guitarist last week. Isn't it amazing to meet again like this? Gotta be fate, huh?"

Phillip squinted at her. "No, I'm sorry, I don't remember you."

"I'm Lily." She looked over her shoulder, and sure enough, there was Eleanor, just coming out of the hall, but way too soon. "Hey, Eleanor," she shouted. "Come on over here. You gotta meet someone."

She turned back to Phillip, about to explode with nerves and excitement. It was going to work, but she had to do this fast. "Listen, Phillip, you know what, when I was on the plane, they gave me this stuff that they said was really old cognac. But I don't know.   Could you try it for me? Pleeeease?" With her left hand in her purse, she shook the bottle vigorously.

Phillip stared at her as if she'd already gone over the waterfall. "Sorry, I know next to nothing about cognac." He turned toward the bar.

Eleanor was approaching fast, but looking around edgily. Anytime someone came close, she shied away, making a zig-zag path through the lobby. She kept her arms out from her side, as if to keep people away.

Aw, man, this wasn't going well. Lily ran around Phillip to block his way. "No, see, if you know *next* to nothing, you're still way ahead of me, 'cause I know *exactly* nothing. Please. I promise I won't bug you anymore."

Eleanor was just behind him now.

"Here," Lily said, putting the bottle in his hand. "Just try one sip for me, okay? I promise you'll be glad you did." She reached out and grabbed Eleanor's hand but didn't pull her forward.

Phillip frowned, hesitated, but took the bottle. He opened it, sniffed, and shook his head. He sniffed again and started to lower the bottle.

Desperate now, Lily shoved the bottle toward his lips at the same time she pulled Eleanor forward and pushed her directly in front of him.

Phillip clamped his mouth shut. The potion hit his lips and splattered outward.

Lily's heart plummeted. He didn't get any of it in his mouth. Then he licked at his lips as if trying to remove something nasty. His Adam's apple bobbed as he swallowed. He choked and coughed, and his head came down, his face twisted in surprise, anger, and distaste, a trail of potion dribbling down his chin, fizzing cheerfully, and a good portion spreading over his shirt. He was glaring like a livid drill sergeant. "What the hell do you..." He saw Eleanor. He faltered at the knees. His aura turned into a swirling rainbow. His face went completely sappy. He stared. His gaze went all mushy. He blinked. "Hi," he crooned. "I'm Phillip."

Eleanor looked around as if expecting someone and said distractedly, "That's nice." She moved off and headed for the elevator.

Phillip trailed after her. "Let me guess, you're a guitarist, aren't you?"

Lily jumped with glee. Like, far out! It worked. He'd only licked his lips off, and whammo, it hit him. He was into Eleanor like a hippie into his weed. Just like when she'd crashed into that George Craig. She knew exactly what he was going through. And all she had to do now was give the other half to Eleanor. Easy job. It couldn't be nearly as hard as getting Phillip to take it. No question, they were in for a happily-ever-after. And all because of her!

She watched him trying to engage Eleanor. Oops, better keep them separated till the other half was done. After all, he hadn't had much; and the way Eleanor was acting, she might just undo the potion with her spiky opinion of men.

Lily ran after them. "Hey, Phillip, was that really cognac?"

Eleanor squeezed into a full elevator, leaving Phillip with his arm outstretched.

Phillip turned back, dazed. He looked past her, jerked his head back and forth a few times, and started toward the front door. After a few steps, he stopped, gazed around as if lost on an alien planet, and turned back to the elevators.

"Phillip," Lily said, standing right in front of him. "Come on, let's go get a drink."

He stared down at her.

"I'm her roommate, you know. I can tell you all about her."

Phillip grabbed her arm and pulled her toward the bar.

20

Ursula squirmed in the presence of *Herr* Barkov, who was sitting opposite her at the supper table, between the girl from Potsdam and another student from Weimar. Even *they* seemed to lean away from him. His hostile, predatory air made her keep her eyes on her plate. She moved the cooling food around aimlessly. Why would such a sour man keep making advances toward her? Did he think she found his hostile face attractive with its thin mouth arched downward like a horseshoe? Did he think no one noticed his wedding band?

He leaned toward her. "You've hardly touched your *Sauerbraten*, *Fräulein* Kimmig," he said in his weasel's voice.

Ursula shrugged and lifted her eyes without looking at him. "I need to prepare for tomorrow. If you'll excuse me..." She shoved her chair back.

He rose from his chair, too, forcing the Postdamer to jump up, knocking over her bottle of soda water.

As she hurried through the dining room, she

glanced back. Barkov was in a tangle with the student, trying to follow her but unable to get around the student and dabbing at his pants, which were spotted with the spilled water. He'd be after her soon. Tense as she was, however, she couldn't help noticing again the difference between their group and the others. They'd been a table of dark silence in the chatting, laughing camaraderie. Maybe they, too, would have chatted, even laughed, if Barkov hadn't been there.

He was so obvious. So disgusting. She'd known men who were probably *Stasi*, but never one so amazingly blatant in using his slimy power to prey on women.

Back in the room had to herself, she felt safe again. She reveled in the silence, the solitude, and the time. If she wanted, she could practice all night for her slot in the first round of the competition. Twelve hours away, nine o'clock, second on the program. The thought made her shake. Now that she'd heard what some of the Westerners could do, she knew she had to find the song, the passion in the music before she went on stage.

Her warm-up scales twanged and echoed about the room unevenly. She set the guitar aside, lay back, and breathed deeply, visualizing herself seated calmly on the stage, the familiar guitar resting against her chest, her right arm draped over the body. She wanted to see herself as Fortier recommended, oblivious of the audience and aware of the composer speaking through her.

It didn't work. She couldn't feel the composer's presence at all. But she could feel Barkov's presence, standing behind her in the convention room, following her down the hall, probably listening outside her door right now. Falling on top of her when they'd checked in this morning.

She remembered the scene after the fall. He'd looked long at her briefcase and her face. Now that she thought of it, he'd seemed almost panicked. Then he'd collected himself and registered the group, making certain she got a room to herself while the other four were paired. He, of course, had a single room, as well. Idiot. Transparent as air.

She got up and retrieved her briefcase from the closet to take out the pieces for tomorrow's performance, though she had them all memorized. She stared at the case and hefted it again before sitting down with it on her lap. It was heavier than she remembered. With a gasp, she knew it was not hers. It was his, the one so much like hers that she'd noticed it at the border. Why had she not realized how heavy it was? Of course, after the fall the porter had put it on a luggage cart and set it in the closet for her.

"My God," she said aloud and threw the case

onto the quilt. Now she knew why he'd been hounding her. He didn't want her, he wanted this. Why didn't he just say there'd been a mix-up and demand his briefcase back? She should run right to the desk and ask his room number, return it immediately. She had absolutely no business with a *Stasi* briefcase in her possession.

Ursula got up but sat down again. Yes, why hadn't he said anything? Now the briefcase radiated danger. What could he be carrying that would make him so nervous and the case so heavy? Not his underwear. He'd had a big enough suitcase for all his clothing. Dossiers on all five of them? A dossier on her? What could possibly be in a dossier on her?

Shaking, she shoved at the catches with her thumbs. They were locked. Would her key work? She fished it out of her purse and inserted it into the hole, hoping it would refuse to turn. It caught at half a turn and she pulled the key out again.

She should stop this right now. Take the case and find Barkov. She stepped to the door and put her ear to it. No sound at all came from outside.

She inserted the key again, turned it to the catching point, and then jiggled it slowly, looking for a place where it would give. The key moved and finished the turn. She opened the second lock and thumbed both aside. The hasps clacked open, the sound loud and accusing, like gunshot, surely audible if he was listening outside the door. She shoved the briefcase under the feather quilt, jumped up and stepped to the window. She waited for his demanding knock.

In a minute she slid the case out again and opened the lid. A pile of papers, released from its confines, rose toward her. Inside the lid was a slot for an identification, and his name was on it.

In the case lay a thick stack of papers, covered by the title page:

PERSONNEL FILE: BARKOV, WOLFGANG.

Ursula gasped. Two realizations struck her at once. This was not supposed to be in his hands. No one ever got to see his own file. Even *Stasi*. Everyone knew that. Which meant he'd stolen the file. She gulped hard. He'd stolen his own file. It must be very damning. Why would he bring it out in public? Her heart raced at the thought. He thought the government would fall. He wanted to destroy the file on himself for all eventualities.

Was it even possible the government would fail? The floor seemed to fall out from under her. How would her country function with no government? No, Moscow would never let that happen. But Moscow was in the middle of turmoil now, too. Still, the government would hang on somehow. The people had been too scared for too long. All they could do in protest was to stand around with a lot of candles.

She stared at the stack of yellowed papers. She should close it again. Not read a single page. Give it back to him with some excuse about noticing that it wasn't hers. Assure him she'd never opened it. This was too dangerous.

But this was *Stasi*. No one ever got to see proof of what they did. If she read it, she could go to jail forever. Or conveniently disappear. Barkov could simply say she'd been killed by street thugs in the West, and no one would know any better.

The papers pulled at her, took control of her hands. She put them both down into the case and lifted the files out.

DEUTSCHE DEMOKRATISCHE REPUBLIK
    STAATSSICHERHEITSDIENST
File date of origin: 17. 7. 1965, 14:33:15 o'clock
Name: Barkov, Wolfgang
Code Name: Orion
Date of Birth: 28. 9. 1943
Place of Birth: Halle
Service Number: 22 19 80 11
Date of entry/recruitment: 18. 3. 1964

A detailed profile of Wolfgang Barkov's life followed, including his parents, friends, education, and activities. Ursula scanned it quickly, surprised to find that he'd studied socialist leadership at the Humboldt University in Berlin, during which time he'd "recruited" two professors and seven students.

Her stomach knotted itself into a tight ball of anger. Even if no one said it, everyone knew what the *Stasi* called "recruiting." *Spitzel*, filthy informer, forcing tepid socialists to be informers, too. Blackmailer.

She thumbed through the detail and found his report on his first assignment as a *Stasi* agent, written in a small, cramped hand.

Date: 01. 06. 1966

Code Name: Orion

Assignment: Bonner, Karl, Supervisor, People's Radio and Television Sales and Service, Halle. Subject known to criticize quality of television sets produced in German Democratic Republic and to boast of receiving transmissions from West Berlin via home-made antenna.

Research showed that subject has daughter with cerebral palsy. Orion reminded him of necessity to demonstrate solidarity with Socialist Unity Party to continue medical assistance received in children's hospital Halle. Further dissidence might result in child's transfer to clinic in Jena, no experts in child care. Antenna surrendered. No further dissidence expected.

The next page was Barkov's supervisor's report on Barkov's report.

Date: 03. 06. 1966
Code Name: Roster
Subject: Barkov, Wolfgang,
Service Number 22 19 80 11
Assignment: Bonner, Karl
Subject contacted Bonner in People's Radio and Television Sales and Service. Assignment successful. Subject also convinced Bonner to alter waiting list for television sets, setting name Barkov at the top. Subject is dedicated enough to be of use but not above using party for own gain.
Recommendation: Observe subject.

Furious, Ursula dropped the old report onto the bed, thumbed through a number of others from all over the country, and noted his rise in the hierarchy of the State Security Service.

About a third of the way through the stack the word *Telefon* caught her eye. The report, a stack in itself, summarized the construction of the telephone tapping installation near Radeberg. Much of it was technical, but Ursula understood enough to realize it had indeed been designed to tape every single telephone call in the country.

One short report caught her eye:

Date: 03.18.71
Code Name: Orion
Assignment: Bloss, Peter
Subject seen and overheard discussing purpose of telephone installation with fellow workers. Demonstrates unacceptable views about necessity for installation and right of government to build it.
Action: Removal

Subsequent to construction accident, Bloss accused and convicted of negligence, transferred to Frankfurt an der Oder.

She read of the chain link fence constructed around the installation in Radeberg, with the rolled barbed wire on the top that kept East Germans out of their own land. The knowledge crushed her and consumed her with hatred. Her hands fell to her lap and several papers scattered to the floor.

She retrieved the files, careful to keep the pages in order, and thumbed through more reports. Weimar and the name Hannelore Holger caught her eye. *Tante* Hanne? Everybody in Weimar called her that. What in God's name could Wolfgang Barkov have to do with Aunt Hanne?

As a young woman she'd been married to a man with epilepsy. During the Hitler regime they'd both been subjected to sterilization and it had broken *Herr* Holger's spirit. He'd died before the end of the war, leaving Hanne nothing but the house they lived in.

For years, Hanne had scratched a living out of the post-war years and the Russian occupation. Finally, she'd had no option but to rent the ground floor of her house to a man with party affiliations. He paid her a pitiful rent for it, but no one wondered why the housing commission let him get by with it. She'd moved to the second floor, where she had two bedrooms and a bath but no kitchen. She'd cooked on a hot plate.

Later, to make ends meet, she'd had to rent the two bedrooms out and move into the attic, where there was no running water, no heat, no electricity. Neighbors had done what they could, sharing hot meals with her; one or two had even offered her a bed in their cramped quarters. But Hanne had held onto the house. She never talked about a pension or any support from the government, but it was rumored she'd applied for it any number of times and been denied. Like so many causes for distress, her plight remained a question no one dared voice. Three years ago old Tante Hanne had been run over by a car, and the house had apparently passed into other hands.

Wolfgang Barkov's hands. He'd bought the house for 9,000 marks, less than the cost of the cheapest car. Why would he want the house? What did he know? Or was he planning to retire into it when there were no more ordinary people to manipulate?

Barkov was a lot worse than Ursula had thought. The worst kind of *Stasi*.

Ursula shook with the realization of the danger she was in. If she gave it back to him, he'd know by her face that she'd read it. He'd find some way to get rid of her. And he'd get away with destroying the damning file.

She couldn't let that happen. Which meant she had to go back to the East when she wanted so badly to stay in the West.

21

November 8, 1989

Lily woke on Wednesday with her left leg and right arm stuck out of the quilt, chilled to the marrow. The rest of her was sticky hot under the feathers. She pulled her cold limbs under for a minute, looking across to see if Eleanor was still asleep. She was gone. Even better. Lily smiled. Eleanor had no idea what a cool surprise was in store for her today!

After she'd zipped up her fleecy robe, Lily grabbed the water bottle out of the duffel bag, where it had lain among her clothes all night.

Her eyebrows shot up and the left side of her mouth turned way down. The potion didn't look good. The oil had separated and coagulated at a slant as a greenish brown mass, with the brandy mix trapped under it. The brandy mix had formed strange little lumps that looked somehow bruised and weary.

She shook the bottle tentatively. Nothing

changed. She shook it vigorously. The oil broke into chunks and then fought with the lumps to get to the top again. The mixture continued to churn after she stopped and looked as if it were building up to an explosive pressure. She ran to set it in the bathtub, just in case. There was no way she'd ever get Eleanor even to put this to her lips. She'd have to make another batch.

"Burn out," she moaned, sinking onto a weird piece of plumbing between the toilet and the tub, beset by the feeling that after the success with Phillip, nothing was going to go the way she'd planned it. Super, cosmic bummer. All she'd wanted in the beginning was to marry Phillip and put some good vibes in the world. She'd botched that. Now she was halfway to getting him matched up with Eleanor, and that was all very cool. But what she really wanted to do was go hunt down that gorgeous George Craig. Well, maybe he was, like, a little scruffy around the collar. And cuffs. Shoes. His socks probably had holes in them. But she was his and nobody else could ever be hers. Maybe she could get him to drink it.

She regarded the churning slime in the bottle. No, no sane person was going to drink that. Anyway, better to concentrate on one thing at a time. She'd have to worry about George later. She just hoped she could get to him before he checked out of the hotel.

Very slowly, holding the bottle steady in the tub, she opened the old mix. The escaping vapors whined and then the mix oozed out like a chemistry experiment gone bad. A stain spread along the bottom of the tub as it made its way into the pipes. The bathroom smelled of rancid ginger and rotting coconut. She grabbed the bottle, flushed the remaining mix down the toilet, and washed the bottle out with a small amount of Eleanor's shampoo.

She showered, doused herself with rose oil, and began the chanting and the concoction, using the brandy and the glass from the bar. Ready to get the tap water from the bathroom, she spied a new water bottle on the dresser. Probably better than tap water, which looked a bit gray, she thought. She screwed the lid open and heard the little whoosh that accompanied the breaking of the seal.

"Hey, weird, they vacuum seal their water around here," she muttered. She poured water into the mix until she thought it looked right, raising her eyebrows slightly when it bubbled. The new potion looked inviting, downright cheery, in fact. Like, wow, maybe this was going to come off better than she thought. She transferred the potion to the old bottle and replaced the cap.

She dressed to go find Eleanor. This time, she

knew, there would be no problem getting them together; Phillip was already hooked and would be hovering around somewhere.

She left the open bottle of water on the dresser, barely glancing at the many little bubbles that rose from the bottom and popped on the top like champagne.

22

Eleanor took her coffee, soft boiled egg, and rolls to the only empty table in the dining room. Fortunately, it was near the door, so the hit man wouldn't have to fire past anybody else. Should she sit facing the door? What would she do if she saw him aiming at her? Would she automatically dive under the table? She sat with her back to the door. It would be soon. Fear alternated with relief. Every few seconds, her mind's eye saw Sylvester Stallone leap into the doorway with a massive machine gun and fire off a round.

She sliced the top off her egg. The soft yolk and the squishy white around it turned her stomach as she visualized it splattering across the room with a bullet that pierced her clean through. She moved it across the table and spread a little butter on a crispy bread roll. Unable to put it in her mouth, she added a spoon of plum jam from the little pot on the table. When she realized she couldn't even drink the coffee, she gave up on breakfast and went down to the convention hall.

She stepped out of the elevator into the lobby and collided with Phillip Redding.

"Good morning, Eleanor," he said, with that same idiotic smile he'd turned on her yesterday afternoon.

She returned the greeting without smiling and moved away. She had to keep distance...

He followed, bent around her from the side like a gangly parenthesis. "Are you going to a master class this morning?"

"No, the competition," she said over her shoulder as she moved away from him.

He curved around her from the other side. "Ah, what a coincidence. I was just on my way there myself."

"Aha."

Phillip followed her into the hall, inanely oblivious of the space she kept trying to put between them. She stopped at in the back row just inside the door.

"There's lots of room. Don't you want to sit a little closer?" he asked, his hand on her elbow, ready to propel her down the aisle.

She regarded the six or eight empty rows in front of them and the hundred or so guitarists who'd crowded close to the front. "No, I like it back here. You go on up." She sat in the chair closest to the door.

He squeezed past her, took the next chair, and

moved it closer. She shifted hers to the left. A moment later he cut the space between them again. He simpered away at her about the concerts and classes. She moved her chair again and laid her purse on the floor between them.

"I'd love to hear you play sometime," he said, leaning across the space.

Eleanor grunted. This didn't make sense. She had met him once before, at his own house, in fact. What was it...two years ago?

She opened her mouth to mention that and closed it again. She didn't want to encourage him in any way. She needed to get him to move away.

"Look, could you..." she started.

"We could go to concerts..." He interrupted, waving his hands in front of him as if her were painting a picture.

She'd been to a *flamenco* concert with Hal about three weeks before they broke up, and he'd talked her into going to the Redding house for a reception. She hadn't wanted to go; she'd heard enough about the Redding receptions to know she wouldn't enjoy one. Too crowded. And they were supposed to get pretty wild as the night progressed. Not to mention Redding himself, whose reputation as a playboy made her disapprove him automatically. But she would've done anything for Hal.

"...enjoy a glass of wine afterwards..."

After what? She and Phillip had been introduced at his reception, and he'd been as aloof as he was yesterday, before Lily dragged her over to meet him. Back then, if she hadn't been so involved with Hal, she'd have been offended.

She ran her hands up and down her arms in her thin silk blouse. The conference room was cold.

"...play any *flamenco* at all?"

What a relief. The performances were starting. He'd have to shut up. Why was he suddenly so interested? He was in danger, hovering over her like an umbrella. A new thought sent a sharp chill down her spine in the cold conference room. Was he the hit man? Eleanor's breath stopped. That would explain such deluxe living without having to work for it. What was he waiting for, then? Was she supposed to give him some kind of signal? A code word? This was crazy. And underneath all her questions lay a quivering gray jelly of fear. She wanted to bolt out of the seat and run away from him.

She forced herself to sit through the first performance, not knowing what was more distracting, his constant focus on her, the prospect of his aiming a bullet between her shoulder blades, or the chills skating on her spine. Before the introduction of the second performer, Phillip turned to her, ready to start blithering again. What an act.

"Excuse me," she muttered without looking at him, fearful of what she'd see in his eyes. "I have to run upstairs and get a sweater. I'm freezing." She was out the door before he could get his suit jacket off and offer it to her. She realized immediately she'd left her purse between the seats, but she didn't dare go back. She grabbed at her pocket to be sure the key was there. At the elevators, she jabbed the up button and paced frantically, jabbing again and again. When the left elevator doors swung open, she strode forward and crashed into a small thin man trying to get out. Automatically, they grabbed each other to keep from falling. They stared. Their eyes popped simultaneously. All breathing stopped.

The scraggly brown hair, the acne scarred face. The twit who wanted to get in the Mafia. Whose initiation had been to hijack her car. Who'd failed.

The elevator doors slid inward, hit them, and opened again, beeping indignantly.

"You," they said in unison. And then, "YOU?!" And then, "Oh, no. Oh, my God."

He shoved her out the door and ran past her. He stopped in the middle of the lobby, spun around, stared back at her with his head shaking, and then ran for the doors, dropping a pink paper on the Persian carpet.

Eleanor stood frozen in front of the elevator.

They had sent him? Not that Redding man? No! He was a total incompetent. He couldn't even hijack a simple car, for God's sake. He'd kill the wrong person. He'd aim at her and miss. Or he'd hit her in the spine and paralyze her for life. From the neck down.

She slammed her hand onto the up button, but the elevators were gone. She ran for the stairs and didn't stop running until she was in her room. The maid had just come in and was about to strip the cover from the feather quilt on Lily's bed.

"Please, come back later," she gasped without thinking. The maid was a small, chubby Turkish woman in a long blue dress under her hotel smock and a gray veil covering her hair. She looked like some kind of nun. She did not understand English.

"*Bitte, machen sie das Zimmer später,*" Eleanor tried again, leaning against the dresser, her chest still heaving. The woman smiled and left, taking the half-empty mineral water bottle with her.

Eleanor grabbed her suitcase and rummaged for the telephone number. Of course, it was in her purse. The purse was downstairs next to that Redding man who wasn't going to kill her after all. She slapped herself on the head.

"That twit of a hit man left the hotel," she muttered. "I think. At least it looked like he was headed for the door. I have to get that... God, what was his name again? Sonny. That Sonny's number. They have to call him off." She took a deep breath. "Don't panic," she said aloud. Then she said it eight more times.

She peeked out of the door and down the hall. It was empty. The stairwell was only a couple of doors away. She went back and changed into her pearl gray turtleneck. If only she had a hat.

23

Ursula stood at the bottom of the steps that led up to the stage. Her heart fluttered so wildly she could barely breathe. Was it because she had to climb those steps and perform for this Western audience or because she knew Wolfgang Barkov lurked somewhere? She looked toward the back.

He stood at the door, his eyes fixed on her like crosshairs. He didn't move a muscle. Was he just going to stand there like a frozen vulture and stare at her during the whole performance?

The coordinator of the competition announced her name and the audience applauded. Astonished, Ursula glanced at them as she started up the steps. At the back of the room that strict American woman with the long bun at the back of her head got up and ran out, right past Barkov, and Ursula wished she'd knocked him over.

Feeling like a moving target, she walked to the stool in the center of the stage. She forced herself to focus on the performance. How often had she played in the towns around Weimar, and not once had there been a single clap of two hands together before she played. The audience usually didn't even applaud after the performance. But these people hadn't been picked up at their workplaces and forced to come here as a civic duty to support art. They didn't withhold applause to show their resentment at having culture shoved down their throats.

Ursula settled on the stool and draped her long black skirt over her knees with shaking hands. The guitar nestled comfortingly on her lap, her right arm in the long sleeved white blouse rested on the familiar bulge of the body. As always, she stroked the strings one last time to be sure none had slid out of tune. It didn't calm her enough. She made a pretense at tuning the G-string, and strummed a B major chord. She sat and breathed deeply for a minute, trying to ignore the audience and concentrate on the music. And then she realized: the audience wished her well. When they'd applauded before the other performances, she'd assumed many had known the competitors. But they'd given her encouragement, too, before she even appeared; they were not her enemy. She looked out at them and smiled nervously. She would give them something in return. The devil take Barkov.

She started the Castellnuovo-Tedesco piece with its dark colors. Her right fingers were sweaty and wanted to jump off the strings before she had them placed for good sound. She reined in her nerves and played deliberately, letting the colors hang in the air. By the time she finished, the fingers were dry and she was calm.

She glanced up during the applause, catching Barkov out of the corner of her eye. She ignored him and tuned the bass string down to D for the Solenkov piece that was so popular in the East with its driving rhythm and its silky, lilting middle section. The audience seemed to love it. The appreciation lofted her spirits into the Bach "Chaconne," and she played every variation like a different letter to the people before her. She missed the fingering in one of the faster scale passages but recovered well.

She let the last note ring till it died, but the "Chaconne" still had her in its grip. She had never played it with so much feeling before. Maybe she had infused emotion into it that Bach would never have approved. The applause rang in her ears for a minute before she stood up. She bowed awkwardly, not knowing how to respond to enthusiasm.

The audience began to disperse for an intermission as she walked down the steps again. She could see Barkov working against the stream and heading toward the stage. Panicked, she searched for a different exit. If he caught up with her, he'd send her back to the East immediately, with a mark on her file that would end all hope she had for any kind of future. If she was lucky.

At the bottom of the steps several people stopped to compliment her on her playing. A smiling face came into focus directly in front of her, hazel eyes over a straight nose and beautiful teeth. Barkov was halfway down the aisle.

"*Fräulein* Kimmig," said the friendly face, "I'm not a guitarist, but I want to tell you how much I enjoyed your playing."

She recognized him—one of the men she'd seen yesterday when she left the hall to escape Barkov. An agent of some sort, surely, especially if he admitted he wasn't a guitarist. What else would he be doing here? She looked into his face. It was not hard and cold like Barkov's.

"Are you all right?" he asked. "Don't faint. You did fine, really you did."

Barkov's head bobbed only a few meters away.

Desperate, she said, "Please, walk out of here with me."

He blinked in surprise but then smiled warmly. "I'd be glad to, *Fräulein* Kimmig."

She shoved her guitar quickly into its case and took his arm.

"Thank you very much for the compliment," she said as they went past Barkov.

Of course, he turned and tailed them up the crowded aisle, practically stepping on her heels.

24

Lily saw Eleanor's purse on the floor next to Phillip, moved behind him, shoved chairs aside and slid into the seat next to him. Weird. Why'd he want to sit back here, practically out in the hall? The distraction almost made her forget her tapestry purse dangling from her shoulder. She resumed rocking it to shake the potion.

Phillip turned toward her with a great big teddy bear smile, no doubt for Eleanor. It fell right off his face when he saw Lily, and he turned his attention back to the guitarist on stage.

Lily faced front and listened. A young blond woman in a white blouse and a long black skirt was playing some moody piece that didn't seem to have any melody you could hang on to. "Far out," she thought. "I think I'll stick to the beginner stuff. At least you can sing along with it."

She watched Phillip out of the corner of her eye. He seemed to dig it. She listened harder. Well, there was a thread of something there, but it was beyond her.

"Where'd Eleanor go?" she whispered.

Phillip put his hand out and slapped gently in the air, telling her to be quiet. Way in front, where the rest of the audience sat, heads turned and faces frowned. Lily sighed. She looked over her shoulder toward the hall for Eleanor but found someone else. A real horror stood at the door, a man with a hatchet face and thinning blond hair. She'd come right past him and hardly noticed. He looked as if he'd have enjoyed the potion that had gone bad. The thought made her shake her purse a little harder.

The concert ended, and the audience clapped wildly; some even stood. The guitarist got up, looking as if the clapping were a complete surprise, and bowed in a couple of body jerks. The applause died and the aisles filled with people chatting about the performances, speculating on the winner. The guitarist left the stage, watching the back of the room anxiously.

Lily looked back at the ferret at the door. He was moving as fast as he could toward the stage, against the current.

Phillip waited in front of his chair, watching for Eleanor. Lily grinned up at the back of his head. Just wait, she thought, picking up Eleanor's purse and dangling it from her shoulder over her own, which she jiggled gently.

Eleanor appeared in the entrance, pale and

tense, struggling against the crowd. Phillip and Lily moved into the aisle to greet her.

"Far out, Eleanor, you look like you just lost your aura," said Lily. "What's up?"

"You really do look like you've been through a wringer," added Phillip. "Is there anything I can do for you?"

"Where's my purse?" asked Eleanor with a shrill edge to her voice. "I need my purse." She squeezed past them into the row, bent over, looking under chairs. She was close to hysteria.

"I got it," called Lily.

Eleanor rushed back to her, snatched the purse, and headed for the door.

Lily grabbed the hem of Eleanor's turtleneck. "Hey, hold on. Drink this. It'll perk you right up."

Eleanor stared at the liquid that was still churning in the bottle. She squinted at Lily in complete lack of comprehension. "What? Now? No, I..."

"Drink it, El," Lily pleaded, still holding Eleanor's clothing.

Eleanor gave her a long stare that started with surprise, turned to suspicion, and then eased into resignation. She shook her head with her lips drawn into a line, but she pointed at the bottle and snapped, "What is this, some kind of tea?"

"Yeah, some kind. Come on, drink it. It's just what you need, I promise." Lily could hardly keep a smile from exploding out of the triumph. This was going great. Two happy people coming up! She shoved the bottle forward.

Just as Eleanor's fingers closed around it, the blond guitarist hurried past, steered by a young man.

Lily dragged Eleanor out into the aisle, right in front of Phillip.

Eleanor put the bottle to her lips and swallowed a fair amount.

Phillip backed away from the swing of Eleanor's elbow and caused the ferret man to change course and pass right in front of Eleanor. He barely glanced down to excuse himself.

Lily saw it happen. Eleanor's eyes locked into the glance and followed the ferret to the door. The ripple came late, but there was no mistaking what had happened. Eleanor stood there as if some cosmic force were trying to tear her body in two. She stared after the retreating ferret. She dropped the bottle, shoved things around in her purse, came up with a small slip of paper, and ran out the door.

Phillip rushed after her.

Lily stood rooted in the empty room, every cell in her body vibrating with shock.

25

Horst watched the pale, frightened face of Ursula Kimmig as they hurried to the elevators.

Two other tight-faced girls got on with them, looking at Ursula as if they expected some kind of explanation for his presence. They must be her colleagues. Certainly they had the veiled, wary eyes of East Germans. They got off on the third floor, glancing back and bending their heads to each other just as the doors closed.

Immediately, Ursula's face lost some of its tightness and her shoulders loosened.

She looked up at him and smiled a little. "Thank you. That was very kind of you."

"Look, *Fräulein* Kimmig, I can see there's something wrong here. Can I be of any help?"

The doors opened and she started down the hall. "I don't think so, but thank you once more."

"Well, would you allow me to buy you an early lunch? I think you at least deserve some kind of special treatment for your wonderful concert."

She started to shake her head as they rounded a corner in the hall.

"I think you'd enjoy it," he said. "I know a fine little Indian restaurant not far from the hotel. It can't be too crowded at this hour. Have you ever eaten Indian?"

She stopped. "Eat away from the hotel? I don't think I'm allowed..."

She gazed at him, but Horst knew her mind was chasing up frightening avenues.

She looked back up the corridor. "Is there another way out of the hotel besides the front door?"

"There must be. Where's the breakfast room? It must lead to an outside exit, even if we have to go through the kitchen."

"On the second floor."

"Let's try that."

Horst seated Ursula against the wall in the *Indien Chai* and sat to her left so that other customers who would surely share the table wouldn't converse past them.

She avoided his eyes and took in the walls decorated with pictures of elephants transporting Maharajahs, alternating with colorful gauzy drapes inset with sequins. Indian music droned lightly from hidden speakers.

"That's a sitar playing, isn't it?" she asked

when he'd ordered for them. Finally she looked him in the eye.

Horst grinned, embarrassed. "I'm afraid I don't know much about musical instruments."

Her eyes hardened with suspicion. "Who are you?"

"*Ach*, please forgive me. I should have introduced myself in the auditorium. Horst Bauer. West Berlin Police."

She looked skeptical and frightened.

"Really." He took out his identification and showed it to her.

Ursula moved as far from him as her seat would allow. "What do you want with me? I haven't done anything."

He laughed. "You stand accused of bewitching me with your music."

She didn't respond to his light tone. "But why were you at my performance?"

"My being there had nothing to do with you, I assure you. I was there for the other concerts, too, while my partner checked the classes. It's strictly police business. Has to do with some man wanted in America."

She nodded knowingly. "Their criminals are everywhere, aren't they? Did it really sound all right?"

"What, your performance? It was wonderful."

She sat back and relaxed.

"You've never been to America, I guess," he said.

"No, have you? You know, I've never played like that before. The audience was so different. I felt I was giving them a gift instead of playing what somebody thinks they should hear." She stopped suddenly and glanced at him sideways. "I shouldn't be telling you this. And I certainly shouldn't be talking just about myself. I'm sorry, *Herr* Bauer. I guess I'm still just caught up in the performance. I've never had a really appreciative audience before."

"Is that what it's like to be a musician at home? Weimar, isn't it? I read everything on the program about you. And don't worry, your secret is safe with me." He touched her hand on the table. She looked at his hand, then at his face, and away, moving her hand into her lap.

The waiter brought a metal plate with a great round flat bread on it and two little bowls with sauces made of yogurt and green relish. He set it down and walked away without a word or a smile. Horst waited for her to help herself.

She touched the stiff, cracker-like bread and put her hand back on the table.

"I guess this pretty strange stuff for you, if you've never eaten it before," he said. "Here, I'll show you what to do with it." He broke off a piece. "I like the green sauce, but you might find it a little spicy." He dipped a piece in the green sauce and bit the end off.

She followed suit. Her eyes flew open as the surprise flavors hit her taste buds.

Horst smiled at her, trying to get her to relax. "You asked me a minute ago if I'd been to America. I have. I spent six months in the state of Colorado working with the police in Denver."

Her face showed no sign of comprehension.

He remembered his own vague knowledge of American geography before going there. "It's in the western half of the country. The capital is at the foot of the Rocky Mountains. I loved it. You can see the mountains from the city, a huge long panorama of them. In an hour and a half from Denver you can be on a mountain almost four thousand meters high and look down on the city."

Ursula had wrinkled her brow the minute he'd said he loved it in America. "But all the criminality, the violence, the race wars."

"Yes, that was bad, although I think the expression 'race wars' is far too strong. But criminality is only a small part of the picture. The people are so nice, so open and friendly. Just for example, the waiters. Watch how this one acts when he comes back. Over there, waiters make you feel welcome; they give you a table for yourself; no strangers come and sit with you. They smile and chat with you. Sometimes I had the feeling a waiter would sit right down and eat with me. They come back often to see if you're satisfied with your meal.   They refill your coffee cup endlessly for free." He grinned. "Of course, the coffee's so weak that you have to drink several cups to feel like you've gotten any."

She finally smiled at him.

The waiter brought their curry dishes and turned away again without a word.

Horst watched the retreating Indian. "See how they do here? Or the clerks in stores in America. They'll demonstrate everything in the store for you, and if you don't buy anything, they still smile and tell you they hope you have a nice day. Anyway, I'm going back there someday."

Ursula shook her head. "I can't imagine that. Our stores hardly ever have anything to sell anyway, and when they do the clerks act as if your asking for help is a thoughtless infringement on their time."   She stopped a moment and then continued, looking at the table. "Everyone who comes back from the West always says the stores here are amazing. I wish...but I don't have time. I have to get back and practice." She took a bite of curry and chewed thoughtfully, apparently focused on her tongue. "This is strange, but I like it. Are there many Indian restaurants here?"

"Some.   And a lot of Chinese, and some French, Italian, Japanese, Turkish. Even Mexican.

I learned to love the Mexican kitchen while I was in America."

"This is delicious. We have a Chinese restaurant in Weimar, but I think it's run by Vietnamese."

"Would you like to try some of the others? I'd be happy to take you."

She looked surprised. "Thank you for the invitation," she said, "but I have to go back to Weimar on Friday morning."

"Well, is there anything you'd like to do before going back to the hotel?"

She shook her head. "I should go to the master classes or look over the music sales and exhibitions. I need to practice the competition piece. Not that I'm likely to have to perform it, because I doubt if I'll make the second round." She stopped took a deep breath. "No. I want to go shopping," she said. "I don't have enough money to buy anything, but I want to see the stores. If I happen to get into the second round, I'll just practice all night. Besides, I'd like to stay away from..." Instead of finishing the thought, she put a new bite of chicken curry in her mouth.

Horst knew she feared mentioning the *Stasi* agent who was obviously after her. "All right, I'll take you where there are a lot of stores, and then at five o'clock I'll meet you again where I leave you and take you back to the hotel. I'd go with you, but I have to get back to work. By now my partner is probably asking himself whether that American felon got to me first and shot me dead."

She smiled at him now, a warm and open smile, only a little timid. "Thank you again, *Herr* Bauer."

"You're very welcome, *Fräulein* Kimmig. I really would like to see you again, you know."

"It isn't going to be possible, is it?"

Horst shrugged. "Who knows? The way things are going, maybe the whole Wall will fall down."

The anxiety came back to her face. "That'll never happen."

26

Wolfgang Barkov had been watching the elevators for an hour, sometimes sitting on the edge of a red chair with his elbows on his knees, sometimes pacing the length of the lobby. Where was that girl? He'd banged on her door twice since her performance. He fiddled with coins in his pocket, shifting the top coin of a small stack to the bottom over and over. His shoulders ached with tension. He took his hand out and ran both over his face. The right one smelled of worthless aluminum coins.

He hadn't slept since discovering the mix-up of the briefcases. His entire circulatory and digestive systems were aroil. He didn't know how to deal with danger in the West. If he made a scene here, his *Stasi* status not only did not make him invulnerable but might even put him in great danger if the girl exposed the file.

He knew for certain she'd read it—that had been obvious in the way she'd attached herself to that young man the minute she left the stage. Who was he? How had she managed that maneuver? It was planned. Clearly, she'd called someone last night. "I must have missed a West connection somewhere," he muttered through his clenched jaw.

Where had she gone? And who was the man who'd suddenly showed up?

She must have returned to her room by now. Maybe they were both there, looking at the files this minute.

His heart racing, he ran to the elevators and jabbed the up button continually until the doors slid open.

On the fifth floor he peered out. There was no one in the hall before it turned toward *Fräulein* Kimmig's room. He walked down the hall, distracted momentarily by the muffled but high pitched voice of that mousy American who was in room 511. She was shrieking, sounded panicky. He dismissed her.

He turned the corner. Toward the end of the hall was the maid, a small, dumpy foreign woman with some kind of head covering, just taking bed linens out of her cart. She went into the room next to *Fräulein* Kimmig's. Wolfgang strode to the guitarist's room and put his ear to the door. He heard nothing but his own pounding heart. They were not there after all. He would get the maid to open the door.

He stomped into 537. *"Fräulein,"* he said angrily. "You have not yet made up my room." He jabbed his finger in the direction of room 535.

She looked up from bundling the old sheets. She'd understood the tone of his voice, but not the words. He took her by the arm and pulled her to the next door. You…make… room…now," he said loudly.

She pulled her arm away. "Make already."

"I don't believe you. Open the door."

"This you room?"

"Yes."

She looked skeptical. "You open."

"I don't have my key. You open it now or I call the manager."

"Yes, you call manager. This room for lady. Not for you." She put her hands on her hips.

"You'll be sorry for this," he hissed. He turned on his heels and strode back to the elevator, more nervous than ever. He stationed himself in the lobby in a chair where he could see all doors. That Kimmig girl would not go unpunished for this. No matter how weak the government got, there would still be some time before there were no more strings he could pull, no more schmucks he could blackmail. There were things that could be done to her own file. She would still apply for jobs. Someday she would want an apartment. She would regret ever taking his briefcase. In the worst case he could...

A movement of drab color near the reception desk caught his eye. The man was too nondescript not to be an agent. His plain, rumpled trench coat gave him away immediately. Dark tan with a stain on the back that looked as if he'd sat in some coffee.

Barkov stood up and backed away, trying to implode himself into the shadows about him. He watched as the man waited to speak to the receptionist, who ignored him. His disguise was so ridiculous no *Stasi* would ever deign to wear it. Or was that costume supposed to throw Wolfgang off? Shaggy brown hair, scruffy shoes. Skinny and puny as an earthworm. Always the most dangerous kind of agent. Out to prove himself. Whose agent was he?

The man cleared his throat with a squeak and asked a question. The receptionist poked under the counter and handed him a small piece of pink paper, holding it between her thumb and forefinger.

When the strange agent turned from the desk, Wolfgang gasped and clapped his hand over his mouth. He recognized the profile. It was a face he knew, but from where? His fist clenched the sweat-sticky coins in his pocket and his head began to throb. They wouldn't send another agent to check on these ninny-guitarists. He could only be looking for Wolfgang himself. They'd discovered the stolen file.

The drab non-entity peered around as if looking for someone he dreaded to see and rushed through the lobby doors.

Barkov stood frozen behind the plant, wondering which direction danger would come from next.

27

Lily slid the room key quietly into the hole and opened the door slowly. Eleanor's voice shrilled through the first crack.

"Don't you dare put me on hold!" she shrieked. "I'm calling from Berlin, for God's sake. He told me to call back in an hour. Put me through now!"

Lily slipped in and slumped onto the bed, hiding behind the quilt. She should leave. Not eavesdrop. But she just had to apologize, explain what had happened.

Eleanor turned from the dresser and stared right past her.

"Sonny? Did you get through?...I know I paid good money...I don't care if you're out on bail and they have their eyeballs up your...Did you call it off?...What do you mean 'you can't?...' 'The ball's rolling'? So stop it from rolling."

Eleanor listened another minute. "Look," she screamed, "I'm the one, the contract. The man you sent is an idiot. He'll do it all wrong. And, besides, I'm in love now." Her face paled and her eyes squeezed shut. "What? I can't believe I said that!" she mumbled, shaking her head in quick, tight jerks. And then she was shouting again. "You have to do something."

She listened again. Her shoulders sagged. She hung up and threw herself on the bed.

Lily wished she could make herself invisible in the silence that followed. It was no good. She had to confess. She got up and sat on Eleanor's bed.

"It's all my fault," she whispered.

Eleanor dragged herself back from far away. "What?"

Lily nodded.

Eleanor drew her face into a lot of wrinkles. "Don't be ridiculous."

"No, really, I made you fall in love. You know that stuff I gave you to drink to calm you down? It was really a love potion."

Eleanor squinted at her like Dumbo in a quantum physics class.

"See, it was like this. I wanted to marry Phillip, so I made a potion for him and me. I drank my half, but then I ran into George Craig in the street and Phillip's half ran into the gutter, all smoky and, like, hissy. Man, I was so bummed out. I fell in love right there. With that George. That's why I'm here, in fact. 'Cause I knew he was coming. I kept thinking it'd wear off and I'd dig

Phillip again, but it didn't. I still got it really bad for him. George. So since I was hooked on him, I thought I'd give Phillip to you, see? 'Cause I decided it was time for me to start doing some good. And for you to have some happiness. I gave him his potion last night, you know, when I introduced you? And it worked just fine. He's dead gone on you, you know. Then I gave you yours, but that man that looks like a vicious undertaker got in the way."

Eleanor's mouth had fallen open about when Lily said "hissy." Now she snapped it closed and then said, "What on earth are you talking about?"

"Don't you see? I made you fall in love. With that potion. No, I don't mean in love with the potion. I mean I used it to make you fall in love." Lily flinched, expecting a tirade from Eleanor.

Eleanor squinted at her for another minute and then shook her head. "Listen, Lily, I don't even faintly believe in love potions, but I'm not going to get into that right now. That's the least of my worries. I have a lot more pressing..."

"Yeah, some contract that fell through, huh? I heard what you said on the phone." Lily sat up straighter and put her hands up, palms out. "I'm sorry, El, I couldn't help it. You were pretty loud."

Eleanor heaved a great sigh. "I was screaming. I suspect the whole hotel heard it."

"So what kind of contract was it? You going

to play a concert or something?"

Eleanor let out a nasal, rather juicy snort. She shook her head and put her lower arm over her eyes. For a long time she didn't say anything, but she didn't shoo Lily away.

Lily waited. When it seemed Eleanor had slid into some kind of unhealthy meditation, she started to get up.

"Wait." Eleanor grabbed her arm. "I don't want you to be in danger."

"Huh? Now what on earth are *you* talking about?"

Eleanor closed her eyes and took a deep breath. "There's a contract out on my life."

Lily jumped up, horrified. "What? No! How do you know? Who'd want to do a thing like that?"

Eleanor swallowed hard. "Me. I took it out."

Lily's eyes bugged wide and she stared speechless for a minute while her face slid into comprehension and then sympathy. "Aw, El, I'm so sorry. You must've been really bummed out to do a thing like that."

Eleanor shook her head. "'Bummed' is a pretty mild word for it, but yeah. I was."

"I never heard of taking out a contract on your own life." She looked down at Eleanor, so lonely, so sad, so...what? Desperate. "Far out," she said, "this is so far out. How are they going to do it?"

A new thought struck her like a car crash test. "Oh, my God. That undertaker guy, I bet he's the hit man, right? Oh, man. Burn out. Burn right out!" Lily moved away, found herself by the window and felt a queasy tingling between her shoulder blades. That guy could be... She moved toward the bathroom.

Eleanor squinted at her. "Undertaker? Never mind. I know who it is, and he's an idiot. They sent the wrong man. I ran into him by the elevator. That little twit. He tried to hijack my car a few weeks ago to get into the Mafia, but I didn't let him."

"You stopped a hijacking? Jeez, Eleanor, you're soo cool! How'd you do it?"

Eleanor sighed and shrugged. "I only did it because I was depressed. I'm still depressed. Anyway, I was on the way home from Boulder one night, trying to drive my car into an overpass on the turnpike. I chickened out. Then I ran over a raccoon on the highway, and when I stopped, this little twit jumped into the car. I just told him to go ahead and shoot me."

"No way!"

"And now he showed up in Berlin. He recognized me, and we both knew what he's doing here. He ran out. I just tried to cancel the contract, but they said it's too late. They can't reach their Berlin contact. He was supposed to leave for

Greece on vacation immediately after the hit man contacted him."

"Heav-ee. What are you going to do?"

"I have no idea. Stay in the room, I guess. Then I'll never see that blond man again," she groaned.

"Listen, did you get a good look at him?"

"Who, the hit man?"

"No, the blond, the undertaker with the ferret face."

Eleanor let her head fall back on the pillow, smiling absently. "Enough. Those blue eyes..."

"Like chips off a glacier. The man is a snake. A weasel. I had a good look at him before the performance was over. Besides, he's on the make for the guitarist who was playing."

Eleanor groaned. Her lip quivered. "I should just go down and wait for the twit in the lobby. Maybe if I go right up to him, he won't miss or kill the wrong person."

"No way, we can't do that to Phillip."

"Phillip? Are you seriously telling me he's in love with me?"

"Yep. That was a great batch." Lily straightened her shoulders and grinned.

"I don't want him in love with me. I can't stand him. Or his type. Never had to work for anything in his whole life. Never did anything useful. He can't possibly have any values. I had to work from high school on..."

"Come on, Eleanor, he's a nice, generous man. Everybody says so. And he has the most gorgeous aura." Lily's stomach growled into the short silence. "Are you hungry?"

"Actually, I am. I didn't eat any breakfast, half expecting to get a bullet in my head."

"Want to share my peanut butter?"

"Well..., what the heck, sure, thanks." She shook her head and almost smiled.

Lily dug in her duffle bag and brought out lunch. "You take the spoon," she said.

"What are you going to eat with?"

Lily brought her tooth brush from the bathroom and dug the handle into the peanut butter.

"Smart thinking," Eleanor said around the peanut butter. "I predict some lucrative career for you."

"Wishful thinking, you mean. I guess my meager bank account was the cause of this whole mess. I just figured that if I could get Phillip to fall in love with me, I'd work hard to be a really good wife to him, but I wouldn't always have to worry about the last five cents in my checking account on the twentieth of every month. I'd find myself, maybe take some classes, and do something worthwhile. I know I sound like a slimy gold digger, but I really wanted to do some good. So I got out the book on witchcraft that I bought from Shalmon and tried out the potion."

"Speaking of potions, did you tell me it made you fall for George Craig? He's got to be a little old for you, don't you think? Of course, Phillip isn't..."

Lily smiled that far-away smile. "I think this one is an entirely different George."

"Why don't you use a potion on him and make it mutual?"

"I figure I have to straighten out this other mess first. After all, I'm the one who screwed it all up. Besides, I realize the potions are, like, too dangerous. One out of three isn't a great track record. But there are other charms in the book I could use if I ever got close enough to him."

"What does he look like, anyway?"

"He's kind of short, barely taller than I am. He has brown hair, brown eyes, and a few scars on his face." Her face started to slide into a dreamy gaze.

"WHAT?!"

"Brown hair..."

"What was he wearing when you saw him yesterday?"

"Hmm, a dark tan trench coat."

Eleanor's face went white.

"What's the matter?"

"Your George Craig is the hit man."

"No."

Eleanor nodded.

"Aw, shit." Lily threw herself back into the quit, fists clenched. The quilt bounced up on both sides of her. She grabbed the feather mounds, drew her legs in, and disappeared like a caterpillar into a cocoon. "Aw, bummer," she moaned. Only a muffled *m* escaped the quilt. She freed her head and beat against the feathers. "Aw, George, you space case, you absolute flake, what do you want to go and do something like that for? Aw, man, just my luck to get myself into it with a loser, an end-of-the-line hit man. Oh, bummer, double bummer, bummer to the nth power."

She sat up again and caught Eleanor's eye. They stared at each other a minute, and then said together, "What are we going to do?"

"Hey, listen," said Lily, "thanks for not being mad at me."

"Don't mention it. I guess there was enough stupidity to go around and we could both learn some lessons from this."

"Yeah."

"What are we going to do?" they asked again.

Eleanor got up and paced between the beds, from the door to the window. Lily slid off her bed, walked on her knees to the window, closed the curtain, and assumed her yoga position on the bed, the quilt puffing up around her. "Let's both try to relax. Sit down and breathe," she said.

"Breathe? I am breathing."

"No, the deep-calm exercise. Get comfortable on your bed."

Eleanor raised her arms like a fitting for a crucifix. "I'm about to jump out of my skin and she tells me to get comfortable." She stretched out on her bed anyway.

Lily began to speak in a voice that emanated from a world of drifting colors and mists. "Now go to the calm place deep inside you. Put all tensions and bad vibrations far from you."

Eleanor sat up slightly and stared across the room. How did this girl think she could shove the bad vibrations any further than her skin? Still, she dropped her head back on the pillow, rolled her eyes, and let the voice take her.

"Breathe slowly, in...*hu,   hu,   hu*... out... *phhhhhhhhh*, in...*hu, hu, hu, hu, hu*... out... *phhhhhh*..."

The room became silent except for the light gurgling of two stomachs working on peanut butter and two sets of lungs deep-calming.

After a while the cosmic voice said, "Concentrate on good vibes for George Craig."

Eleanor started to say something, but changed her mind and sent out a thought that was not directly lethal.

"Why does George want to do this?" asked the voice.

"Because he thinks it'll make him rich,"

answered Eleanor.

"Why does he want to be rich?"

"Because now he's poor."

"Money is just a surrogate. He needs love."

"He needs a swift..."

"If he were in love, it would change his karma."

"So?"

"He would focus on other things."

"Aha."

"He could be influenced by the person who loved him."

"AHA!"

"Yes!" The cosmic voice was gone and Lily was full of her own presence.

They both sat up and stared at each other again. Lily dove for the duffle bag and seconds later she was waving *Parsley, Sage, Rosemary, and Mandrake Root* under Eleanor's nose.

"What's that, your potion book? Oh, now, wait a minute. Another potion..."

"No, I know, it has to be something else. The way things are going, we'd end up with George in love with the ferret, too. Or you. That's what's great about this book, it's got lots of different charms. Let's see if we can find one with all the instructions intact."

Eleanor reached across and held the book where she could see the cover. "*Witchcraft from your Windowsill*?" Are you kidding? Is this where you got the potions?"

"Well, sort of. I improvised a bit."

"You impr...!? Girl, are you sure you're not the hit man? It's a wonder you haven't killed us all. What did you put in my drink, anyway?"

"Only natural, wholesome ingredients. Aloe, zinc, ginger, brandy, you know."

"No, I don't know, but maybe it's just as well."

Lily flipped through several pages. "Here, look at this one." She punched at a left page. "'Make a braid of hair and bits of personal belongings of the one wishing to be loved. Rub with rose oil while chanting some practitioners have tried belladonna but have found it too...' What? Oh, the bottom of the page is missing. I was reading the page before that. '...while chanting...' O.K., chanting. Next page. 'Tie onto the beloved's penis while he is in a deep sleep, again intoning the above chant. At his first physical contact with the person whose charm he has received, he will fall forever in love with her.'"

Eleanor stared at her, mouth agape.

"Yeah, I know this is pretty far out. But it's really simple, don't you think?"

Eleanor jumped from the bed and paced, her arms flailing. "Simple?! You have to tie this on his... anatomy...while he's sleeping. Do you even know what room he's in? Did you consider how you might enter the room? How you were going to get him into a sleep deep enough that he wouldn't notice you fooling with his...with his thing?"

"We can work that out..."

Eleanor reeled from her path to the door. "What do you mean 'we'?"

"...and it doesn't call for complicated ingredients. Besides, it'd be specific to me."

"What about the chant?"

"Oh, that. I've just been doing the only one I know. The *ah*, *oom*, remember?"

Eleanor stepped to the wall between the bedroom and the bath and leaned her forehead against it, as she sometimes did when the fourth student in the same class asked the same question. "You can't possibly be serious," she whispered to the textured plaster. Still resting on the wall, she turned her face back to Lily. "Can you?"

Lily smiled apologetically. "You have a better idea?"

Eleanor thought for a minute. "I don't have *any* ideas," she admitted, turning back to the room. "So how do you go about it? Please note the use of second person, *you*."

Lily stepped into the bathroom, washed off her toothbrush handle, and brushed her teeth. "Always helps me think," she said, returning to the bedroom, running her tongue over her front teeth.

"I'll have it in a minute." She assumed her yoga position on the bed again and seemed to disappear.

Eleanor stared for a minute, shrugged, and brushed her teeth. Before she could settle on the bed and wait for the cosmic voice or the second insight, Lily jumped up.

"Phillip," she yelped.

Eleanor called silently for help from the ceiling. "Neither of us has even the faintest interest in Phillip!" she explained.

"No, we'll get him to help us. I tell him what to do, and he'll do it for you."

"Oh, no, I'm not going to use him. I'm absolutely not going to stoop that low."

"Come on, Eleanor, it's not all that bad. All we have to do is ask him to watch for George Craig and get him drunk somehow. I'm sure that's something he can do easily."

Eleanor paced again, shaking her head. "There's got to be some other way. I can't believe this. It's too stupid to contemplate. Completely hare-brained."

Lily was pulling things out of her duffle bag. "Here," she said. "You wear this. We'll disguise you and go find Phillip."

Eleanor stared at the long rose and gray wool skirt and the faded turquoise sweatshirt. She froze while Lily put a huge tam on her head, covering most of her face. "Wait," she stalled, looking at her watch. "It's got to be right in the middle of the afternoon classes and competition performances now. We'd have to haul him out of something. Can't it wait till around five?"

Lily started to protest.

Eleanor cut her off. "We could have some real lunch. We could call down for room service."

Lily's head came up from the duffel bag. "Room service?"

"Yes, my treat, you can order anything you like."

"I can't speak German. You order for me."

"Okay, what do you want?"

"Anything. Just not meat."

They sat on their beds and waited for the trays to come.

"Listen," said Lily, "don't call him a twit any more, okay?"

"Whom?"

"George. He's the man I love, you know."

"I'm sorry. I didn't know at the time, and I didn't say it to make you feel bad."

Lily sighed. Tears formed and rolled through her lashes. "I'm in love with a man who might go to jail, I don't even know anything about him, he might be a real rat, and I'm stuck with him. Damn that potion. No, damn me. It's my own fault," she wailed.

Eleanor sat next to her and put her arm

around Lily's shoulder. "Look, I guess he's just a man down on his luck and looking in the wrong places to bring it up again. He certainly wasn't an experienced car-jacker."

"You really rode down the turnpike with him? What was he like?"

"Let's see, what did he tell me about himself? I wasn't concentrating much on him at the time, just on myself. I think he said he'd worked in a shoe store and gotten laid off or something. He doesn't have much self-confidence."

Lily hung on to every word. She wiped her face. "Do you think love can cure that?"

Eleanor looked at her with real affection. "Don't set your heart on it, Lily. People don't change much, and we should never get involved with them on the assumption that they will." She sighed. "I know one of my lifelong faults has been setting my standards too high and waiting for others to change so they could measure up to them. At least I've learned by now that no one's under any obligation to be what I want him to be. I just don't know whether I can change my habits to be more accommodating."

"Yeah, change is hard, isn't it?" She looked down at her skirt. "I know all this old hippie stuff isn't me anymore, either. I just don't know what *is* me. So changing it is pretty scary."

"Yes, well, we can both worry about that

later."

"Hey, listen, El, I'm going to get all this to work out. I promise."

"I may be more afraid of that than the alternatives."

28

Ursula entered the hotel with Horst Bauer just after five. She was still dazed. Those stores, the colors, the lights, the incredible variety, the racks jammed with things you could buy and take with you right now. All afternoon she'd thought of the two dress shops in Weimar, which received their "new" fashions on Thursdays. How many times had she stood in line from ten o'clock until the opening at noon, and then bought a dress she'd have to alter to make it look different from the hundreds of others all over town.

Herr Bauer said something, but she focused on him too late to understand. Blinking, she came back to the present in the crowded hotel lobby.

And the present included *Herr* Barkov, who was just standing up from one of the red chairs to the right, more tense than ever. He was surrounded by guitarists and looked like the Grim Reaper at a happiness convention.

Ursula's hands began to sweat.

The door to the conference center opened. The

competition coordinator stepped out and tacked a sheet of paper on the bulletin board. From all over the lobby, contestants flocked to see whether they were on it.

"Looks like they've posted the finalists," said *Herr* Bauer. "Come on, let's see if you're among them."

Ursula hung back. "I'm sure I'm not..."

Herr Barkov elbowed his way to the board. He checked the list, turned, looked directly at her, and walked toward them. "My congratulations, *Fräulein*, you made it to the finals. I would like to talk to you." He reached for her arm, glowering.

Ursula backed into Horst and he put his hand on her shoulder. He turned her toward him so that his arm was between her and *Herr* Barkov. He smiled down at her, a glowing, warm smile, and said, "Congratulations, *Fräulein* Kimmig, I told you your concert was wonderful."

Despite Barkov at her back, Ursula filled with warmth and amazement, both at the impact of his smile and the recognition of her performance. Feeling as if she could simply levitate off the floor, she smiled back. "Thank you."

He moved her toward the elevator, saying loudly enough for Barkov to hear, "Can I have dinner with you before I take you back to your room?"

She glanced up at him and back at Barkov,

who stood where they'd left him, his disbelief in her audacity written darkly in his eyes.

Herr Bauer laughed. "I know you have to practice, but you have to eat sometime."

"Well, yes, I guess I do. All right." They took the stairs to the second floor dining room and Horst steered her to a table where two others were already sitting so there'd be no room for Barkov.

Barkov ate at a nearby table, dividing his stares between them and the entrance, his face taut with angry frustration—and something else. Each time he checked the door, he looked almost fearful. What on earth could Barkov have to fear? Unless the government fell, he had all the power, and she had a briefcase that might as well be a noose around her neck.

It was too late now to give it back to him. Besides, she didn't want him to destroy it. If the government actually collapsed, she had proof of what the *Stasi* had been doing all these years. And if the government didn't collapse—well, she could forget everything she'd hoped for.

He followed them to the elevator afterwards, but *Herr* Bauer turned to him, took him by the arm, and steered him away a few feet. After a few words from the policeman, Barkov puffed out his chest and appeared to protest something. *Herr* Bauer took out his police identification. Instantly Barkov blanched, backed away, and headed for the stairs.

Ursula stared after him. "What on earth did you say to him?" she asked when Horst returned.

"I just told him he was obviously *Stasi* and could be detained in the West. I expected more resistance, but I think now he'll leave you alone." He shook his head. "It's pretty clear what he's trying to do. Would you like to talk about it?"

Ursula wondered whether Barkov might try to hurt *Herr* Bauer. It was more likely if Barkov thought *Herr* Bauer knew about the personnel file. She shook her head. "I can't."

Herr Bauer started to say something but gave it up. They rode up to the fifth floor in silence.

At her door, Ursula put her key in the lock but turned back to him before opening it. "I had a wonderful day. I don't know how to thank you, *Herr* Bauer."

"You could call me Horst."

She flushed. He wouldn't say this unless he wanted to be long-term friends with her. Or more.

His face reddened and he shifted on his feet. "Well, no need. Maybe we're a little faster with familiar forms of address on this side of the Wall." He smiled sheepishly. "Or maybe it's just a tendency I brought back from America, where people speak to each other on a first name basis all the time."

"Horst is fine," she said, shaking his hand.

"I'm Ursula."

He didn't let go when the ritual handshake was over. "You know," he said, still smiling, "we really ought to drink the customary glass of wine to celebrate this, but I suppose you want to get at your guitar."

Ursula nodded and gently pulled her hand free.

Horst backed away a little and stopped. "I just have to say this before I go. Don't let that old lecher make you nervous. I don't think he'll bother you anymore."

Ursula's felt her face redden. "He doesn't want what you think. I'm sorry, I can't explain, but I do thank you for keeping him away from me...Horst."

He gave her that warm smile again. "I have to be back tomorrow. We haven't spotted our man yet. What time do you eat breakfast?"

"Around eight. Then I have to practice all day. The final round is tomorrow evening."

"Shall I pick you up here at eight?"

She hesitated.

"Is Barkov going to be around tomorrow?" he asked.

"Yes."

"Well, let me take you to breakfast then."

"All right, and thank you for your concern."

He stood awkwardly for a minute and then

put his hand on her face. "Lock your door. Good night, Ursula, and good luck," he said.

Ursula closed her door and leaned against it with her hand on her cheek where his had been. He was so nice, the last kind of man she'd ever expected to meet, a West Berlin policeman who made her feel sheltered. Not at all like a *Vopo*, like Joachim, who made her feel watched and edgy. *Herr*...Horst...was too kind, and she couldn't let him care for her. More than ever after the wonderful master classes, she wanted to stay in the West, but she couldn't endanger the one person she'd met who could actually help her.

What would he do if she showed him the file? He didn't have authority to hold it as evidence when Barkov's crimes were committed in the East and were legal for *Stasi*. Certainly he couldn't arrest Barkov. Or could he do anything he wanted, like a *Vopo*? One way or the other, though, he'd try to do something. He could probably arrange for her to be taken off the bus at the border crossing. The vision sent her heart into a tempo it had never beaten before.

Stay in the West. Her blood rushed through her whole body. No, she simply couldn't use him in such a base way. She'd never want him to think he was no more to her than a ticket out of the East. There had to be another way to stay in the West. On her own. But then, what of the file?

She sighed. Who would've thought a Westerner could be so nice? But it was a friendship that would last barely another day. If only she didn't like him so much.

29

Eleanor closed the door and quickly slipped after Lily to the stairway. Lily's black tam flopped over her ears and covered her French bun completely. The hem of the gray and pink wool skirt scratched her calves. The "Let it all hang out" sweatshirt constricted her neck, pinched under the arms, and barely reached her waistline.

In the lobby they concealed themselves behind a post and a fern to wait.

Hardly a minute passed before Eleanor spotted the KGB agent in the middle of the lobby, nervous as a music student at his first recital, his eyes flitting from the elevators to the front door, the conference hallway, and the bar.

Lily poked her elbow. "See, I told you he looked like a vicious undertaker."

Eleanor tried to ignore the squishy wave of yearning that rolled through her and see his face objectively. Okay, Lily was right. He was the poster boy for all the drabness and suspicion of the East. Probably *Stasi*. Good God. The yearning wavered a bit and then sloshed against her insides again. She moved trance-like toward him.

Lily yanked her back, hissing, "Come on, El, we got to keep our minds on Phillip."

The conference doors opened and the guitarists crowded the bulletin board, where an official was tacking up a list.

"Psst, watch now," Lily whispered.

Eleanor forced herself to watch, between strayings of her eyes to the *Stasi* man, who was scanning the guitarists, too.

When Phillip emerged and started toward the board, Lily dragged Eleanor into the open and stationed her so that a column obstructed Eleanor's view of the nervous ferret.

Phillip noticed Lily, did a sharp left turn, and headed for the front door.

"Phillip," yelled Lily, turning heads all over the lobby.

He stopped dead.

Eleanor turned toward the elevators, too mortified by her own appearance and by what she knew about Phillip to look him in the face.

"Hi, it's us," Lily called, pulling Eleanor into Phillip's field of vision. "Me and Eleanor."

Phillip bent a little and peered under the tam.

Eleanor memorized the lobby carpet.

"What on earth are you got up like that for?" he asked, smiling thinly.

Eleanor started to turn and run. Lily's hand clamped her wrist like a bear trap.

"Why don't we go somewhere and we'll explain it to you," offered Lily.

Phillip gave the suggestion considerable thought before agreeing, his eyes shifting from one woman to the other. "There's a bar around the corner. Strange people hang out there, but it's very dark inside. I'll meet you there in ten minutes. It's called *Das Grab*."

"'The Grave'?" muttered Eleanor. "Naturally. What else?"

She studied the pavement while Lily led her to the bar and seated her in a black-leather, semi-circular booth at the end of the room.

Phillip joined them a few minutes later.

A cadaverous waitress in a hooded black robe asked for their order.

"What would you like?" Phillip asked.

"Brandy," said Lily.

"No more brandy for you," said Eleanor.

"Okay, a Bailey's Irish Cream."

Phillip stretched his hand toward Eleanor but stopped short of touching her skin below the too-short sleeves of the sweatshirt. "What about you, Eleanor?"

"I don't know. Is a Wallbanger anything like its name? I think that's what I need."

Phillip looked up at the waitress, ordered for

the women, and added a whiskey. He glanced at Eleanor. "Better make that a double."

The waitress turned and melted into the decor.

"You really dig Eleanor, don't you, Phillip?" Lily began.

Phillip squirmed.

Eleanor flushed so hot the tam felt like the lid on a witch's cauldron. What on earth had she been thinking? This was insane. She was never going to let Lily lull her with the stupid *ahing* and *ooming* again. What she really ought to do is jump into a taxi, go to the airport and fly out on the next plane. Why didn't she think of that sooner instead of falling into this absurd plot?

Phillip looked desperately around the room. "Well, yes, I find her most...I'd certainly like to...although I've always disliked..." He stopped. He lifted the edge of the tam but let it go again. "And of course, I don't know how you..."

Eleanor pulled at the neck of the sweatshirt. Her head sank lower and the tam brushed the table. She slid her hips as if to get out of the booth, but Lily was in the way on one side, Phillip on the other.

Lily shoved at her under the table. "Well, see, Eleanor needs a favor. Actually, I do, too. There's this man, and he wants to, like, hurt Eleanor. He's really a nice man. I think. He just has this thing, see? And we need you to, like, get him drunk so we can fix him, uh, fix it so he won't hurt her."

Phillip backed away and frowned. "Why would anyone want to hurt Eleanor?"

Lily swallowed loudly enough for Eleanor to hear but didn't answer.

Eleanor mumbled, "I don't want to talk about it."

The waitress materialized out of the darkness, set their drinks down, and evaporated again.

Phillip took a large gulp of whiskey then curled over the table to see Eleanor's face. "Is that why you're dressed up in this costume? If you don't mind my saying so, the schoolteacher garb suits you better."

Eleanor stalled with a sip of Wallbanger.

Lily jumped in again. "And it's all my fault."

Phillip kept his eyes, clouded with confusion, on Eleanor. "I don't get..."

"It's pretty hard to explain," said Lily. "But you know Eleanor is a wonderful person and wouldn't ask you to do this if it weren't absolutely necessary, don't you?"

Phillip's eyes darted back and forth between them.

Eleanor relaxed a bit. He wouldn't do it. Thank heaven. She'd just take care of her problem on her own, which she should have done in the first place. How could she have let herself get suckered into this whole moronic scheme?

Lily wasn't ready to let it go. "I know you know that, Phillip. Couldn't you just trust her and do it for her?"

Phillip sat for a minute rolling a stray beer coaster back and forth with his thumb and index finger. He turned until he was facing Eleanor, put his arm around the top of the booth, and drew the tam to the other side of Eleanor's head. "Do you really want me to do this thing for you?"

Eleanor looked him in the eyes and then stared into her lap. She opened her mouth to say no.

Lily hit her hard in the hip and pulled her over. "Come on, El," she whispered. "It's George Craig we're talking about. Please. Remember? I'm, like, completely around the bend here."

Eleanor clenched her jaw. Swallowed more Wallbanger. And then, against her better judgment, even against her worst judgment, she said, "Yes. Please. I'm sorry." She gave him the best smile she could drag out from under the layers of shame.

Phillip's face glowed with his answering smile. Still he hesitated. He fiddled with the beer coaster again while he considered. After a minute, he let it drop back to the table, rapped on it with his knuckles, and said, "Well, all right then, if all I have to do is get him drunk." He looked hard at Lily. "You're not planning to do him any harm, are you?"

Lily put her palms toward him and shook them back and forth. "Oh, no. Nothing worse than giving you the brandy from the plane."

"Well, I seem to have survived that. I think. I'm not giving him your weird brandy, right?"

Lily gave him a sunbeam smile. "Oh, no. Just whatever they have in the bar."

Phillip leaned forward to look under the tam. "Glad to help out, Eleanor. What's this guy's name, and where do I find him?"

Eleanor stared at him. She couldn't imagine herself doing the same thing for anyone. She had no idea how she'd ever be able to repay him. She finished the Wallbanger in one gulp while Lily gave him the information about George Craig, hit man.

30

Martin Girelli dragged himself from the dark, wet streets of Berlin into the hotel, carrying a black doctor's bag and a soggy manila envelope. The ache that started in his damp feet spread to the top of his head. He was cold to the marrow, and his stomach had gone from growling to burning. With no money, he'd have to wait till tomorrow morning to eat again. He would clean out the whole breakfast buffet.

For now, all he wanted was to pick up the clunky key from that snooty mannequin of a receptionist and hit his room for a hot shower and a clean bed. That job he had to do—well, he'd worry about the woman in the morning. After he'd fortified himself with a huge breakfast.

He hadn't made it to the reception desk before a tall man with a kind of button nose ran into him, knocking the bag out of his hand. It clanked dully on the thin carpet but didn't open. Martin snatched it up.

"I do beg your pardon," said the tall man. "I

should have been more careful."

Martin moved away, a little comforted by his own language, and said over his shoulder, "Okay."

The man fell into step with him. "Uh...You look a little bedraggled. Berlin weather isn't the greatest, is it?"

Martin shook his head as he reached the desk.

"Why don't you have a drink with me and take off the chill?"

Martin froze with his hand over the reception bell. A drink? Why would this guy want to have a drink together? Maybe he was a fruitcake. Maybe even a cop. Martin's heart stumbled over that thought. He opened his mouth to say, "Naw, thanks," but clamped it shut again. He could out-fox the fuzz any day, right? And a drink would go right through his empty stomach, send some warmth to his bones. He just couldn't afford one.

"I'm buying," said the tall man. "It's the least I can do for running you over."

"Okay, thanks." Determined to keep his mouth shut, Martin followed the man into the bar, sat on the manila envelope, and put the doctor's bag on the chair beside him. It poked into his hip.

The stranger reached across the table to shake hands. "I'm Phillip Redding, from Denver, Colorado."

"Mar..." Oops. Damn, he had to keep his wits about him when he was on a job. What name had he signed on the registration form? "Ah, George. Crane."

Redding frowned. "Crane?"

Martin's heart accelerated. He stalled. "Crane? No. You must have heard wrong." The image of the poster at the end of the reception desk flashed into memory. "I said Crag. Craig."

Redding stared back like he was having a hard time processing the information. He checked out Martin's trench coat and then shrugged. "Looks like you had a rough day, George."

"Two days. I had this...ah...contact to meet yesterday on *Breitenhof* Street. At the desk they told me to take subway nineteen. I must have taken it in the wrong direction. I ended up at the Wall, and somebody said the other side was Potsdam. Then I didn't have any more German cash. Somebody told me you can ride the subway free, if you don't get caught. So I got on again and ended up at some train station called Frederick Street or something. I had to walk back and keep asking people where the hotel was. I wasted the whole damn day. And that was only yesterday."

The Redding man tsked and shook his head. "It can be really hard in a foreign place, I know."

"I'll tell you one thing. I was in parts of Berlin they don't show the tourists. Some definite weirdoes out there, believe you me. Punkers like we haven't had in Denver for years. But real hostile. Black leather everything, boots that would kick your brains out in one swing. Nazi medals. Man, give me the Denver Bloods any day." A shiver vibrated through his whole body.

"Drink right up," said Redding, nudging his glass. "There's nothing like a good whiskey to provide a little internal cashmere. Did you ever meet your contact?"

Martin took a good swallow and choked a bit as it burned down his throat. "Yeah, late this afternoon. I decided to take the bus this time so I could see where I was going. I had to transfer four times, and twice got on the wrong bus. My God, this is a huge city. Then my contact was furious. I caught him on the way out the door to go someplace. Turkey or Greece or something. By the time I was...uh...finished with my...um...business, it was dark and raining. I was out of cash again and had to walk." He took another big swallow.

Phillip put his hand up for the waiter and indicated another round.

Martin burped slightly and sighed. He put his right foot up on his left knee away from Phillip and subtly examined the sole of his shoe. The hole under his bunion was larger than ever and it wouldn't be long before his sock was on the pavement. He took another swallow.

"Ah, that really does feel better. I think my feet are thawing out."

"Have another."

"Well, thanks."

"So. You're from Denver, too. What a coincidence. What business are you in?"

"Uh, shoes." Martin leaned back and rested his head on the chair.

"There are a couple of ladies from Denver here, for the guitar convention that's going on. We should all get..."

"No!"

"No! You're right. What was I thinking of? Here, have another. Let's drink to no ladies."

"Right." The whole glass went down easy this time.

"When are you going back to Denver? Is your business finished now?"

"No. I don't know. I'm not sure if I can do this deal. It could be the end of me." Martin drained the last drop and another glass appeared in front of him. He was beginning to slope toward the floor.

"Well, sometimes it's best to cut your losses and walk away. There's always more business."

"I think that may be the problem." His speech faltered at his front teeth. He shored it up with another belt. It eased the chills but didn't close the huge crater that opened in his head with the thought of more business.

"Have one more, and I'll help you up to your

room," Phillip said.

"Yeah, one for the e'evator," Martin muttered, the possibility of fruitcake or cop forgotten.

31

The telephone rang. Lily and Eleanor leapt for it and bruised each other scrambling for the receiver. Lily stopped.

"You get it," she said, as the phone shrilled again. "He really wants to talk to you anyway."

"Yes?" said Eleanor into the receiver.

"It's me. Phillip. Mission accomplished. Good grief, I sound like the worst kind of juvenile spy movie. I've done what you asked. We're in room 518 and I guarantee he won't wake up for hours."

"518?!" gasped Eleanor. "He was right down the hall the whole time?"

"Looks that way. Listen, I don't think he could possibly be out to get you. He makes a pretty sorry impression."

"I know. Thank you, Phillip. Can you wait there a little longer to let Lily in?"

"Sure."

Eleanor shook her head as she hung up. His voice had sounded unexpectedly pleasing.

Lily's face was drawn. She had already

showered and woven her hair with the colorful wooden rings. "Well, there's no point in putting it off, is there?"

"No, his deepest sleep is probably right now."

"Okay."

"Okay."

"You wouldn't have a few candles, would you?"

"No."

Lily went to the bathroom and came back with her hair brush. She began to pull hairs from it and to chant. She stopped.

"All of a sudden, this makes me feel way out stupid. Chant with me or I won't be able to get into it with you watching."

They both started again with the *ah*, avoiding each other's eyes, struggling not to giggle. Lily pulled several hairs from her head.

"Fresh ones," she explained between syllables. *Oom*. She went into the bathroom again, never stopping the chant, and came back with several short, crinkly hairs. "Only fair," she inserted into the chant. "Considering where they have to go."

Eleanor rolled her eyes to the ceiling.

Lily started to pull a few threads from the wool skirt, which was lying on the bed. Eleanor grabbed her hand. "I was wearing that," she injected into an *oom*.

Lily dropped it, reached down, and caught up

the hem of the paisley skirt. She drew out a few threads and the side seam frayed open. She pulled up her blouse and unraveled about two feet of white cotton.

She lined up the ends of the hairs and threads and offered them to Eleanor to hold while she braided, still chanting. Eleanor ran to the bathroom and came back with a sheet of toilet paper, folded it around the ends of the strand, and held tightly without missing an *ah*.

Lily braided, working the short hairs in as she went. She tied both ends into knots. She took her rose oil from the duffle bag. It was nearly empty. She held it toward Eleanor, her face asking whether she had any.

Eleanor shook her head and *oomed*.

Lily shrugged. She dripped the oil onto the braid and then let a couple of drops fall on her arms. She massaged the ends of the braid from the middle out and then rubbed the last drops into her arms.

"Okay, that's that," she said.

"Well, go to it. Good luck," said Eleanor.

Lily's eyes grew large. "You have to go with me. I may need help. Anyway, the vibes are that much stronger with two."

"Uh-uh. What if he wakes up and sees me?"

"He won't, and even if he did, he'd be too zonked out to do anything."

"What if he ended up falling for me?"

"He can't. This charm is only good for me."

"I can't do it. Mess around with his body."

"Me neither. Come on, Eleanor, I really need your help. And it's your life I'm trying to save."

Lily set the tam back on Eleanor's head and towed her into the hall.

Phillip opened the door almost before they knocked. They scooted through it and stopped. George Craig lay flat on top of his quilt, snoring like a bulldozer. The trench coat hung over the foot of the bed.

"Thanks again, Phillip," said Lily.

"Yes," said Eleanor.

"You can thank me by having breakfast with me," he said to Eleanor.

"I can't, he may still be after me."

"He won't be up before noon, believe me. He's not used to drinking. Anyway, you can wear your disguise again. He'd never recognize you."

"Well, if you're really sure."

"Great, meet you in the restaurant at eight. Shall I save you a place, too?" he asked Lily.

"Yeah, thanks."

"So what are you going to do here?" he asked, smiling at Eleanor.

Eleanor smiled back. "You don't want to know." She closed the door behind him, feeling guilty. Was she being unfaithful already? She was deeply in love with the blond who looked like an angry scarecrow.

Lily was already standing at the bed, gazing down at George, her face beatific. "Isn't he wonderful?"

Eleanor looked down at the thin frame in the damp, rumpled clothes, the haggard face with pale dirty-brown stubble, the battered shoes. "Well," she said, "if a ferret of a KGB agent can look wonderful, this George Craig is an Apollo among men."

"Does he look like you remember?"

"He's definitely the one."

"What did your George Craig look like?'

"You're stalling."

"I know."

"Go ahead. Undo his belt and pants."

"I don't suppose you could do that part."

"Not a chance. I'm not touching him. I'm just here for the chant, remember? *Ah oom, ah oom...*"

Lily chimed in and pulled gingerly at the belt. The leather was torn and let the pin slap through to the next hole. She jumped, took a deep breath, puffed out, and tried again.

George snored a ponderous rhythm and the chant fell slowly into it.

The belt was free. Lily lifted the corner of the pants closure and the button flew off. She pulled the zipper. It was skewed to his right. He was wearing boxer shorts. Neither the bottom hem nor a strategic opening was visible.

Lily straightened up and scratched her head. "Aw, bummer. We have to pull the pants down."

"Not me, I'm not laying a finger on him."

"Well, could you just pull on his pants while I try to lift his hips?"

Eleanor went to the foot of the bed and picked the pants legs up with her thumbs and forefingers, the other fingers extended like a cock's comb.

"*Ah...oom...*"

Lily tried to lift him, then had to raise one hip at a time.

George snorted and stirred. He opened his eyes.

Eleanor let go and dropped to the floor.

One of his eyes stared at the wall to his right, the other seemed to be searching for the dresser on the other wall.

Lily froze.

The right lid closed, then the left. He relaxed and took up his old rhythm.

"Come on, he's out...*oom...*"

Eleanor stood up. She pulled the right leg and then the left.

"I don't believe this," sighed Lily.

"Am I mistaken, or does he have his shorts on backwards?"

"He must, like, really be having a hard time. Didn't you ever put your bra on backwards when you were stressed out?"

"No, but once, after one of my many break-ups, I sprayed deodorant all over my toothbrush. And that was after I'd smeared my underarms with toothpaste."

"Once I dialed my social security number trying to call my folks from San Francisco. After an earthquake."

"We're stalling," they said together.

Lily pulled at the tired elastic. It would not give enough. "We have to pull again. Grab the shorts."

Finally he was free. They both flushed.

"Chant," said Lily. She took the braid out of her waist-band, let it loop under him, and gently worked it toward the top of his manhood with a series of little jerks and upward slips.

"Do I use a bow or a knot?" she asked.

"How would I know? I guess a knot is safer."

"I think it's long enough for both. A bow looks nicer, don't you think?" Lily knotted and bowed her braid with a flourish, drew a pentagram over it, and *oom*ed a last time.

"Are you going to put him back together?"

"You think I should?"

"He'll probably just think he got up to go to the bathroom when he wakes up."

"Yeah, right."

Lily laid his trench coat over him, tucking it around him gently. She reached to touch his face, smiling wistfully.

Grabbing her arm, Eleanor hissed, "Come on, let's get out of here before some other mishap occurs."

They tiptoed back to their room.

32

Thursday, November 9, 1989

Ursula rode down in the elevator with Horst, feeling ill-at-ease. She should have told him she couldn't see him again. Not only did she not want to use a man she liked so much, but she didn't even want to like him this way. The friendship was a dead-end-street with the end only hours away. Besides, he certainly couldn't follow her back into the East, where she had no protection from Barkov, who was suspicious and ruthless. Back home, there was no limit to the possibilities open to him for making her pay for the mix-up with the briefcases.

Horst's easy laughter caught her attention. What had he started telling her about? His first ski lesson?

He was watching the floor numbers above the elevator doors. "...first thing they teach you is how to fall down in such a way that you don't hurt yourself. Well, I can tell you, falling down is the one part of the lesson I ever mastered."

Ursula laughed in spite of herself. It was so refreshing to meet someone who could make fun of himself.

"...and Scott's seven-year-old son was having his first lesson at the same time. I spent the whole day with my nose in the snow, and every time I looked up, little Scottie was gliding by in a great wide wedge, waving at me and yelling, 'Hi, Uncle Horst, look at me.' I wanted to answer him with my ski poles..."

Ursula was laughing again as they walked into the breakfast room, enjoying the easy humor of this man who made her feel so comfortable.

The first person she saw was Barkov, sitting alone, glaring at the entrance. Her laughter caught in her throat. She paused in the doorway.

Horst took her elbow and steered her toward a

table at Barkov's back. "Don't worry, there's not a thing he can do. And see, nobody likes him. Not one person is sharing his table. Looks like a gargoyle, doesn't he?"

Ursula shuddered. "If gargoyles get distemper. You know, horrible as he is, he must be lonely."

"Well, don't waste your sympathy on him, and don't let him spoil your breakfast."

They ordered coffee at their table and collected rolls and then browsed the buffet.

Ursula pointed at something in a fruit basket that looked like a brown, fuzzy egg. "What is this?"

Horst looked around until he found a garnish on a platter of Danish rolls. "This," he said, pointing to a green slice with black seeds in a circle. "It's a kiwi. It comes from New Zealand, I think."

Ursula blinked in surprise. "All the way from New Zealand? Do you eat it?"

"Yes, take one. Or better, here." He picked several slices from the plate. You can see if you like it before you take a whole one."

"Thank you. Oh, look. These are American, aren't they? Have you ever eaten any of these 'corn flakes'?" She pronounced them "flah-kes."

"Oh, sure. And a lot of other 'flah-kes,' too."

She watched him for a second. "Oh, well, are

you going to have those now, or are you going to have something to eat first?"

Horst laughed his easy, warm laugh. "What I'd really like is an American weekend breakfast—thin bacon, eggs, toast. But I'll settle for rolls and coffee. I still have to work today." He escorted her back to the table. "Come on, sit with your back to Barkov. I'll keep an eye on him."

Ursula started buttering her roll, deeply conscious of hostility at her back and warmth across the table. She smiled across at Horst. "I'm very grateful to you."

"For what? Interfering with that hyena? Actually, I'd find that very satisfying by itself, even if it didn't mean the pleasure of your company. I'll pick you up at your room for lunch, if you like."

She would tell him no, stop this right now before it became any harder. "Yes, please, I'd like that very much. I'll need a break by then. Do you know any other exotic restaurants near here?"

"I have an inexhaustible supply."

Ursula waved a slice of kiwi on her fork for a minute. "This is wonderful. I've never tasted anything like it."

"I'm glad you like it," he smiled without deriding the fact that such things were unknown in the East.

They ate in silence for a minute. Her heart began to weigh in her chest again.

"Maybe I shouldn't...," Ursula started.

"My, God, look at those two," said Horst, motioning toward the door with his head.

She turned and stared. "Americans?"

"Well, yes, but not like any I've ever seen before."

The taller woman was wearing a black hat that drooped over her whole head, a pink and gray plaid skirt cut on the diagonal, and a faded green blouse with tattered lace at the cuffs and collar. She walked with her shoulders hunched. The other was in a peasant blouse and a flimsy skirt partially torn at the side seam with thick tights under it. They made their way to a table where a man had saved two places with his jacket and a folder.

"That's odd," said Horst.

"No, I mean the woman in the hat. When she went by Barkov's table, she stopped, and I swear she wanted to sit down and talk to him. Then the younger woman pulled her on."

Ursula turned again. "Why would anyone want to talk to him?"

The two women were sitting down with that nice American guitarist who'd tried to talk to her before the conference started.

Eleanor sat down facing that man by the door, the one she couldn't ignore despite his jackal-face. The minute she'd seen him, she'd been jolted back to that piercing glance yesterday as he pushed past her in the concert hall. Phillip said something. She tore her eyes from the blond for a second, long enough to say, "What?" and was riveted again.

"Good morning," said Phillip loudly enough to be heard several tables away.

"Good morning," chirped Lily, kicking Eleanor under the table.

"Oh, good morning."

"Did you get your man 'fixed'?'

Eleanor glided back into the conversation. "Who?"

"Oh, yes," interjected Lily. "We, uh, I think we got that problem all tied up." She giggled and Eleanor bit her lip.

"So, what are you two going to hear today?" he asked, opening his folder. "There's the Begner class on modern music, the Wilovski seminar on eastern music,..."

"We're going shopping," said Lily.

Even Eleanor snapped to attention.

"Eleanor can't stay here till we know for sure that George is...um...neutralized."

"Shouldn't you...check on him? Soon?" asked Eleanor.

Lily shook her head so hard the little beads woven in her hair rattled. "I can do that later. Best we get you out of his way. Maybe get you a better disguise. I really don't want him to hurt you."

Eleanor turned to Phillip. "She's right. Anyway, I don't care much for modern music or that other lecture. It would be best to get out of the hotel for a while. Besides, Lily's never been to Berlin before, have you, Lily? She should see something besides a hotel."

"You can come, if you want," said Lily.

Eleanor kicked her.

Phillip shifted toward the backrest of his chair and put his hands out, palms out. "No thanks, count me out. Even modern music sounds more appealing."

Across the room the guitarist from Weimar who had made it to the finals got up from her table, and a young man followed her out. The blond man left immediately after them. Eleanor swiveled to watch him go.

Phillip waved his hand up and down in front of her face. "Hey, here we are!"

The blond disappeared through the door and Eleanor turned back.

Phillip looked a little desperate. "At least go to the competition finals with me, and maybe we can find a place to go dancing afterwards. It's our last night here, you know."

The upheaval over the thin blond subsided, and without the interference, Eleanor made herself focus on Phillip. There was a certain kindness in his gray eyes, even if he did have the air of a moron. She smiled a little. "Well, all right. It probably is my last night." And then the old wish for the real last night echoed sharply from her heart.

33

Hideous, deafening droning. There were two dronings. Martin moved his head slightly and set off a frontal earthquake. One of the dronings increased its volume to one decibel below splitting his skull. It turned slowly into an agonized groan.

"My God, it's me," he tried to mouth, but the words merely warped into blobs of sound and blended with the other droning. The one that wasn't him. What was that? He opened his eyes, looking for the source.

There was a door in a dresser. That was all right. He closed his eyes and opened them again. Now the door slid away and stood itself in a wall. Well, that was all right, too. Where was the other drone coming from? It was the door droning. No, doors could stand in walls, but they didn't drone. It was outside. He closed his eyes. The drone came from outside. A mammoth vacuum cleaner was going by on Seventeenth Avenue. Okay.

His stomach lurched. He was freezing. He

opened his eyes again. It was a hotel. He was in that hotel in Berlin. He was lying on the bed with his trench coat half under him and half trailing off the bed onto the floor. There was something he had to do today.

A volcano in his stomach was about to erupt.

Bathroom! He rolled over and stood up, holding his head and that of the bed. He took a step, tripped over his own pants around his ankles, and fell on his face. Searing, blinding pain exploded behind his eyes.

The thin carpet scratched his stomach. A chill shook his whole body and he realized his legs were even colder than the rest of him. He turned on his side, looked down, and screamed. A rat was crawling across him. Horrified, he slapped at it. "Ow," he yelped. The stomach was coming up. He crawled as fast as he could to the toilet.

In a few minutes he stood up, grasping anything solid that came under his hands. Something was tickling him. He looked down and screamed again. It was the rat. Not falling off his body. He tried to brush it away, but it hung on. He shook his head. He turned on the water and splashed it cold on his face. He looked down again. It was still there. Not a rat, some kind of rope knotted around him. Long black fibers and some white stuff. Braided and tied in a bow. He stared at it a long time. With thumbs and index fingers he grasped the ends and pulled.

It loosened easily until it came to a knot. There was no zap. It didn't blow his privates across the room.

He undid the knot and brought the rope up to his face. What had he done to himself? Why had he done it? A faint smell of flowers wafted into his nose and eased his headache for about a second. He stared again. He looked in the mirror. Perhaps he had become someone else. The face was the same. Shaking his head slowly lest he set off the earthquake again, he laid the rope on the bidet and reached for the shower tap.

In a minute he was under a trickle of warm water. "Niagara," he moaned at the droplets exploding against his skin. After the shower his head cleared. He squinted a last time at the rope and threw it in the trash basket next to the desk.

He'd planned to eat a big breakfast at that buffet this morning. His stomach heaved wildly at the thought. So much for that. His digestive system was strictly a one-way street, and that way was up.

What time was it? He pulled the curtain aside.

The blinding light of an overcast November day stabbed right through to the back of his skull. He knew now how the edges of the tectonic plates felt during an earthquake. He yanked the curtain closed again. No way to tell what time it was. If only he hadn't sold his watch to come here. Now he had nothing. That dumb woman. It was all her fault. He ought to kill her just for getting him in this mess. His hands shook. Killing.

"I can't do this," he said aloud in a voice that sounded like a rasp against a square mile of rusty sheet metal.

"You have to," said a voice in his head that sounded like Sonny. "You got nothing left but a ticket home, and what's waiting for you there is no job, no money, and no future. Besides, the broad was already trying to off herself when you met her. Remember? You'll be doing her a favor."

"Her, maybe. What about me? I'd be a murderer."

Desperate, he reached for the phone to call Sonny and back out. He'd just have to stiff the hotel for the international call.

Sonny answered after the ninth deafening ring, breathless, his voice smooth as heavy molasses. "What you want, Marty? You're interrupting something here. You take care of that business yet?"

"That's what I wanta talk to you about."

Sonny's voice turned sharp as broken glass. "So what's to say?"

"Listen, Sonny, I don't think I can be a murderer."

"Hang on."

Martin heard a door close. The broken glass voice became a lethal shiv. "Well, let me put it this way. You rather be a murderer or a murderee? 'Cause that's what you'll be if you come back and you ain't carried out your assignment. I'm the one sponsored you, so I got my reputation riding on this. You screw up and they'll come after me, too. Now, you call me the minute you get back. Or don't you never come back. Don't never show your sorry face any place the Family's liable to stumble across it. And if they don't find you, I will!" He hung up.

Martin gulped, but his tiny bit of spittle didn't make it past the back of his tongue. His heart was banging out of control against his bones. He had no choice now. He looked at the medical bag and the manila envelope on the dresser. There was not much use in checking the photograph in the envelope. He knew who it was. Better to look anyway. He'd really be in a mess if he took out the wrong person on an assumption.

He tore the envelope open and that schoolteacher's face emerged smiling as if she were almost human. He had a better picture in mind— her with her nose all red and her eyes shiny from crying, like he'd seen her the first time. He snarled at the glossy photograph, ripped it to shreds, and started to aim at the trash basket. The rope caught his eye. He squinted at it, shook his head, and threw the shredded picture on top of it.   He opened the bag and dumped the contents on the bed.

A small brown bottle with some German writing on it rolled to the edge and he barely caught it. He peered at the writing for a familiar word. Well, he couldn't use that, not knowing what it was. It could be an explosive, a poison, an acid. He set it on the dresser. He still had a twelve inch knife left, as well as a gun and a silencer. He laid the knife next to the bottle. No way was he going to get that close to her.

He picked up the revolver, astonished at the weight. He took the silencer.   His hands were shaking so hard it took several attempts to screw the silencer into the gun. The thing was heavier than his weights at home. He raised it at arm's length and tried to aim at a flower on the curtain. His arm strained and his hand wobbled. The gun let out a pffft and jerked his hand. Two feet to the northwest of the flower, a hole the size of a volley ball opened in the plaster wall, exposing ridged reddish brick with a mangled bullet stuck in its center like a bull's eye. The plaster clattered to the desk in a white cloud. Martin jumped and looked around, but there was no one who might have heard, and the vacuum cleaner was still droning in the hall. "Jeez," he muttered, "I'm not cut out for this."

He shrugged into the trench coat and slid the gun into the huge left pocket. With his shoulder drooping, his coat hanging four inches lower on the left than the right, and his thigh being pummeled by metal, he made his way to the elevator.

34

Eleanor was exhausted. All morning they'd wandered through the stores, *Karstadt, Kaufhalle, Neue Mode*, where Lily had been intrigued by the elbow-to-elbow crowds in the aisles, the snooty help, the extravagant prices, the stylish shoppers. Neither of them had spent a *Pfennig*. A doomed expedition when one had no money and the other no attractive future for the attractive clothes. They'd finally made it to a second-floor café on the *Kurfürstendamm* where they could look down on the street.

It was long past the normal lunch hour, and they managed to find a table at the window. Only one other customer occupied it, a frumpy smoker who fed every other bite of her *Torte* and whipped cream to her fat long-haired dachshund. Although she'd fixed the hand loop of his leash under the leg of her chair, little brown *"Liebchen"* obviously wasn't interested in running off when there was chocolate cake coming down.

Sitting across from Eleanor, Lily moved her

eyes over the menu without comprehension. "You order for me, okay? Just so it doesn't have any meat in it."

While Eleanor perused the menu, she found herself yearning for an American restaurant, where they wouldn't have to share tables. Even a hamburger joint would beat eating at a table with this stranger, who'd obviously resented their intrusion. A dark hole opened in her mood. Surely not homesickness when there was nothing at home for her. It was the old black depression, sapping her energy and the last tatters of hope. She should just march back to that George's room when they got back and let him have at her.

Lily stared at "*Liebchen*" and shook her head, apparently surprised at finding a dog in a restaurant. She turned and gazed out at the blackened stones of the old the *Kaiser Wilhelm Gedächtniskirche* next to the blue glass of the new tower and church. "Look at that, the tower's so old it's black. I still can't believe I'm here, in Berlin."

The waitress approached, stared at their clothing, sniffed, and exchanged a disapproving look with the other diner.

Liebchen's Mutti returned the sneering smile. "*Amerikaner kenne ich schon, aber diese zwei...sie grauen einem an, gell?*"

Eleanor jerked herself out of the black hole and repeated the slur to Lily. "'I know Americans, but these two...they're horrid, aren't they?" Indeed. She glared at both the waitress and the other customer. *"Wir moechten beide gemischte Salatplatten,"* she said loudly.

Lily's eyes grew large in resentment of the exchange. She added her own glare and a very disapproving fanning of the woman's cigarette smoke.

A hostile silence arced between Eleanor and the woman until the waitress returned with their meal.

Lily turned her attention to the salad. "That was such a pretty robe in that last store, and it looked so warm," she said as she speared a lettuce leaf. "Why didn't you buy it?"

Eleanor paused with her fork stuck in the cucumbers. "I don't know. Maybe I still don't believe I'll be here tomorrow to wear it."

"Yes, you will. I promise, as soon as we get back I'll ferret George out, even if he's, like, hiding in a bottom drawer. We already did the critical part. Now, all I have to do is zap him." Lily thrust her hand across the table and poked Eleanor's arm with her index finger. "Bzzt."

Eleanor grinned at the image. "I'm not sure I even want you to go near him. I know where we put that thing, but who knows where it actually worked, if it worked at all? Maybe it fried his brain. He could turn on you. Did you ever think of that?"

Lily's hand froze with a fork full of some white, shredded vegetable. Her eyes popped wide. "No."

"If he ever finds out you did it, he'll shoot you for sure."

"Okay, I'll worry about how to zap him safely later. You said maybe. Was there more to the answer?"

"What answer?"

"The robe. Why you didn't buy it."

Eleanor laid her fork down and gazed toward the street, but all she saw was the darkness that was eating at her. "You want the marrow out of my soul, don't you? Okay. I didn't buy it because nothing's changed, really. There's no more chance that I'm ever going to be happy than there was a week ago. Or a month. Or ten years."

Lily nodded. "Maybe we have to do the changing ourselves."

"I know that. I just don't know how."

"Well, you said you were always too rigid in your standards. And it shows even in your clothes. Like that gray suit you were wearing yesterday. Don't get me wrong—it's real pretty, but it's so...what? Straight. Like, strict, maybe. All the lines are perfect, parallel or symmetrical or something. I don't know. But when you look at that suit, you can tell a school teacher is wearing it." She shrugged apologetically.

Eleanor winced inside. "I just like clean, uncluttered lines. Besides, is it so bad to be a schoolteacher?"

"No, but what if you wore something with a ruffle or a flowered print or a lace collar? Would it hurt?"

"No, I guess not."

Lily obviously wanted to say more.

"So what else?" Eleanor asked, glancing at *Liebchen's* owner to see whether she was following the conversation.

The smoker merely took another bite of the chocolate torte and said in German as she chewed it, "You'll get the next bite, *Liebchen*, Mommy's going to give you a nice big piece with icing."

Eleanor ignored the need to gag and looked back at Lily.

Lily hesitated, biting her lip. "Well, your hair. It doesn't do your eyes or nose any good pulled straight back like that. It looks sort of...forbidding. A little body around your face would look so pretty."

Embarrassed, Eleanor ran a hand over her hair, looking for stray ends. "Really?"

"Listen, why don't we spend the afternoon loosening you up a bit? Get some frilly clothes and a new hairdo? 'Course, I know it won't make any difference for your future. It'll just make you feel good inside right now, like a new woman. Or even a new girl. It's a place to start."

Eleanor pressed her lips together. Tears started.

No, she wanted to say, I'm not going to spend a lot of money for stuff that means nothing and changes nothing. But Lily was staring so hopefully, waiting for an answer. And suddenly Eleanor realized that Lily actually cared what happened to her. Briefly as they'd known each other, Lily had accepted her and tried to help. Eleanor felt a rush of friendship for this little hare-brain, whose pleading smile was something to hang on to. They shared an experience, even if it was the most idiotic one she'd had since the witchcraft class.

Lily's shoulders dropped after the long wait, her frown showing her fear of a negative response. "Hey, I didn't mean to hurt your feelings. I could use a lot of making over, too. You're not the only one."

It wasn't enough, of course...one friend when she already had friends. But Lily would be hurt if she refused. She didn't want her last act to be hurtful.

Eleanor sniffed and swallowed hard. She'd just do this and when she got back, she'd put herself right in Craig's path somehow. "Okay, then, I will if you will."

"Me? I don't need any loosening. If anything, I probably need tightening."

"We can do that, too."

"Look at me, Eleanor. You know what I own in the world? A ticket home. Did you see the prices on the stuff we looked at? I couldn't afford one price tag, much less a whole wardrobe. Or a trip to the beauty shop. Especially not a European one."

Eleanor looked straight in her eyes for a minute. "Let me do it for you."

Lily's head rose slightly and her eyes widened. She sat back and put her hand up, palm out. "Uh-uh, no way. Thanks, but I can't accept that. I'll work it out somehow."

Eleanor laid her fork on the plate and put both forearms on the edge of the table. "Listen, Lily, all my life I put my money aside because I thought one day I could buy things for my children with it, or pay for a nice wedding, or guarantee myself a comfortable old age, none or which I'll ever have. The only things I ever bought with it were these occasional linguistic pilgrimages to Germany and new cars when the old ones rusted around me."

Lily started to say something.

Eleanor put her hand up to stop her. "When you contemplate suicide, money loses all value because there's no future. You don't even want to buy a bar of soap you won't use up, or a box of cereal you'll never finish. You can't imagine a future any different from the unbearable present. Right now, to me, this day is all there is, present and future; and I realize that what I wasted was all the scrimping. So on this day I want to enjoy my money for a change, and I can't think of anything more fun than a wild shopping spree for both of us."

Lily stared at her shredded carrots. Then she looked up, doubt still in her eyes.

Eleanor cocked her head to the right. "Come on, Lily, do it for me. Think of yourself as the daughter I never had. One spree isn't going to break me." She grinned. "You could do it as repayment for all that chanting I did for you."

Lily laughed but the doubt came right back. "I'm just not comfortable letting you spend money on me."

"Okay, if you ever have some extra money lying around, you can give me some of it back. I really understand how you feel. I'd feel the same way. Let's just do it and let the devil take tomorrow."

Lily thought another minute and then shouted, "All *right*, far out!"

Liebchen's owner jumped and glared at them. She reached down, no doubt to calm the panic in her dog.

"Sorry," Lily said to the whole café. She

turned back to Eleanor. "I tell you what, you choose stuff for me, and I'll choose stuff for you. Agreed?"

Eleanor bit her lip and reached her hand across the table. They shook on it.

"We're not going to touch your hair, though," said Eleanor. "I just love the way you do it. It makes you look like some kind of hand-woven Cleopatra."

"Really? Well, thanks."

Fully energized, they bolted down the rest of the salads, left the café, and headed back to *Neue Mode*.

35

Ursula lifted her right hand from the strings and let the last chord, the only harmonious one in the competition piece, die slowly in the narrow room.

As discordant as the piece was, she'd found memories from the grave in the music; she'd played reflections on growing up; yearning to amend mistakes; anger at being dead; sorrow over loved ones left behind; and finally, in the last harmony, peace and resignation. She'd given the piece a certain unity despite its disparate elements and had almost come to like it. The question was whether the judges would accept her interpretation. Her heart faltered at the thought of the final round, only two hours away now.

She polished the guitar with a soft cloth, laid it back in the case, and picked up the new set of strings Horst had given her when he'd taken her to lunch.

He'd slipped them from his pocket, looking a little embarrassed. "I bought them from one of the vendors here, so I hope they're a good brand. At least I'm sure they're for classical guitars."

Such a kind gesture. She hadn't dared put them on the guitar, however, being unfamiliar with the brand and not knowing how long they'd have to be played before they held their tune.

She held the flat, square packet against her cheek for a minute and slipped it back into the case for luck. She'd never see him again after tonight. His kind face returned with all its warmth, and his willingness to protect her without even knowing why Barkov was after her.

Barkov. She'd almost forgotten him. He was paler and more tautly drawn into himself every time she saw him, clearly furious at Horst's interference.

She looked under the bed. The briefcase was still there.

Barkov knew now that she knew what was in it, and he'd stop at nothing to get it back as soon as Horst wasn't around. He would hound her when they returned to the Democratic Republic. Or worse. He was ruthless enough, that was clear from the files. Old *Tante* Hanne. Most likely she hadn't died soon enough to suit him and he'd had her run over out of sheer impatience. The look on his face when she'd come back from lunch with Horst was nothing short of bloodthirsty.

She could ask Horst to hide her after tonight's

performance, to help her petition for asylum. The thought of him brought a warm feeling, a smile in spite of her dilemma. He was so kind and she was drawn to him. He would be happy to have her stay. No, she couldn't use his kindness like that.

But she couldn't go back with Barkov. He would ruin her and her family.

Grief for her country overcame her again. She could not stay in the West after all. The hope that had shone like a beacon in her head went out. She had to get the files back to the German Democratic Republic and make her people see what snakes like Wolfgang Barkov, code name Orion, did to them. They had to know how they had been used. Her stomach lurched and her heart beat heavily. How could she publish the files? She would find a way and it would land her in jail. She swallowed hard and took a deep breath. Perhaps if she won the competition, the small fame of it would protect her until she found a way to get out.

She showered, did her hair, put on her long black skirt and a white blouse. She slipped the little West money she had into the pockets of the skirt, along with her identification.

Horst knocked at 6:45, just as he said he would. "You look wonderful," he said. "If you don't win the competition, I'm sure they'll give you the beauty prize."

"You certainly make me feel good," she said,

smiling and feeling guilty about it.

"Ready?"

"Yes." She picked up the guitar case and her folder with the new score. She stared a minute at the briefcase, its corner still peeking out from under the bed. She grabbed it, too. Barkov could find a way to get in and take it while she was performing.

"Why are you taking this?" Horst asked, taking the briefcase out of her hands.

"The stuff in it is—valuable. I can't leave it here."

He took the guitar also, letting her carry the folder.

He put everything down at the door, ran his hands through his hair, and said, "Ursula, may I ask you something?"

"Certainly."

"Did you ever consider staying in the West?"

The beacon of hope flashed on for a second. She looked at his kind face and knew she could come to love him. How badly she wanted to say "yes."

"I'm sorry," he said when her agonized silence grew too long. "Bad question or bad timing. It's just my selfish wish. May I at least give you something for good luck?" He caught her hands in his, and she felt his shake just as hers did. Then he kissed her and touched her face again.

A tear rolled from her left eye.

He frowned. "Was that so bad?"

"It wasn't bad at all. It was worth the whole trip to Berlin. Thank you. Horst."

36

Phillip sat as long as he could in the new music seminar and finally walked out between speakers, longing to reach down and massage his sitting muscles. Instead, he strode through the front door of the hotel and walked fast down the *Kurfürstendamm* to loosen things up. His thoughts went back to Eleanor and the crazy outfit she'd had on at breakfast. Obviously the clothes had belonged to that girl. What was her name again? Lisa? No, Lily. What a little fluff-head. Why on earth had he let her talk him into that ridiculous escapade last night? The memory embarrassed him.

Why was he suddenly so attracted to this old schoolmarm, a type he could hardly bear? Not just the type, the archetype. Lord knows, he'd had enough of them after him. He peered mentally under the tam again and saw the unhappy, humiliated face and felt his heart go out in spite of his better judgment. If only she didn't look like some sixth grader's stereotype of a schoolteacher. Somebody whose name ought to be Miss

Satchelback. He sighed.

Maybe it was just the Berlin air. Or two strangers in a foreign land. When they got home, it'd all settle down and be forgotten. Still, it made him feel so happy when he saw her, even dressed like a refugee. Allison would be delighted, but Roger would laugh until glass biodegraded if Phillip bit the bullet at last.

This inexplicable infatuation would pass. It had to. No, he would make it pass. He squared his shoulders and stalked back to the hotel.

By quarter of seven he was waiting impatiently in the lobby, pacing and keeping an eye on the elevator. As he made a turn, the opening of the front door caught his eye and two women entered. After a glance, he turned to the elevator again.

"Hi, Phillip," said the chirpy voice of Lily behind him a minute later.

He turned. "Lily, is that you? I didn't recognize you. Where's Eleanor?"

"Here," said Eleanor at his left elbow.

He turned and gasped. Oh, God, he thought. That's it. I'm done for.

Eleanor waited with a half pleased, half fearful expression on her face.

"Don't you like it?" she asked, smoothing her hair above her blushing face.

Phillip forced himself to sound normal while

his nerves tried to push his voice pitch up to soprano. "You look wonderful." His heart soared and did loop-the-loops around the chandeliers.

Eleanor turned to show off her new outfit, a dusty rose wool suit with an open jacket. Under it she was wearing a pale pink blouse with layers of lace hanging from the stand-up collar. Her hair floated about her face and over her shoulders in soft curls.

"Thanks, I feel wonderful," she said. "What do you think of Lily?"

Lily turned around in her medium blue, calf-length wool dress. She was wearing a pale blue scarf etched in silver that seemed to float around her neck and over her hair. It billowed below her waist in the front and the back.

"You both look incredible, I would never have recognized you."

"Well, I'd better go up and see if George is still tied up..." started Lily.

"I doubt that'll be necessary," said Phillip. "No one would ever recognize either of you. Anyway, I'll keep an eye out. I'm not going to let him get near you," he added, taking Eleanor's elbow to steer her toward the conference room. She rewarded him with a warm smile.

The elevator opened and the East German guitarist got out, along with her friend from breakfast. They headed toward the conference room. In the corner, the blond weasel stood up, scowling, and started after them. Eleanor's eyes shot to him. She turned and followed him, glancing back and smiling apologetically at Phillip. Lily's shoulders drooped and she plodded into the hall. Phillip scratched his head and followed Eleanor. Well, hell. Unhappy schoolmarm or not, this new Eleanor had him, and he knew he'd just looked into the face of his future. So why was she after that obvious Communist agent? And what could he do to win her attention?

From behind a fern in another corner of the lobby Martin stepped out and joined the throng streaming toward the conference room for the final round of the competition. He went to the far door and stationed himself just outside, where he could watch the target. His stomach growled. His hand wrapped itself around metal and began to shake. He revved up his anger to the point of determination. The hand quieted.

37

Ursula was sitting to the left of the stage in the front row that was reserved for the finalists. Across from her and two rows back, Wolfgang Barkov lurked in an aisle seat, a coiled viper of desperation and hatred. She could feel his eyes stabbing through her right temple. He would detain her after the concert. It was his last chance, since their van was scheduled to leave by midnight. She looked to the left, hoping to see a side aisle where she could elude him. There was none. The chairs had been placed right to the wall. She glanced around.

Horst smiled and waved from his station near the door, where he'd gone to watch for the American criminal after he'd escorted her to the front. He set the briefcase on the floor to his right.

She smiled back.

Barkov turned and saw the exchange. Of course, he noticed the briefcase. He paled and glared at her with venom in his eyes.

Ursula tried to swallow, but her mouth was

dry as driftwood. She'd put Horst in danger now, too. What would Barkov do to him? No doubt the *Stasi* had agents in the West, ready to carry out any directive. She'd have to figure out what to do when her performance was over.

Her head was throbbing. She tried to concentrate on the first finalist's rendition of the competition piece, rubbing her hands to warm them in preparation for her own performance. The cacophonous music barely penetrated the waves of frustration and fear that rose from her stomach. The files. A burst of applause startled her. She was next. She would never be able to rush out with the guitar case after her performance. Barkov would see to that. The competition coordinator called her name and the audience applauded. She stood up, lifted her guitar from the case. Barkov. Horst. The files. The competition. Her parents. Stay in the West.

The audience was looking forward to her, wishing her well. She had chosen such a unique interpretation. She knew it was good. They deserved to hear it whether she won or not. She couldn't give up her small chance at winning. The files. Her only chance to take them back was to run now, when he least expected it. Get across the border before he could catch up with her.

She threw the guitar back in its case and bolted up the aisle without it. Out of the corner of her eye she registered Barkov's shock and the first motions of rising from his seat. He was only centimeters behind her. She reached Horst and snatched the briefcase. "Please, stop him," she begged, and raced out the door.

Stunned, Horst reacted swiftly but off balance. His foot shot out, Barkov fell headlong and Horst fell on him without control. Barkov turned their tangled bodies, shot his fist under Horst's ribs, and was up again in an instant.

Eleanor watched the girl's flight, gasping with the rest of the audience. That blond weasel's pursuit felt like a slap to the heart. Without thinking, she leapt up and began working her way out of the row, yanking her hands away when Phillip on one side and Lily on the other tried to hang on to her. At the door she nearly collided with the guitarist's friend just getting up, and they dashed through the lobby together.

"Damn it all," said Phillip, standing up and crashing out of the row after Eleanor.

Martin's hand fell into spasm as he ran after Eleanor. He tried to yank out the revolver with the silencer on it. The butt caught on the inside of his pocket, dragging the whole side of the dark tan trench coat up to his chest.

Lily joined the exodus, treading on several feet. As she dashed up the aisle, she caught sight of her George Craig passing the exit on the run, flapping the right side of his coat about. She darted through the lobby behind him.

Ursula ran to the taxi stand outside the hotel. She jumped into the first one. "Drive!" she yelled. "Get away from here fast."

Tires screeched and the taxi lurched forward just as Barkov reached for the door handle. His cold, furious face streaked past the window in a blur. Ursula watched out the back window. He jumped into the next taxi and it pulled into traffic two cars behind them.

"Where to, *Fräulein*?" asked the driver.

Ursula glanced at the dark, foreign face in the mirror and realized suddenly she didn't know where a border crossing was. She had no idea which crossing the van from Weimar had used. She'd heard of Checkpoint Charlie. That was supposed to be for Americans. There was a train crossing somewhere, but she didn't know the name of the station. Of course—"The Brandenburg Gate," she said. It was right on the line between East and West. There had to be a crossing there. She looked back at Barkov's taxi.

Eleanor ran to the third taxi. *"Folgen Sie die vorderen zwei,"* she commanded, and the taxi took off.

Horst, still holding his side and panting from the blow, jumped into the next taxi and was just about to order the driver to follow the others when a small man with brown hair shoved two other people aside and jumped in. "Follow that cab," he yelled in a squeaky voice. The taxi lunged forward.

"You!" said Horst. "We look since three days for you."

Martin tore his gaze from the taxi ahead and stared at him, stunned. "Who're you?"

"West Berlin police. They want you for questioning in Denver. You will not to carry out any contract here, understand?"

Martin tried a bluff. "I don't know what you're talking about."

The cop's face showed it didn't work.

Martin shrank into the corner of the seat, and shoved the pocket-gun-tangle under his leg.

Horst looked to the front again as the Eleanor's taxi careened around a corner after the first two. "Don't lose them," he shouted at the driver.

There was only one taxi left. Lily and Phillip piled in.

"*Ja, ja, folgen,*" said the driver, and tires squealed again.

"Do you know what's going on?" asked Phillip.

Lily was sitting as far forward as possible, her hands on the back of the front seat. Her blue and silver scarf had fallen around her neck, and she was twisting the ends of it into a knot. "Not even, like, faintly."

The string of taxis tore through the crowded streets, heading East.

Ursula strained forward, as if that would put greater distance between her and the taxi behind her. She gasped with relief when the Brandenburg Gate came into view behind the Victory Column, then the huge white signs warning in German, Russian, and English that this was the end of the West Sector. All of it was only dimly visible in the dark. She reached into her pocket and threw all the West money she had onto the front seat.

"This is as far..." the driver started. The taxi hadn't fully stopped before she shoved her door open and flew out. She raced for the Gate across the wide expanse of pavement, clutching the briefcase with both hands in front of her, peering through the darkness for a guard house or an opening in the rolls of barbed wire she knew were there. She could barely see. Why was there no light?

Wolfgang leapt from his taxi without paying and raced after Ursula, vaguely wondering why there were no lights on the Wall. The angry taxi driver sprinted on his heels, yelling in Turkish.

Eleanor threw some money at her driver and tore across the pavement in her new pink suit. Cascades of lace flopped over her left shoulder and tapped her back like a reminder of some insanity. "Why am I doing this?" she wondered. Why, indeed? She slowed down and let the blond gain ground. His presence still tugged at her, but not as strongly as yesterday. She shook her head. She'd been listening to Lily's silly drivel too much.

Horst's taxi careened to a halt behind the others, barely avoiding dented fenders.

"*Bleiben Sie hier, Sie sind verhaftet!*" he shouted at Martin, forgetting to arrest him in English. He dug in his pocket and thrust his police identification in the driver's face. "*Polizei, warten Sie!*" He threw some money over the back of the front seat. "*Sie auch,*" he ordered Martin, poking him in the shoulder. He leapt from the taxi and disappeared into the darkness. In a few seconds he overtook Eleanor.

Wondering what the German man had said, Martin jumped out behind him. So what if he was some kind of cop. He didn't have Sonny and the whole Family breathing down his throat. Martin snarled. The woman hadn't fooled him. She couldn't put on some frilly costume and think he wouldn't recognize her. This was his last chance. The darkness was perfect cover. He had to do it. They'd kill him if he didn't. But somehow he couldn't make his feet speed across the pavement the way they should.

Phillip and Lily joined the parade a few

seconds later.

Ursula was in panic. The first rolls of barbed wire were faintly visible now. Why was it so dark? When they'd come through on Tuesday the border crossing had been brighter than day. There had to be an opening somewhere. She veered to the left. She was close to the rolled wire now. Where was the?...suddenly there was light and she was blinded. Behind her something thudded behind her, like several laundry bags hitting the ground, but she kept running.

"Ursula," Horst's voice came from far behind her. "Get down!" She turned slightly, not breaking her stride. Barkov was on the ground, looking around, terrified. The lights. If the lights were on again, they could be shot. She fell to the ground holding the briefcase under her.

Horst turned. Why were all these Americans running toward the no-man's-land? "Fall down," he yelled, falling and rolling to one side. "You'll be shot."

Eleanor stopped. Her new suit. Slowly she sank to her knees and lowered herself gently to the pavement. Lily went down like a paper airplane, Martin dropped with a metallic thud. Phillip and the taxi driver dove into a puddle.

They were frozen in an eerie silence. They waited. Slowly Horst belly-crawled around Barkov, who was watching in the direction of the lights, and headed for Ursula. No one else moved.

Then, in the silence, a man climbed over the Wall and came straight toward them. He began cutting the wire. Behind him another climbed over, looking dazed and half-afraid, as if he had just been given a new pair of eyes. He walked slowly after the first man, hunched over a little, looking back often. Then came two young women and a man, none of them wearing *Vopo* uniforms.

Lily looked around. Behind them traffic was beginning to stop near all the taxis. People were leaving their cars in the middle of the street and walking slowly toward the barbed wire. She rose and, ignoring her new pure silk stockings, walked on her knees to where Martin lay balled up like a doodle-bug. She took his hand. "George," she said.

"My name is not...." He started to raise himself on his elbow. Suddenly every cell in his body detached itself from all the others. The space between cells filled with some new vapor that flowed from this girl's hand into him, a vapor light and open as mountain air in the spring, as sweet as a flower he'd smelled recently but couldn't remember. He floated like a summer cloud. Perhaps a second passed, perhaps a year. The cells returned to their original configuration and weight. Now butterflies raced up and down the north-south axis of his torso. Or were they hornets? He fell back and his head slammed onto the concrete.

Lily took his other hand and flapped them both up and down. "It's not? I knew it. I knew you couldn't have such a...pedestrian name."

Martin wondered if he'd gone schizoid and skipped something important. "Who in the hell are you?"

"I told Eleanor you couldn't be George Craig, playing such a mean trick on her. What is it, then?"

"What?"

"Your name, your real name."

"Martin. Girelli. Who the hell are you?"

"I love it. Lily. Marcuso." She smiled.

Martin felt the butterflies and hornets accelerate to unbearable speed, reach his heart and other parts of his anatomy, and buzz there in a frenzy. He knew that in some way he was lost.

Lily put an index finger on his chest. "Listen, I know about the contract on Eleanor. You aren't really going to try to pull it off, are you? Because if you do, love or no love, I'm going to, like, rat on you."

"Love or what love?" The pavement rocked beneath him.

"Ours."

"What?! I've never seen you before in my life. I don't..."

"Can you really deny it? I saw it happen. Tell

me you don't love me."

Martin's mouth opened and closed to the rhythm of his racing heart, but no sound came out. He stared up at her and knew his future was smiling back.

"See? We're stuck with it. I have to be honest with you, I'm not much of a catch. I have about as much to offer you as you do me. So let's just make the best of it. No, better yet, let's make the best of each other."

Martin rose to his knees, thinking to walk away, get a little distance.

Lily put her arms around him while they still knelt, and his frenzied parts exploded around them. He stared into her eyes until he thought he'd hit the other side of infinity there, and finally put his arms around her. As they hugged, they both shook their heads. Then they moved back, looked at each other again, and laughed.

Lily swallowed hard. "I love you, Martin," she said.

Martin nodded seriously. "Give me a few minutes to get used to this, okay?"

"I'll give you a whole lifetime," she said as they stood up.

Fifty feet away, Phillip started crawling toward Eleanor.

She had one arm under her face and the other over the back of her head.

He put his arm around her shoulder.

She jumped and went rigid.

He started to remove his arm and then pressed harder, almost angry in his determination to make her feel safe. "It's okay, Eleanor, it's me, Phillip."

Slowly, she turned to him. "You. Your arm. Across my shoulders." The pressure went right through to her heart and squeezed all other feeling out of her.

Phillip winced. He hadn't thought he might be annoying her. "Sorry." He started to move it. "I was just trying to protect you."

Eleanor smiled then, the first smile not distracted by that blond man or whatever other sorrow she carried around like a cannon ball in her heart. "Don't take it away. It feels good. Thank you, Phillip."

"Do you think I might keep it there while standing?" He helped her up.

Horst stood and helped Ursula up. "Do you realize what's happened?"

She looked around. From both sides people were moving toward them. Behind the stone portals of the Brandenburg Gate a cheer arose. Then there was another from the no-man's-land.

"The Wall has fallen!" shouted Horst. "It's over. The Wall is over!" He grabbed Ursula, lifted her and whirled her around.

Ursula looked down at her spinning friend,

dazed.

During the second revolution, she saw Barkov crawling toward the briefcase at Horst's feet.

She pushed herself out of his arms. She snatched the case just as Barkov reached it. "*Stasi*," she yelled to the East Berliners. "This man is a *Stasi* agent. He built the telephone monitoring system in Radeberg. He manipulated an old lady into starvation to get his hands on her house. He's a *Spitzel*, an informer!"

Barkov was suddenly surrounded by men without uniforms.

"Let's see how he likes his jails," said one of them.

Ursula started to give the East Berliner the briefcase and then stopped. "I want to see this through myself," she said, looking up at Horst.

The crowd was growing and getting louder.

A man in a grey mechanic's jumper, who had Barkov by the collar, yelled, "Somebody take this man to the jail."

"Ha," yelled another in a business suit. "I'm not going back now. I just got here after twenty-eight years."

The man with the wire cutters pushed through the men surrounding Barkov. "Let's just build him a cell right here," he cried. He shoved Barkov to the barbed wire and had the others hold him while he cut enough wire to make a tight, double high circle around Barkov. They spread the word and left him standing in the "jail" while the celebration whirled around him. The crowd jeered.

Ursula threw her arms around Horst's neck. "Can this really be happening? I'm so glad."

He picked her up again, and the briefcase flopped against his back.

"So that's what Barkov was after. But why on earth did you run for the Gate?"

"I wanted to take the file back and let people know how they'd been lied to and manipulated and controlled all these years."

"How were you going to get across the Wall? There's no crossing here."

"There's not?" Ursula's eyes opened wide. "If the lights hadn't come on..."

"I wouldn't have let him hurt you."

Someone from the West side came with champagne and the bottle circulated.

"Come on," yelled Horst and dragged her toward the Wall in front of the Gate.

People were climbing on it. Someone hauled him up and he reached down for her.

Ursula straddled the Wall in her long black skirt, looking East and West, laughing and crying and cheering and singing. "I'm not afraid," she shouted, grabbing Horst's hands. She looked left and right and felt the weight roll from her. "My whole life has been controlled by a fear I didn't even know I had." She sobbed, thought of her parents in the crowded, dreary apartment, and grabbed Horst's hand.

He looked down and put his hand on her face. He was crying, too.

Eleanor stood with Phillip's arm making a warm cushion across her back and watched as the East Germans built a kind of barbed-wire cage around the blond man. *"Stasi,"* the girl had shouted. A sense of panic and pity nearly overcame her. She forced her eyes away and turned slowly to Phillip. Briefly she thought of Lily's confession about the potion, but the pull of emotions toward the man in the coiled wire had lessened. Silly, the whole thing was too silly. But Phillip still had his arm around her shoulder, pulling her to him, pressing exactly into the spot that had always been in her dream. She smiled up at him. He wanted to protect her. That was a value, wasn't it? And she had said he didn't have any.

She looked around at the jubilant crowd. The Wall had fallen. They were in the middle of one of the most dizzying moments in the history of the Twentieth Century. She wouldn't even be able to tell her students she had lived it. She was playing hooky. From somewhere a champagne bottle was pushed into her hand. She took a swallow and handed it to Phillip.

"Let's go up to the Wall," he said, pulling her by the hand.

A jackhammer battered away at the Wall from the other side, its noise nearly drowned by the cheering crowd. Suddenly the point bit through and chips of the Wall began to hit the ground. Through the hole a young *Vopo* and a young uniformed West Berlin policeman shook hands.

Lily joined Eleanor and Phillip. "Guess what, his name isn't George Craig. It's Martin."

Eleanor jumped at the sight of him. He put his hands up, palms toward her.

"It's all over, ma'am. I think I always knew I wasn't cut out for that kind of work. I guess you were safe from me all along. I mean you no harm anymore, I promise. And I apologize." He held out his hand.

Eleanor started to back away but saw the plea in Lily's eyes and slowly offered her hand from as far away as possible. Phillip shook his hand as well while maneuvering himself in front of Eleanor.

Lily made introductions all around in the din and then screamed, "This is really something, isn't it?"

"That's putting it mildly," Eleanor shouted in her ear. "This is the most amazing moment in recent history. It's the culmination of a bloodless revolution."

Lily looked down at the chips of the Wall falling at her feet. "Then these ought to be worth something someday, wouldn't you think?"

All four sets of eyes opened wide. "Not someday," shouted Phillip. "Now."

Suddenly they were all scrambling on the ground, filling all their pockets with pieces of the Wall. Lily, who had no pockets, just stood after a minute with full hands. Eleanor picked up the hem of Lily's new, medium blue wool dress and made a lap bag for her to fill. The wide stocking runs at the knees and her new silk and lace slip peeped out at the revelry.

The first pieces in Martin's huge pocket clinked against metal, but even he didn't notice.

38

July 23, 1990

Ursula poured away the last bucket of water and cleaned the brush she had been using for two days to repaper the wall in the living-dining-music room. She went back and regarded her work critically. The lighter paper, available in huge quantities now that there was free trade between East and West, made the room look a little larger. It had been expensive, and she'd been surprised that in a few places the glue was inconsistent. In fact, it was second-rate merchandise. Her suspicion that the East was being used as a dumping ground for inferior goods from the West angered her. Still, it was no worse than the materials that had been produced in the East, and at least there was a great deal of it.

She went into the bathroom, lit the gas water heater, and ran a bath. She bathed and washed her hair in the tub, dreaming of the shower in Berlin. It was so easy, so relaxing. All you had to do was turn the tap to the right setting; the water sprayed out at exactly the temperature you wanted, and you could stand under it as long as you liked. Such a luxury.   After her bath she drained the water from the tub, brushed her teeth over it and then scrubbed it.

She dressed in a new pleated gray and white skirt she had bought last week when she and her parents had taken the train to Fulda for a day, a week after the currency reform.   Though it was their first time in the West, her parents had refused to go to a bank and get their *Begrüssungsgeld*, "welcome money," a gift of 100 Marks from the West German government to every East German who could come to claim it.   They both thought it patronizing.   And since, after all the debate, the government had credited them with one West mark for each old East mark in their bank account, they didn't feel they needed it.

They'd spent a long afternoon wandering through the stores.   No one had said much, not in the city nor on the way home.   Goods were coming into the East now in a steady stream, too, but there was still nothing to compare with the stores they'd seen in Fulda, much less the ones she'd visited in Berlin.   On the ride home even Ursula had been lost in thought about the degenerate materialism she had always been taught to repudiate in Westerners.   Why, if their materialism was so reprehensible,   did   they   look   happier   than

Easterners? Was the inability of the East Bloc's industrial complex to satisfy even the basic needs of the populace the reason why Easterners were not materialistic? Were they content with what they had simply because they could not have more?

But that was a philosophical discussion she'd have to have with herself later. Right now, she had to get ready. She checked herself in the mirror, straightened the skirt, brushed her hair harder than she'd ever done, and checked again.

Horst was coming. Her heart fluttered at the thought. They had written often and he'd called twice in the eight months since the Wall fell, but they hadn't managed to see each other again. And now he would see how she had lived, meet her parents.

That thought made her hands shake. Her father was becoming bitter about "these *Wessies*," the westerners who came in with their noses in the air, wanting to show the "whining *Ossies*" how to do everything. Would Horst be condescending like so many of them?

She glanced at her watch. He would be here for afternoon coffee at four. She still had an hour to run to the Aldi tent-store, one of the new *Wessie* supermarkets that had sprung up like mushrooms. Her mother had asked her to pick up some whipping cream for the cake she was going to serve.

The doorbell rang before she could get her sandals on. Her heart skipped a beat and she squeezed past the corners of her bed and the piano to shove the curtain aside. There was a *Wessie* car parked across the street. She hurried barefoot through the maze of furniture to the door.

Horst was still stripping the wrapping from two beautiful bouquets of flowers. He smiled above the red carnations, tore the last bit of paper off in order to hand her the flowers without the wrapping. He wadded the paper up and held it behind his back. Then he brought it out again and stuffed it under his other arm to free his right hand. He handed her the carnations.

"This is for the lady of the house with my thanks for inviting me," he said, "and this is for you," he added, handing her a bouquet of roses, daisies, asters and delphiniums. "And this, too." He reached down and picked up a small basket filled with kiwis.

Ursula laughed and immediately all the jitters about seeing him again were gone. "Come in," she said, opening the door until it hit the china cabinet. "I'll show you something." She drew him into the kitchen, thanking him for the flowers. On the floor in the corner was a cardboard box filled with kiwis. Horst stared and started to apologize.

"No, let me tell you about it. I guess we still

have a lot to get used to. A few days ago I was in the new Aldi store and saw some kiwis. Of course, I remembered them from Berlin, so I bought one for each of us, and my parents liked them. The next day my mother went back and bought a box of a hundred because she thought they would disappear and we wouldn't see any more for ages. We've been eating kiwis for every meal, giving them to the neighbors, trying to find recipes for kiwi preserves...."

Horst laughed. "And here I come with my proud contribution. Do you think you'll ever get used to the easy life?" he asked, stroking her face. He was not patronizing, he was just laughing with her. "I apologize for being early," he went on while she busied herself with finding and filling vases. His strange, sweet presence surrounded her in the small, primitive kitchen. "I allowed myself plenty of time because I wasn't familiar with the roads or with Weimar. I guess I should have driven around for a while first."

"I'm glad you didn't, but I'm afraid you'll have to come shopping with me."

"I'll be glad to. Shall we take my car?"

"We'd just have to wait in line to get a parking place. It's not that far if you don't mind the walk."

As they left the building Ursula could sense Horst's attempt not to stare at the door hanging from its one remaining hinge. "I'm sorry about the door," she said, "It's been broken since the year before last. The supervisor always said he was waiting for a replacement hinge, but then after the Wall fell no one knew what was going to happen to the building."

"You don't need to apologize for anything," he said, putting his hand on her shoulder. He turned back to look at the façade. "Is your building caught in the returning-refugee dilemma?"

"Yes, I guess you know the policy."

Horst nodded. "Restore the property to its original owners rather than compensate them for it. *Rückgabe vor Wiedergutmachung.*"

"People here resent that. The way we see it, refugees left decades ago of their own free will and have a good life now. When the buildings were abandoned our government legally took them over and the people in them now have lived there for a long time." She looked up at him and realized she sounded preachy. She softened her voice. "Anyway, about our building. The former owners settled in Hamburg. And there's a big dispute over the inheritance of it that'll have to be settled in court, so no one knows exactly who owns it now or when they might be willing to have things repaired."

Horst shook his head. "I guess I can understand the old refugees' desire to return to their homes, but I think you're right. If I had any property in the 'new states,' as they're calling the East, I'd just sign it over to whoever was living in it before the Wall fell. It's been too long and there are enough problems without the time and money it's going to take to get that all sorted out."

"Not many *Wessies* feel that way." Some of her father's bitterness crept into her voice. Horst glanced at her and looked away again.

They walked past the line waiting for shopping carts at the Aldi tent. "All I need is some whipping cream," Ursula explained to the offended customers.

Horst looked stunned. "This is your supermarket?" he cried. "I saw tents with hundreds of cars parked around them in several towns, and I just assumed they were circuses or something."

Ursula smiled. They went past the vegetable section. Horst stopped and looked. He picked up a wrinkled green pepper; turned it over in his hand, frowning, and laid it back on the pile. He inspected the tomatoes, the cabbage, and the limp carrots. "I don't spend a lot of time in supermarkets," he said, "but it looks to me like you're getting stuff that was moved out of stores because it wasn't fresh anymore."

"I know. We're supposed to be glad we at least can buy these things whenever we want. And we're not supposed to complain if the prices are higher than in the West." She knew she sounded sarcastic and could sense a rift widening between them. "Come, let's get the whipping cream and go home."

They waited twenty minutes in the check-out line. As they approached the cashier, Horst stared at the register with its little glass window for scanning the bar codes. "We don't even have that everywhere in the West yet," he said. "Most stores in Berlin still have the old fashioned machines where you have to punch in the numbers."

"Oh, they send us the latest technology, all right. We're a regular money faucet that's barely been turned on. They just don't send us the freshest goods or buildings to put them in."

"Come on, you can't expect buildings to go up overnight. Surely there are plans for them."

"Of course, it's just that the Reunification has turned out to be more of a takeover than people here...Well, I won't talk about it. I'm afraid my father will tell you eloquently enough how we *Ossies* feel."

"That sounds ominous. You think he won't like me?" He looked genuinely concerned, and Ursula put her hand on his arm to try to bridge the rift.

"He's a good man. I think he'll try to get to know you as a person, not as a *Wessie*," she said. They smiled at each other and her hand slid briefly into his.

Conversation around the table was not going well. Ursula tried to mask the uncomfortable silences by refilling plates with almond spice cake or pouring more coffee.

"*Herr* Kimmig," said Horst after refusing a third piece of cake with whipped cream. "Do you happen to know anyone who has a *Trabant* for sale? I'd like to buy one."

Herr Kimmig frowned. "Why?"

"Well, as a collector's item, I guess. Since they aren't going to be made any more, they'll become more valuable as they disappear from the market. Most people I know think they're..." Horst looked down at his hands.

"They're what? Pathetic imitations of cars? Lawnmower motors with fiberglass bodies? Blue dragon's breath? They're cars, *Herr* Bauer, they get people where they want to go." He clamped his mouth shut and shook his head.

"I didn't mean...."

"You shouldn't discount the *Trabi* too much, *Herr* Bauer," *Frau* Kimmig broke in gently, laying her hand on her husband's arm.

"Please, *Frau* Kimmig, I don't discount them at all."

Frau Kimmig went on, "My brother had one that he paid seven thousand marks for. He drove it for seventeen years, and then sold it for six thousand."

Horst's eyebrows went up and he whistled. "That's quite a record for longevity. I don't understand how he could sell it for so much after seventeen years, though."

Herr Kimmig said with effort, "I beg your pardon, *Herr* Bauer, I didn't mean to attack you. As for used cars, they often fetched a higher price than new cars because they were available when the buyer wanted them. You understand, of course, that there were never many of them around. An owner never sold an old car until he was at the top of the waiting list and knew when the new one would be delivered."

"Horst has been to America," Ursula inserted to change the subject.

"Just a minute, Ursula," said *Herr* Kimmig. He turned back to Horst. "I do happen to know a man who may be interested in selling a *Trabi* within a few weeks. He has a brother in Nuremberg who's keeping an eye out for an Opel or a used Audi. It'll wipe out his bank account, but the fool thinks Chancellor Kohl can keep his word."

"Papa..."

Herr Kimmig was in full swing. "Remember his promise that no one in the East would be worse off after the Reunification?"

"A lot of West Germans believed him when he said there would be no new taxes to pay for it, too," said Horst with the edge to his voice that Ursula had dreaded.

"He made it sound so easy, didn't he?" she said. "It seems...." She couldn't find words to ease the tension.

The ringing of the doorbell fell into the silence that followed. *Frau* Kimmig, the only one at the table who could move freely to the door, got up to answer it. *Herr* Kimmig, Horst, and Ursula looked at the streaks of whipped cream and the cake crumbs drying on their plates.

"Peter," *Frau* Kimmig exclaimed. "What a surprise. We weren't expecting you until Saturday."

She ushered Peter into the room. He was the image of *Frau* Kimmig, but he looked pale and shaken. Ursula automatically left her chair and sat on the edge of the day bed to make room for him. Horst stood up and extended his hand.

"Bauer," he said.

"Markert," said Peter, taking the hand with an air of surprise and distraction.

"This is my uncle," said Ursula.

"*Herr* Bauer is Ursula's acquaintance from Berlin," explained *Frau* Kimmig to her brother.

Herr Markert said nothing. He sat down on *Frau* Kimmig's chair and she moved to the one Ursula had vacated. She started to pour coffee for him, but he put his hand over the cup.

"What's the matter, Peter? You look terrible."

"Robotron's going to close." Everyone but Horst gasped. "It's the currency reform. Our main customer was the Soviet Union, of course, and the Russians can't afford to buy from us now that they have to pay with West marks. Nor any other East Bloc country. All the industries that sold to the Warsaw Pact will close within a few months. There will be tens of thousands out of work."

Shock settled over the room. Horst stood up. "I'm terribly sorry, I'm here at a bad time. I'll leave now."

"No, wait, let's go for a walk," cried Ursula. "Do you mind, Uncle Peter? Horst has come all the way from Berlin..."

He looked at her and shook his head.

They walked all the way to the park on the outskirts of town without speaking. At the edge of the park they passed an old bombed out church with a birch tree and grasses growing high up in the remaining stonework. They found a bench in front of a statue of Shakespeare and sat down. On the grass before them children ran half-heartedly at a soccer ball in the muggy July heat.

"See the building over there?" Ursula asked.

Horst looked across at the tall wooden house and nodded.

"That's Goethe's summer house. He kept his

mistress there, I think."

"Ah, right. Goethe lived in Weimar, didn't he?"

"Schiller, too."

"What's Robotron?"

"Our computer manufacturer. They had plants in several places. My uncle works in Jena."

"I wish I knew what to say."

"It's not just Robotron that's bothering him. He looked like such a shell of a man when he came in. I wish you could have known him even a year ago. He was the kindest man I ever knew. He was a real socialist. My parents, too. And they feel the collapse of the whole system was their failure. They've had their ideals snatched away and held up in front of their faces as shams and delusions."

"I guess they weren't all Barkovs." Horst leaned forward and put his elbows on his knees.

"And then there was his wife. She had nagged at him for years to get out. She wanted a better life. She gave up hope for it here a long time ago. Of course, he didn't tell us that until a few months ago. I guess none of us have gotten used to talking freely yet. I have a strange feeling telling you all this, even now. You know, after I got back from Berlin I heard my parents talking in their bedroom for the first time in years."

He turned to look at her and shook his head.

She went on. "Anyway, I don't think Aunt

Inge waited two weeks after the Wall fell. She left
for Freiburg and is staying with a sister or
somebody. By that time she thought Uncle Peter
such a fool that she didn't even suggest he might
go with her."

"So he's lost his ideals, his wife, and his job in
the space of a few months. That's awful, Ursula. It
hits me hard, too. I can't imagine I'd survive it."
He sat back with his elbows on the back of the
bench and stared across the park.

"It's what's going on everywhere. My friend
Dieter was a teacher of socialism in our elementary
school. He was so full of ideals, a real
humanitarian. He has no job any more, even
though he taught math, too. All the principals will
be out of work in the fall. Our whole school
system has to be overhauled according to the
Western model, even though there were some very
good things in it. At the very least, it was more
democratic than yours. Of course, no one dares to
say things like that these days, for fear of being
viewed as a die-hard socialist. None of our
teachers are qualified in your methods. Nearly all
our textbooks have to be thrown out and there's no
money to buy new ones. So we're being 'adopted.'
I know the town of Offenburg has 'adopted'
Weimar and is supposed to send thousands of
used books to our schools. Can you imagine how
that makes us feel?"

"Like poor relations, foster children. I never realized before how different the two Germanys had become. What about your parents? Will they lose their jobs, too, if they were party-line socialists?"

"No one knows yet. Maybe not. Unless the Music Academy closes. Their talents are not easy to replace."

"Didn't you tell me you had a friend who was a *Vopo*? What was his name?"

"Joachim. I don't know. No one knows what will happen with the *Vopos*. He's so bitter he says he might as well become a punker, although I don't really think he will."

"I guess you've heard how strong they're getting in Berlin."

Ursula nodded. "Dresden, Leipzig, too. Lashing out at everything, especially foreign workers, in pure frustration. It's as if the lid has been blown off. Nobody fears the government anymore, but it was the fear that kept us safe from each other. I think maybe that's what horrifies us the most these days. The criminality. The fact that our streets aren't safe anymore. We never had robberies or muggings here." She almost laughed at the thought. "No one had anything anyway, and even if you did get your hands on someone else's money, there was nothing to buy with it. So with fear and deprivation, we were at least safe in our homes."

"I'm so sorry, Ursula. If I can do anything to make things easier, at least for you and your family, please tell me."

"Thank you, Horst. And I don't mean to paint an entirely bleak picture. Some people are doing well with the change. I even think my parents are finding each other again."

"Things will get better. It will just take some time before life in the East and the West really converge, don't you think?"

"If you're speaking of time in terms of generations."

Horst looked out at the children playing almost silently and their parents watching without smiles or encouragement. He sighed. "I'm afraid you're right. What about you, Ursula, what will happen to your career plans? What does all this mean for us? Can we remain friends? Or more?"

"Friends, certainly. More? I don't know." She put her hand on his arm. "But I love the question. We'd need more time together. As for my guitar career, I realized in Berlin that something's missing from my music. I can't learn it here. Maybe by next fall I'll be able to study somewhere in the West."

"Berlin, I hope?"

"I'll have to see who's teaching there."

"Who's a big name in guitar? I'll arrest him

and hold him in Berlin."

Ursula laughed. "You mean your police have that much power, too? But, thank you, Horst, for wanting me there."

She smiled into his eyes. He put his arm around her shoulder.

When they returned to the apartment the table was still littered with the coffee service. *Herr* Kimmig was playing the piano.

"Your mother's gone for a walk with Peter," he said. Silence followed. "Do you play the piano, *Herr* Bauer?" he asked after a long pause.

"No, I'm embarrassed to say I'm not at all musical. But I enjoy listening. Could you play again? It sounded wonderful."

Herr Kimmig thawed somewhat and began a Mozart Divertimento. He had shifted to a Satie Gymnopaedie when *Frau* Kimmig and her brother returned.

"I have to be going now," said Horst as soon as he could without being rude. "I wish you luck, *Herr* Markert." He shook his hand. "*Frau* and *Herr* Kimmig, I hope you will accept my invitation to visit me in Berlin as soon as possible. I think you know I'm very fond of Ursula and hope to see her again."

"We appreciate the invitation, *Herr* Bauer. Perhaps toward the end of the summer. Before classes start at the Academy. And thank you for the flowers," said *Frau* Kimmig.

"We will try," added *Herr* Kimmig. "Please forgive my outburst, *Herr* Bauer. These are trying times for us, you understand."

"I do, and no offense was taken."

Ursula walked down to his car with him. His arm around her shoulder triggered a memory. She reached up and touched his hand. "I don't think I ever thanked you enough for getting between me and Barkov in the hotel."

"By the way, what ever happened to him?" he asked, standing by his open car door. "You wrote that you had handed his file over to the new state governor's office, but you never said whether anything came of it."

"Our illustrious state governor is just an old Socialist Unity Party factotum who knows how to play the game right. Months later he sent someone around to question me, but I doubt very seriously that Barkov will be punished. He'll find his way into the current regime and use it for his own gain, too. It makes me so angry."

"Do you think he can still get at you in any way?"

"I don't know. I don't think so. I still know what was in the files."

He cupped her face in his hand, glanced up at the windows of her apartment, and gave her a quick kiss on the mouth. "I meant that about coming to Berlin, you know. For your parents, too. I want to stay in touch."

"I know. I do, too." She smiled up at him.

As he drove away, she leaned against the frame with the broken door, waving until the car swung around the corner.

39

Friday, November 9, 1990

Eleanor ran a comb through her hair, barely shoulder length now, with a soft wave that swept back from her temples. She pondered her face in the mirror. It smiled back at her, gentler than it had ever been, and almost pretty, all the self-doubt and fear of the black dream gone. "Mrs.," she said aloud and shook her head.

The doorbell sounded and she left the bathroom. She checked her loosely pleated wool skirt and the pale blue silk blouse in another mirror in the hall. The smell of dinner enveloped her as she neared the living room. She went to the buzzer and pressed it to let Lily in downstairs, then detoured to the balcony and opened the doors to air out the apartment for a few minutes. She checked the dining room table again, smiled at the flat runner of red roses in the middle, and went into the hall to wait for the elevator to open.

Lily stepped out and ran toward her, smiling

as she came.

"Hey, you look great," they said simultaneously into a big hug. Lily's hair was short, too, a profusion of black curls around her face, and she was wearing her old gray and pink wool skirt with a plain pink turtleneck. Hanging from a black leather thong around her neck was a piece of the Berlin Wall.

"Mmmm, smells great, I hope that's coming from your kitchen. What is it?" she asked.

"*Fleischrouladen*, meat rolls. Come on in and I'll tell you how they're made. I'm sure Martin will love them. I know Phillip always does. But I made a vegetable casserole, so you don't have to eat them, if you don't want to."

They went to the kitchen and Eleanor took the lid off the pot with the meat rolls.

"Mmm, I may have to try one, vegetarian or no."

"They're made from very thin slices of top round, about as big around as your hand. You spread ground brown mustard on each slice, then place a half strip of bacon, a strip of onion, and a quarter of a dill pickle on one end, roll it up, and fasten it with a toothpick. You brown them on all sides. They splatter all over your stove, but they're worth the mess. Then you add water and let them simmer. The gravy is wonderful. I always thicken it a little and add some sour cream at the end.

Come on, we have a few minutes before Phillip gets back. Let's go chat."

They went back to the living room. Lily stood for a few minutes examining the collection of antique and bizarre musical instruments that hung on the wall above the sofa. Then she looked around.

"This place is just huge. What is it, the whole top floor?"

"No, only half. The other couple up here have their entrance at the other end of the hall."

"Don't you ever get scared living this far up and not having any other exit?"

"I never think about it. I guess the concept of 'up' wasn't in my head for so long that it seems nothing but positive to me now. But tell me how you're doing. How's Martin? How's the Coffee-osity Shop going?"

"We're fine. I guess we're both working harder than we ever have in our whole lives. But it seems to suit us. He's really okay, you know. There's a lot of kindness in him. He just made a big mistake. He said he kept having doubts even before he got to Berlin and tried to ignore them. And I think he's finally found something he likes. He turned out to be really good at collecting junk from garage sales and flea markets and fixing it up. You can't imagine how much stuff we manage to sell in the coffee shop or the things people will pay good money for."

"So the shop's going well?"

"Considering what amateurs we are, yeah. And Martin's taking some business classes at Opportunity School, which should help us run things smoothly. But the shop wouldn't be going at all if Phillip weren't letting us use his old house rent free. And of course, we wouldn't have had the money for any inventory or the coffee shop fixtures if you hadn't given us all the bits of the Wall that you collected. You could have made thousands if you'd kept them a little longer, you know." She grinned. "Almost enough to make up for that shopping spree."

Eleanor reached across the couch and touched Lily's hand. "We don't need thousands, Lily. Why shouldn't you have them? It saved us the extra weight in our suitcases, not to mention the worry over where to put them when we moved."

Lily laughed and looked around. "Yeah, right. So considerate of me. How are you two getting along, anyway?"

Eleanor smiled, but it was a minute before she answered. "It's wonderful, Lily. Every time I look at myself in the mirror, all I can do is shake my head. I mean, even I can see that I'm a different person. And every day I see something more in Phillip that I admire. He's so generous, so helpful to other people." She stopped.

"I hear a 'but.'"

"There's no 'but' about Phillip. It's just that I always have a little tinge of fear that this can't be real or that if it is, it can't last forever." She smiled sheepishly and looked toward the fireplace. "Are you sure potion you gave him isn't going to wear off? I mean, mine surely did."

"Oh, man, El, when I look back on that and realize what an absolute idiot I was... Of course I'm not sure it's permanent. I can't believe any of them worked then, it was all so far out. Still, mine hasn't worn off. But even if Phillip's does, he's so much into being married to you by now that he'd never dream of leaving. Don't you think?"

"I hope so, but I'm not taking it for granted. I don't think I've ever tried so hard to make something work in my life. It's not that I try to make myself into the person I think he wants me to be. I just keep focusing on the things I like in myself and letting them guide me. It seems to be working. Not that there aren't little problems from time to time, but I've never been so happy in my life. And I think Phillip is, too. Maybe that's the real miracle. It's just..., well, a school-teacher is the absolutely last person he ever thought he'd marry. His sister-in-law kept playing matchmaker with her colleagues, and he couldn't stand any of them."

Lily laughed. "A sure sign that it was the potion. Does he know about that?"

A key turned in the door and Phillip came in carrying the wine for dinner. He kissed Eleanor on the forehead and caressed her for a second between her shoulder blades.

"Hi, Lily," he said. "It's good to see you again. How's stuff?"

"Great, thanks."

"Lily and I were just talking about the love potions," said Eleanor. "She wanted to know if you knew about them." She turned back to Lily. "He does, and about the contract, too."

Phillip shook his head and cuffed Lily lightly on the shoulder.

She grinned at him. "Listen, I did you a big favor. Look what you got."

"I know."

"In fact, if the coffee-curiosity shop fails, I'm going to buy a vending cart and sell potions on the Sixteenth Street Mall."

Eleanor laughed. "Heaven forbid! You'd have the whole city of Denver so cross-wired it'd blow like an overloaded computer."

"You know," said Lily, "I never did figure out why your potion didn't work like the others. I mean, theoretically you ought to be somewhere in Germany right now trying to rescue that hatchet-faced ferret."

"Perish the thought. Did you make mine like all the rest?"

"Yeah, of course. I think so. Let me see, it was the morning after I zapped Phillip. I got up. You were gone. I took the water bottle off the dresser—no, wait! That's it. I used tap water for all the others. But the Berlin tap water was so yucky and looked kind of gray. So I used the bottled water in the hotel."

"You used *Sprudel*?"

"No, I didn't use *Strudel* in any of them."

"Not *Strudel*, *Sprudel*. That's what the Germans call mineral water. Carbonated mineral water."

"Carbonated!? Well, that's the answer. That stuff'll kill you! No wonder your potion wasn't as strong and didn't last. You ought to try putting a plastic spoon in something carbonated, like a Coke, overnight sometime. You know what happens?"

"No, what?" asked Eleanor and Phillip.

"Twenty-fours later the plastic spoon is eaten away. Gone. Dissolved. Disappeared."

Eleanor sat back in her chair and shook her head.

"Well," said Phillip, "that settles that. If I ever have a Coke in my stomach for twenty-four hours, I'm sure not putting any plastic spoons in there. What happens with Zinfandel?"

The doorbell rang and in a few minutes Martin joined them.

"We were just talking about Lily's finagling

with our lives, plying us with potions," explained Phillip, pouring wine into four glasses.

Martin looked embarrassed. "Consider yourselves lucky you just got a potion. I got some hairy rat tied to my...me."

Everyone laughed and he grinned in spite of himself. "You think that's funny, huh? You should just wake up with a roaring hangover someday and find hairy things that you can't explain hanging off your privates."

"Well, it's your own fault," said Lily laughing. "If you hadn't taken on that..."

They all looked at the off-white carpet.

"It's okay, let's get that out in the open," said Eleanor.

"You know, sweetheart," Phillip mused, "I can almost understand your taking out a contract on your own life, but I can't quite see you finding the right contacts to do it."

"Yeah, I've often wondered about that, too," said Lily.

Eleanor looked at Martin and grinned. "I'll tell how I got that far if you will," she said.

"Not much to tell about me. I lived right around the corner from the car parts place. I'd seen a lot of people going in and out who weren't buying anything. They looked way too fancy for the neighborhood, and at first I thought it was a drug front. Which it probably was, too. I figured there had to be something organized there, like the Mafia. Then when I got laid off and couldn't find a job for so long, I thought about going in and asking them for one. Of course, I knew you don't just go in and fill out some application form for a Mafia job. So I started watching the people who went in and out. One day this guy came out that I used to go to school with. I badgered him till he finally took me in and introduced me to Sonny Levinsky."

"What's going on with the investigation, by the way?" asked Phillip.

"Well, I know they got Sonny and tried to offer him a reduced sentence for fingering others. I don't think he did, though. I guess he was more scared of them than of doing a few years. So come on, Eleanor. Tell us about you."

"You had it so easy," she said. "And you were the one who put the whole idea in my head, by trying to hijack me. I figured Colfax was the place to start, too. I went down the same night I met you and walked from Josephine almost to Broadway looking for a likely hit-man hang-out. I was scared to death and felt like the very invitation to rape or murder. But I was determined to go through with it. I didn't even get up the nerve to go into the raunchiest places though, so the next night I rented a costume and dressed up as a man. I wore dark glasses, inside, at night, which I hate to do. It nearly drove me crazy. And being dressed like that only made me stand out. Not to mention the women who accosted me. So the next night I dressed as a prostitute and nearly got arrested. After that I was a bag lady. I got some clothes from the Salvation Army store and ran over them in my car a few times. I went from bar to bar and cheap hotel to hotel for several nights, watching people. I was scared all the time, but I kept telling myself the worst anyone could do was kill me, and that's what I wanted, anyway. Actually, nobody showed the slightest interest in me as a bag lady.

"After almost a week I heard scraps of conversation from two men behind me in a bar that led me to believe they were Mafia. Of course, I could have paid any punk to kill me, but I didn't want it to be messy or in the streets of downtown Denver. I wanted to have the guitar conference in Berlin to look forward to, so the Mafia seemed the only viable place to turn.

"As soon as one of the men in the booth left, I scooted into it and said what I'd come for."

Her face drooped at the memory of the hideous depression she hadn't been able to shake and the week of looking into the garbage can of life.

Phillip moved to her and put his arm around her. She looked up and in a minute she smiled.

"The thing to do now," he said, "is drink to the changes that can happen in a year. Here's to accepting new directions, no matter what propels you into them."

They all lifted their glasses, smiled into each others' eyes, and drank.

"Come on, Lily, help me serve dinner," said Eleanor and led her into the kitchen.

Lily watched her closely as she stirred her meat dish and checked the casserole in the oven. "You're okay now, aren't you, Eleanor?"

Eleanor leaned against the tiles on the stove island for a minute. "The depression? Yes, it's really all right now. The memory makes me sad, so I keep looking forward. But you know, it's not just that I love Phillip or that I've quit teaching and we're planning to travel a lot. That's all wonderful. There's something else. I just feel I want to fight something."

"I don't get it. Fight what?"

"Well, fight isn't the best word. I want to...what? Iron out a wrinkle in society."

Lily waited.

"It's just that women of my generation were brought up to get married. Maybe not like the women of a hundred years ago, but we learned early on that getting a boyfriend, then a steady, a fiancé, and finally a husband was what life was all about. And if you didn't...well, there was no worth in you, you must be flawed somehow. And, believe me, I told myself often enough that that was a lot of bunk, that my value lay in me, not in being somebody's wife. But still, the first time I signed my name 'Mrs. Eleanor Redding,' something rolled off my heart. A weight I'd carried around all my life. And I know it's gone for good. Even if for some reason I end up alone again, and even lonely, that one absurd abbreviation will always be a wedge between me and the ultimate desperation."

"Wow, that's great!"

"Well, it is and it isn't. I mean, I knew in my head all along that I was a worthwhile person. But I had—millions of women have—this emotional submission to that one word that stands for female status."

Lily stood looking at her.

Eleanor shrugged and smiled. "Which isn't to say that I'm not intensely happy now. I've just had a lot of sorting to do."

Lily smiled back. "Me, too, about getting serious about life. About responsibility. About how lucky we all are that I didn't make a huge mess of things."

"Are you happy with Martin?"

Lily looked in her eyes for a long minute. "Yeah, I am. Just not the way I thought I'd be. It's more like being together and working to make something—a business that will provide us with a decent living, a marriage, a family."

Surprised, Eleanor glanced up from the mashed potatoes she was turning into a serving bowl.

Lily put her hands up, palms out. "No, not yet. Maybe in a year or two, when we get established."

"I'm so glad."

Phillip and Martin walked out onto the balcony for a few minutes in the cold of the November evening.

"This is nice," said Martin, looking past Cherry Creek far below to the lights of downtown. "You think I can ever live like this?" he asked.

"Do you want to?"

"Well, when I compare this apartment," he turned back to look into the spacious living room for a moment, "to the apartments that Lily and I had—there's something so calm and easy about it. I don't mean to sound ungrateful, but even the upstairs of your house doesn't have this...what? It's just a glimpse into a kind of life I never touched before. I'd sure like to be able to offer Lily something better than a shaky business and someone else's real estate."

"Don't place too much value on circumstances and surroundings, Martin. I know a certain amount of comfort is important. And of course, that'll come if you keep at it. But what you have together is a lot more important. I was well off and could buy anything, do anything I wanted. I knew it was pretty empty, but I kept women at bay because I got stung once and preferred comfort to risk. So concentrate on what you have, not on what you don't have. The rest will fall into place."

Martin leaned on the railing and watched his breath pulse into the cold air against the city lights. "Yeah, I know you're right. It's just such a hell of a lot of work."

Phillip waited.

"Not that I would trade it for anything in the world."

"I think the CBS special about the fall of the Wall is coming on. Let's look at the beginning of it over dessert." said Phillip, laying his napkin next to his empty plate.

He turned on the television while the others settled in the living room. They watched as the events of late 1989 unfolded once more. The camera focused on the Brandenburg Gate briefly.

"Well, I'll be damned," said Phillip. "Isn't that the guitarist from Weimar on the Wall? I wonder why she bolted just seconds before her performance."

"You're right," said Eleanor. "I wonder what happened to her and that *Stasi* man and the young man she was always with. Let's watch the faces.

Maybe she came back for the anniversary celebration."

"I can't imagine picking her out in that crowd," said Lily. "I don't even really remember what she looked like."

The camera came back to the present, panned the area around the Gate and then zoomed in on it. Eleanor was the first to gasp. "It's her, look, on that ledge on the right end. And the young man is there, too. I can't believe this."

They watched, spellbound, as the report moved from the euphoria over the demise of the Wall, to the Reunification barely five weeks old now, and the problems that had arisen during the year: the claims of old refugees on the property they had left behind, the near ruin of the East German economy, unemployment, resentment on both sides.

"What do you think, Eleanor? How long will it take before you can't tell any difference between the two Germanys?" asked Phillip when the half hour was over.

"A couple of generations, I'd say. You have to understand that the East Germans lived under the same kind of regime since the time of Hitler. And before that, the country had been in dire straits since 1914. There's hardly even anyone alive there who can remember a time of freedom and prosperity."

"God, there's a lot I don't know," said Martin.

Eleanor and Phillip went out on the balcony to watch their friends leave. Far below Lily and Martin walked out of the building, looked up, and waved with both arms, walking backwards toward the sidewalk. As they turned, Lily began shaking her hands up and down, then mimed pouring something from one hand into the other, then drinking from a glass. Martin threw up his hands. She moved closer to him, put her hands on his shoulders from behind, and gave a little jump. He turned around and put his arm around her waist and they walked on toward the bus stop on Lafayette and Speer Boulevard.

Phillip put his arm around Eleanor's shoulder. They were both shaking their heads, smiling. She reached up with her right hand and stroked his hand, then let herself drift into the warm pressure between her shoulder blades, into the dream, the one of the kind man who made her feel sheltered, not alone. Only now he had a face.

Other books by Margaret Bailey

Diamond in the Sky
Two lovers in Leadville, Colorado, will lose each other if the spectacular Ice Palace built to help the silver mining town through the bust of 1895 melts.

Waves of Amber, First Wave
A fictionalized memoir, this story reveals how Hong, a Vietnamese refugee, and Margaret, an American teacher, manage to become family to each other despite cultural and age differences.

Waves of Amber, Second Wave
Four more refugees join the fragile family life of Hong and Margaret and nearly tear them apart.

Waves of Amber, Third Wave
Another wave of refugees throw the now enlarged

family into chaos again. Only love, loyalty, and determination can hold them all together.

Stephanie's Search

A man disappears into the Colorado Rockies, and two broken people try to find him, thinking he holds the key to solving their problems. Their paths cross like two strands of barbed wired, but perhaps they will find something they weren't looking for. All proceeds from the sale of this book are donated to the Summit County, Colorado, Search and Rescue Group.

Father President

Father Paul Greer bolts from the priesthood with no idea where he's going or how he will live. A drunken brother, a flaw in the constitution, and a natural disaster propel him in directions he never dreamed of. His traveling companion is Emma Light in the Lodge, a Native American and radical Earth Rights activist. Neither knows how to survive in Washington. And Washington may not survive them, either.